Obsession

Some passions are meant to consume.

Shayne McClendon

Obsession by Shayne McClendon
Copyright © 2010-2017 Shayne McClendon

Published by Always the Good Girl LLC
www.alwaysthegoodgirl.com

All rights reserved.

No part of this book may be reproduced or transmitted in any form or by any means, electronic or mechanical, including photocopying, recording, or by any information storage and retrieval system without written permission from the author and publisher.

This is a work of fiction. Names, characters, places, and incidents either are the product of the author's imagination or are used fictitiously, and any resemblance to actual persons, living or dead, business establishments, events, or locales is entirely coincidental.

ISBN-13: 978-1548746841
ISBN-10: 1548746843

Dedication

Pain is pain.

No matter who you are, what you are, or how you walk through your day…pain is an equalizer.

It's unlikely you'll make it through your life without scars. Improbable that you'll take your last breath on this planet without regrets, trauma, or pain in one form or another.

No matter the source, you can survive your pain. You can make it through a journey over broken glass and to the other side where there's green grass and cool streams.

Holding on, keeping on, moving on.

Take your pain and put that shit in a box. Slam the lid as tight as you can and keep slamming it when it tries to break out. Find your focus. Find your tricks to making it through because you damn well can.

Your pain doesn't control you. It doesn't dictate the life you live from this moment. Believe in your power.

Right now. This minute. Breathe it your power and hold it close. Nothing strips it from you…but you.

Fight, then fight some more.

Pain is a little bitch.

Much love,
Shayne

Table of Contents

Prologue _____ 1

Chapter One _____ 12

Chapter Two _____ 23

Chapter Three _____ 28

Chapter Four _____ 35

Chapter Five _____ 46

Chapter Six _____ 52

Chapter Seven _____ 62

Chapter Eight _____ 69

Chapter Nine _____ 80

Chapter Ten _____ 91

Chapter Eleven _____ 100

Chapter Twelve _____ 105

Chapter Thirteen _____ 112

Chapter Fourteen _____ 118

Chapter Fifteen _____ 126

Chapter Sixteen _____ 132

Chapter Seventeen _____ 142

Chapter Eighteen _____ 148

Chapter Nineteen _____ 157

Chapter Twenty _____ 164

Chapter Twenty-One _____ 171

Chapter Twenty-Two _____ 182

Table of Contents (continued)

Chapter Twenty-Three	189
Chapter Twenty-Four	199
Chapter Twenty-Five	206
Chapter Twenty-Six	215
Chapter Twenty-Seven	225
Chapter Twenty-Eight	234
Chapter Twenty-Nine	243
Chapter Thirty	249
Chapter Thirty-One	259
Chapter Thirty-Two	273
Chapter Thirty-Three	284
Chapter Thirty-Four	295
Chapter Thirty-Five	304
Chapter Thirty-Six	315
Chapter Thirty-Seven	323
Chapter Thirty-Eight	334
Chapter Thirty-Nine	345
Chapter Forty	363
Epilogue	370
The Barter System Series	377
About Shayne McClendon	379
Also by Shayne McClendon	381
Special Acknowledgments	383

Prologue

January 2009

He picked up the phone on the first ring. "Hyde."

"Hollow."

"You have an assignment?"

"Yes." There was a pause. "I heard you were back from the Middle East. Everyone alright?"

"As well as we can be. The Ghonims went above and beyond after the dust settled." Hyde cleared his throat. "We're good. Back to work. Tell me."

"This is an unusual mission. Outside your usual wheelhouse. It would require *years* of commitment for your entire team. Perhaps a decade." There was a long pause. "Hyde. It could end up being a retirement position."

Such a thing was practically unheard of in their circles.

Lowering to the bumper of the Humvee in their loading bay, Hyde frowned. "Who has the *resources* for a long-term hire of that scale? Have you explained our *rates*?"

Hollow grunted. "Yeah, I explained them and even bumped them a bit. It's for Samuel and Monica Fields."

Hyde whistled low. "They consider your rates a *bargain*."

He said firmly, "It must be for their child."

"What makes you think that?"

"They employ dozens of men already. Several I've trained myself in various organizations. I've kept in touch. Why hire a dedicated team if it isn't to protect their most valued asset?"

"You're right. They require a unit concerned with their daughter's safety only. Her name is Elliana."

"How annoyed will I be?"

The silence drew out. "She's grounded, Hyde. I've met her several times. She's…different."

"How old?"

"Eighteen."

"Why now?"

"Ellie's a freshman in college. Her parents aren't handling it well. They've chosen not to share the extent of the threats with her. They want her to feel normal."

"Does she know about a new team?"

"The Fields have men with her now. They want you to observe before you make a final decision. Due to the length of the contract, they want assurances regarding your commitment. Your rates plus a bonus whether you take the job or not."

"Salt Flats. Call me back with a time we can meet."

"Done."

They disconnected and Fiaaz approached. "New job, boss?"

"Maybe. Not sure it's really up our alley."

The others came out of the barracks and he explained the parameters without specifics. All of them were intrigued.

Si shook his head in confusion. "Guarding a girl on American soil? How much danger could she be in?"

"She's the only child of Samuel and Monica Fields."

All of them went still and Bianca murmured, "Whoa."

"A decade. That's what they want."

Absolute silence.

Then Fiaaz said quietly, "They want to pay *all of us* for a *decade* to guard their daughter?" Hyde nodded and his driving expert said quietly, "Man. They could buy a country with that cash."

Bianca elbowed him. "They already did. Not worth much if they don't have anyone to carry on their work."

The full bio of their possible charge downloaded to his phone and he was surprised that it didn't include typical spoiled heiress photos.

Almost all the ones of her taken in public were at children's charity events, dressed in shorts and t-shirts, running shoes. There weren't many of her in formal attire.

* * *

A week later, they assembled in the Salt Flats to meet with the parents of young Elliana Fields. The meeting was done at midnight and the couple arrived via helicopter to the coordinates Hyde provided.

Introductions were made and he got right to the point. "Trial period of six weeks. Anything discussed, reported, or observed is highly classified." He crossed his hands at his back. "That discretion applies to *both* sides of this arrangement."

As the team stepped from concealment, Monica Fields' eyes widened and Samuel Fields opened his mouth to speak and quickly closed it.

After a long pause, she stared at Hyde and inhaled carefully. "Agreed."

"Agreed." Her husband asked, "You've read Ellie's dossier?"

Hyde nodded.

Mrs. Fields folded her hands. "You must be *gentle* with her. I agree to your terms during the six-week trial period. At the end of that time, you'll tell us what resources you're willing to commit to our daughter."

"We'll have no contact with Miss Fields during the observation period." He gave her a small smile. "Unless we see we're needed. Then we'll *definitely* make contact."

"I appreciate that." Mr. Fields held his gaze. "Your group comes highly recommended through channels we trust. It's my understanding that you've trained some of our best men?"

"I have."

"The security staff on the estate might not make the right judgment call if there's a situation. They're accustomed to responding with Monica and myself as their focus. I need your people to watch *Ellie*, to protect *her*, no matter what else is happening. She has to be your *only* priority at all times."

"I hate that she insisted on an out-of-state college. So many things have already gone wrong in her first semester." Mrs. Fields shook her head. "She's our *only* child. To us, she's so much more than our sole heir. She's our miracle."

Her husband growled and clenched his fists at his sides. "Ellie's listed on an international sex trafficking website. She's been there for several years. Even her eighteenth birthday didn't see the end of it. We've offered to pay the bounty ourselves to see her safe but it changes *nothing*."

The implication was clear.

Elliana Fields was a medically confirmed virgin. It raised her value substantially for the type of men willing to do anything to add such a trophy to their collection.

A virgin worth billions was a target many who existed in the underbelly of humanity couldn't resist.

"Our dossiers are encrypted and classified to the highest levels of government." He handed the couple a laptop. "You can only open them on this. They're viewable for twenty-four hours. Long-term, if we accept, we prefer to fill key positions. It will appear at all times that I'm her sole bodyguard."

"I like that. It won't make her feel so smothered." The

woman lifted her eyes. "We can be overprotective. She's been trained to assist in her defense but I-I'd love it if she didn't have to."

"Understood."

"Thank you, Hyde."

"Ma'am. Sir."

The team watched as the Fields returned to their helicopter and flew out of sight a minute later.

Bianca murmured, "A *sweet* heiress? Is that even possible?"

"I guess we'll see," Hyde responded. "Let's go over some specifics." For the next hour, they finalized details of the trial period for covering Elliana Fields. "We'll rendezvous on her campus before her arrival. Let's lock down headquarters."

* * *

The first day Hyde shadowed Ellie, he realized she was far different than even he'd assumed. She had two speeds. Walking slowly with her eyes in a book or running.

He kept his distance but it was easy to see that the security assigned to her struggled with the common distractions found on a college campus.

They regularly lost track of her, found their eyes drawn to random sounds, and repeatedly broke cover.

Fiaaz posed as a member of campus security and twice interacted with Ellie until her team could reassemble.

Si took over the campus café kitchen and monitored her

food personally after he identified two separate chemicals in specific drinks she always ordered.

As an assumed housekeeper for Ellie's dorm, Bianca removed cameras hidden in her air vents and two bugs from beneath her bed and in the small attached bathroom.

Their observation period neared its' end and Hyde allowed her to glimpse him as he took up a closer position. He'd been noticing several boys who seemed intent on her attention but the men officially assigned to her protection hadn't intervened.

She jogged every morning with headphones in her ears. She loved to run. He paced her at forty feet and was amazed at the way she tuned out.

On one such morning, as she entered the lightly wooded area on the trail, the idiots he'd been watching ambushed her.

Baiting her verbally, she maintained her poise and logic in her responses, attempting to reason with the men. That she wasn't screaming or crying spoke highly of her character.

One of them lunged for her and she punched him in the throat with a simple but powerful move. Returning to a calm stance, she again tried reason.

The second hit the ground when she took out one of his knees. She again gave them the opportunity to walk away but a third man attacked.

She feinted with one leg while the other came up to rack the man in the balls.

Hyde stood a dozen feet away, amazed at the physical ability of a woman who was always calm and studious.

He moved to intervene when a fourth man tackled her in a football play. She hit the ground *hard* and Hyde saw red. The others went to their hands and knees around her like a pack of wild dogs, pulling at her.

Entering the scuffle, he ended it quickly and *painfully*.

Five minutes later, her attackers were restrained and campus security arrived on the scene. He stood within one foot of her at all times. She wasn't hysterical or demanding.

Hyde took her gently by the upper arm and returned her to her dorm without a word. One of her team was unconscious at the head of the trail, having been struck in the head with a rock. Si knelt at his side.

Another was on the verge of a nervous breakdown trying to find Ellie and Bianca calmly explained who they were and that she was safe with their team leader.

The other security people were too far away to recognize the trouble. Fiaaz worked to rally everyone to a central location in the quad for briefing.

Ellie stared at everything going on with wide eyes. In her room, Hyde dropped all the shades and called her parents. She lowered herself to the edge of her bed and watched him in silence. He appreciated her restraint.

When a police photographer arrived, Ellie was asked to remove her t-shirt so they could catalog her injuries. Standing in a sport bra and running shorts, the woman turned on all the lights in her room and began snapping photos.

Hyde ground his teeth at the bruises and abrasions she'd received. Her parents entered as they took pictures of the back of her body.

After answering questions asked by the local police department, Ellie went to shower and her mother insisted on staying with her.

Samuel Fields asked him to talk in the hall.

Hyde wasted no time. "We'll assume Miss Fields' protection."

"That fills me with relief." It was apparent on the man's face.

"Did you find a secure location? This dorm isn't going to work. There have been too many breaches into her personal space already. Too many people have access."

"You'll have security clearance in a place by tomorrow morning along with the rest of your team. Outfit it in whatever ways you deem necessary. I own the building and the staff has been informed of your status."

"You were confident."

"Hopeful. My daughter is…unique. I hoped her gentle nature would inspire your team to agree." He shrugged. "It makes her an incredible asset in our charity work."

Hyde's smile was slow. "Well done."

"Thank you. Ellie's assistant Padme will be joining you. I sent you her bio and qualifications."

Hyde nodded. "Si knows her. He vouched for her skills. I need three days to secure the residence. We'll require a dedicated armored vehicle."

"Done. We'll keep her at our hotel until your team finishes upgrades to the apartment."

Hyde turned to leave. "Hyde?" He glanced over his shoulder and Samuel Fields smiled. "Thank you for being there, for stepping in."

Turning back, he chose his words carefully. "I waited one minute to see if her detail would appear and evaluate her skills."

"Your verdict?"

"Your daughter is smart, quiet, and kind. You should be proud of her ability to keep her head and I was impressed that when given no choice, she used force."

"You agree to the length of the contract?"

"We'll commit to one decade as her personal protection detail. You have the details. Should any of the team be unable to fulfill their obligation, I'll personally train a replacement. I'll see you in three days, Mr. Fields."

Back at the hotel, Hyde stared out at the California sunset.

Elliana Fields was lovely. Over weeks of surveillance, he'd started to feel protective of her on a personal level. It wasn't an emotion other clients inspired.

He dialed a number he'd come to know well over the years.

"Hollow."

"We've taken the assignment."

There was a long silence. "You committed to a decade?"

"Yes."

"Your entire *team*?"

"Yes."

"The Fields offered to make a *substantial* donation to the organization if you took the job. Did you know that?"

"No. It wouldn't have mattered."

Another protracted silence. "You like her. Ellie."

"I want her safe," Hyde hedged.

"Do you need me to send Red out to coordinate the systems? She and Padme have worked together before."

"I'll need her for two days. Fiaaz returns tomorrow with Bianca. They're on their way to shut down headquarters and move everything here. Gear and Finn are bringing you a few things we no longer need."

"Presents? I *love* presents." The line was quiet for almost a minute. "This will be good for you, I think. All of you. You've been in the field too long."

"She's different than what we're used to."

"Different is so often an omen for amazing things."

Staring at the photo of Ellie in her bio, he allowed himself a small smile. "I think you might be right."

Chapter One

Being Elliana Monica Fields, the only child of Monica and Samuel Fields, means I live an odd life.

My parents are incredible. They don't mean to smother me.

They tried to have children the first dozen years of their marriage without success. They adopted a little boy a decade before I was born but he died of a genetic lung disease when he was a toddler.

Afraid to risk losing another child, they resigned themselves to a life of childlessness and threw themselves into their businesses and charities.

I was such a surprise, she was five months along before Mom's doctor considered giving her a pregnancy test. Everyone thought she was going through early menopause.

As the sole heir to the positively massive fortunes they hold individually and as a couple, *highly protective* doesn't begin to cover their concern for me.

The world sees my mother as a pocket Venus but she's really a petite Amazon warrior. Barely five-two with blonde hair and violet eyes, she's continually underestimated.

In comparison, my father towers over her at six-one. With deep brown hair and green eyes, leanly muscled and fit, he looks as if he could take up a weapon to defend me.

They're determined to live forever so I'm always protected. I also hope they'll live forever but I wish they didn't always have to worry about protecting me.

I'm a physical blend of my parents. Five-five with mahogany brown hair that tends to gain blonde highlights during the summer. My eyes are a darker violet than my mother's.

Though I've always been athletic like Dad, the way I deal with others is like Mom.

I like the description of *coltish* my parents' friends used to describe me. Built for speed and endurance, stronger than I look, with a love of running and a hint of wildness.

It fits me.

Wanting to attend college in another state resulted in a battle of epic proportions that wore me out the entire summer before I embarked on my first sojourn outside their line of sight.

I was in the second semester of my freshman year when I realized the man I'd noticed watching me was an additional bodyguard they hired.

It became obvious when a group of men waylaid me on my daily jog around the campus.

I'm trained in self-defense. Since I could walk, the panicked discussions between my parents ensured I'm able to assist in my own protection.

However, no matter how well-trained I am, the sheer

number of large males intent on making the *rich little virgin play nice* would have overwhelmed me eventually.

I tried to reason with them. Their mistake was in coming at me one at a time. *Idiots.* That never works in Kung Fu movies. I ended up taking out three with blows to throat, knee, and balls but they tired of waiting.

As one tackled me painfully to the ground, a man landed in their midst, sweaty from his jog not far behind me. He wore running shoes and basketball shorts.

Despite the situation, I found myself *stunned* by the site of his bare chest, lean muscles, and body movements as he took down the rest of my attackers.

He'd been magnificent to watch.

Only when all seven were cuffed with zip ties pulled from an ankle pouch did he call campus security. They arrived and took my statement without seeming all that concerned.

He guided me gently but firmly to my dorm room and I wasn't surprised that the team I'd taken when I left Texas seemed lost and overwhelmed at the top of the trail.

I recognized several people I'd interacted with in the past weeks dealing with my staff and knew they belonged with the man beside me. In my room, he made a call and kept me away from windows and doors.

With nothing better to do, I studied his physique. *Outstanding.* It was the word that played through my mind as he worked to reassure my father over the phone. Well-defined muscle covered in beautiful golden skin enthralled me.

His voice was like honey and though I couldn't place his accent, it caused a shiver up my spine.

I knew I'd never tire of staring at him or listening to him. He didn't leave my side until my parents arrived hours later.

I was glad.

A few days later, my parents escorted me to the luxury high rise my father purchased the summer before not far from my campus and handed me the keys to the six-bedroom, four-bath penthouse equipped with everything one could need or want.

Stepping from the dedicated elevator, my new protection detail stood waiting to meet me.

Unlike the other men and women assigned to me over the years, they wore casual clothes. Mostly jeans and t-shirts.

My eyes met those of the man who'd saved me and it was the first time he allowed it. His eyes were a lovely blue-green. I swallowed hard as my face blushed hot.

"Ellie, this is Hyde. He'll be your personal bodyguard. He and the rest of his team will live here with you."

"H-hello. Officially," I managed.

"Hello, Ellie."

He smiled and for the first time in a long time, I felt my age. Living with me, going everywhere with me.

That wouldn't be distracting at all.

My dad made introductions, unaware of the instant visceral reaction I had to the man who led them.

"This is Fiaaz. He'll be your driver."

I recognized him from a couple of interactions on campus. He was really lean and elegant with a beautiful face, dark hair, and pale green eyes. I nodded shyly.

"Si will be your personal chef."

I grinned. A few weeks before, he'd started serving me personally in the school café. Only a couple of inches taller than me, nothing was wasted on his frame. Sparkling black eyes matched his smile.

"Your new housekeeper is Bianca."

Her body told me she'd use the in-home gym more than I ever would. She looked like a model from Northern Europe. Very tall, lean, and stunning. Blonde hair and ice blue eyes completed a lovely package.

I smiled. "You've been around the dorm the last weeks.

"Some bugs and cameras. All sorted." Her voice was flavored with a lyrical South African accent.

"Naturally, we brought Padme to maintain her function as your personal assistant. We thought a familiar face would help you feel more comfortable in a new place with a new team."

I was happy to see Padme again. She was with me through high school. I pretended not to know she was as proficient with guns as she was with technology.

Her prominent almond-shaped brown eyes and glossy black hair were nothing compared to her ability to look elegant in any situation.

Mom told me happily, "Ellie, this is *your* team. The men and women assigned to your protection exclusively. No more cycling unfamiliar faces through your life all the time. You can get to *know* them. Won't that be nice?"

Nodding, I took a deep breath. "I'm sure hanging out with a teenager is going to provide levels of adventure previously unimagined."

Feeling strangely stressed, I took in the men and women who were still and quiet as they watched me.

"Thanks for being here. I'll try not to be any trouble. You're obviously good at what you do but your lives are about to get *really* boring."

I rubbed my palm over my heart and said quietly, "I just wanted to go to college like a normal person. I should've stayed in Texas." Shaking my head, I dropped my hand. "You didn't have to do all this, Dad. I'll go home if you want."

"No, Ellie." Dad held my shoulder and lifted my face. He was always gentle with me. "You were *right* to want to spread your wings. It was wrong of us to fight you. We can't keep you locked away on the estate."

He stroked my hair back and kissed my forehead. "Resisting the knowledge that you're an adult now doesn't make it any less true. Let us keep you safe. That's all I ask."

"This is fine. This is good. Thank you."

"It's going to be so much *fun*, Ellie," Mom said.

I rubbed my temples. "Your optimism is kind of daunting, Mom." Turning to the men and women watching me, I said, "I'm glad no one's wearing tactical gear or suits. It'll make it easier to pretend I was the underdog picked to lure the awkward nerd demographic to some reality show."

"Ellie!" My mom looked horrified.

"Trust me, it's better."

"Elliana Fields! You are *not* an awkward nerd."

"I love that you can't see it. Look."

I went to stand in front of my team and turned to face my parents. Padme and Si were the closest to me in height but all of them were at least ten years older with incredible good looks and an air of capability.

Shrugging, I told her, "It's all good, Mom. We'll blend a little better. Walking into poles and stuff while I'm reading probably won't change."

To Padme, I said, "Do you need to brief me on my new schedule?" She nodded. "Give me an hour and everyone feel free to relax."

I gestured for my parents to show me around. "Let's check out my new room. This place is lovely. I like what you did with the light and color."

Rattling on without listening to my questions or the answers, I let them show me to my bedroom. It had an office space to one side.

When we were alone, Mom asked, "Are you alright?"

"A little tired but everything is great. Don't worry."

Dad offered, "Let us take you to dinner…"

"I can't get any further behind. Let's do dinner tomorrow."

The moment Mom and Dad took their leave, I went over my itinerary with Padme and synchronized our calendars.

I grabbed my laptop and went downstairs. Sitting cross-legged on the floor in front of the long balcony wall, I got to work.

"Ellie?" Hyde's voice made me swallow hard before I glanced up. "Do you have any questions?"

Shaking my head, I told him, "I know the drill. I won't leave alone and no one will show up. Just…do whatever it is you usually do."

He crouched beside me and it was disconcerting to have him so close. "I imagine you've seen a lot of staff in your life."

"Yes. I…new people every year." His hair was gilded from the sun. I was completely flustered.

For a long moment, he didn't say anything. Simply watched me. He maintained incredible stillness.

"We're with you at least ten years."

Nothing could have shocked me more. I whispered, "Really?" He nodded and I glanced down at my notebook, tapping my pen against it.

"That will be different. Padme has been with me for four years. That's the longest other than my martial arts instructor. H-he died when I was a sophomore in high school." I swallowed hard. "He trained me from age three."

"That explains your skills."

I met his eyes, taken aback by the compliment. "He wasn't with me all the time. I trained with him twice a week."

The smile he gave me was slow. "We'll be spending quite a bit more time together than that. I'll let you get back to work but let me know if you need anything."

I nodded with a blush and watched him stand. "Hyde?" He paused. "Where are you from? I can't place your accent."

Tilting his head, he replied, "Originally Australia. I haven't thought about it for a decade."

"You must have traveled a lot. Now that I know, I can hear it." I cleared my throat. "Thanks. I get a paragraph about everyone but it's all about skills." Shrugging, I added, "I don't care so much about that. You wouldn't be here if you weren't skilled and everything. I was…curious."

"Feel free to ask me anything, Ellie." He smiled. "I'll leave you to it. I didn't mean to distract you."

Then he was gone and I found myself staring out over the city without seeing it. I wondered where my parents found the people they hired.

As with everyone who came before my current team, I was given a single paragraph and told they *checked out*. As if their criminal background or level of training were all I'd find interesting.

Australia. It explained why Hyde looked like he'd just come in from riding the waves.

Ten *years* with the same staff never seemed possible. I felt such relief, I couldn't have explained it if asked. I got back to work and tried not to dwell on my new bodyguard.

Padme touched my shoulder after several hours. I was surprised to realize the sun had set. I blinked dazedly.

"You need to eat, Ellie. Are you at a stopping place?"

I nodded and shoved everything into my laptop bag. She led the way to the dining area. A single place was set at one end of a table that sat ten.

I whispered, "Five other people living here but eating alone anyway. Okay."

"We thought you'd want privacy, Ellie." My assistant frowned.

"Yeah. I don't have enough of that. It's fine. Thanks." I picked up the plate. "I'll just, I'll work in my room. I need to finish this essay anyway."

"Ellie…"

"I'll see you later. Tell Si thanks for making dinner." I walked to my room and closed the door quietly.

I managed to eat some of the food but waited a long time to take the plate to the kitchen. I didn't want to run into anyone. Dumping the uneaten food, I washed my plate, took a bottle of water from the fridge, and returned to my room.

After wrapping up my homework and a long shower, I turned in for the night. It took me forever to fall asleep.

* * *

The next morning, Padme knocked on my bedroom door and murmured, "Are you awake, Ellie?"

"Yes."

"Breakfast is ready when you are."

With a sigh, I met her in the hall and followed her downstairs.

Turning the corner to the dining room, I was shocked that every member of my staff was present. The table was filled with food and a place was set for each of us.

They felt sorry for me. I knew that but I didn't care. I was stupidly grateful for the company.

Loneliness was my constant companion.

Taking a seat, I greeted each person softly and they returned it. After filling a plate, I ate quietly.

Unless one of them spoke to me directly, I was happy to listen to them, to watch them interact. Each of their tones and accents were so different. They were at ease with one another and within ten minutes, I knew I'd like them as people.

It was my first day living with my dedicated security team.

Their leader was the source of an outrageously inappropriate crush on my part that started the day I first noticed him.

This new arrangement should be interesting.

Chapter Two

May 2009

Settling into a routine with five highly-trained mercenaries was easier than one might imagine.

I maintained a heavy course load in hopes of achieving my dual masters in political science and social work within four years.

The moment Mom and Dad agreed to let me attend the college I wanted, I was determined to make it as quick and painless as possible for them.

Academics came easily to me and I gave the credit for that to my smart parents who hired multi-lingual nannies and other staff always willing to make learning a game for me.

Fluent in Spanish and French, I utilized language in the work I did for my parents. I'd held a formal position within the umbrella organization since I was sixteen and it wasn't done for appearances. I knew the corporate workings inside and out but my strength was the charity division.

Since I was very young, being part of the efforts with those less fortunate gave me an insight I might have missed otherwise.

I was glad for the knowledge.

Working with children has always been a special joy of mine. When my official freshman year came to an end, I was excited to get back to it full-time.

My team shut down the penthouse for the summer and we traveled together to my childhood home in northeast Texas.

Elysian Fields was a captivating estate.

Designed to mimic the multi-winged homes made famous during Regency England, it wrapped around a central courtyard that was part garden, part driveway.

Soft ivory stone gave it a castle feel and the wide stone balconies on every floor lent a welcoming air.

I was shocked but pleased to learn my parents had commissioned a large guest house almost a mile from the main house for my personal use.

It wasn't easy for them to grant me such freedom and I loved that they went to such lengths to compromise.

Having Hyde's bedroom right outside mine was a new form of torture. I came to see it as a good kind of pain.

If I couldn't sleep due to a thought racing around in my brain, I'd head downstairs and enjoy the media room my parents were thoughtful enough to include in the house plans.

Often, Hyde ended up startling the shit out of me by appearing at the end of the couch. The conversations that followed on such nights were always similar.

"Are you alright, Ellie?"

"Yes. I couldn't sleep. You don't have to stay up. The guys

secured the downstairs."

"Are you going to watch a movie?" I always nodded because while I might not watch television, I was a movie junkie. Then he'd come around and take a seat at the opposite end of the sectional. "I'll watch with you."

"I don't want to keep you up, Hyde. You can't work around the clock because my brain doesn't shut up."

He'd smile, place his weapon on the cushion beside him, and say, "What are we watching?"

Sometimes I'd fall asleep and wake up to him crouched beside me, pulling a blanket over my body. Knowing he'd return to the other end of the couch always made me pretend to go right back to sleep rather than go upstairs.

I'm a silly woman-child.

For the most part, I settled smoothly into my life on the estate. Riding, swimming, and the charity work I loved filled many hours and my team could relax a bit more on the secured grounds. I loved that they laughed more and teased each other.

Si offered to teach me to cook and I blushed as I told him, "I've never cooked anything."

"I can change that. It's relaxing to prepare food. I think you'll enjoy how it makes you feel."

With a smile, I told him, "I'd like that."

The man was beyond patient as he explained basic terms other people probably knew by the age of ten. He was right that I enjoyed the learning that was so different from what

I was used to trying to master.

I messed up a lot and even set the oven on fire once. He'd wink and tell me, "We will start again."

Hyde and Padme usually joined us in the kitchen and my assistant laughed more than I'd ever heard and it made me happy.

Having my bodyguard in my peripheral vision was when I made my biggest mistakes. He so easily distracted me.

The first time I completed a fully edible meal, I thought I'd throw up waiting for my team to taste it. Wringing my hands, I lowered carefully onto the edge of my chair and watched as they sipped the French onion soup.

"Holy shit, Ellie. Wonderful." Bianca winked at me and the others all nodded in agreement over my simple accomplishment. "Did you make the bread, too?" I nodded. "It's delicious."

When everyone looked close to done with the soup, I jumped up and ran in the kitchen to grab the second course of blackened mahi-mahi steaks I flew in from Florida.

Plating each serving from the warming oven like Si showed me, he joined me to help and bumped my hip with his. "It's all good, Ellie. Breathe. It's just food."

"I'm so nervous. No one has ever eaten food I made before and…" I giggled nervously. "Okay. Breathing."

He grinned and we took the plates to the dining room. Everyone moaned in pleasure.

"It's official, Ellie," Padme said as she chewed slowly.

"You're good at anything you put your mind to."

I laughed. "Hardly."

"Eat, Ellie. Everything is outstanding." The words from Hyde made me look at him.

In a whisper, I said, "I'm nervous. I'll eat later. I want you guys to eat."

"Have you tasted it yet?" I shook my head. He picked up my fork, cut a piece of the fish on his plate, and held it out for me. Eyes wide, I leaned forward and ate it. "Excellent, right?"

I smiled shyly.

"Enjoy the fruits of your labor." Over my shoulder, he nodded at Si. A filled plate was placed in front of me. "Eat with us, Ellie."

I felt like someone handed me something I didn't know I needed as I ate a meal I prepared with the men and women who kept me safe.

Most of the time, I thought of them as my friends. Sometimes, I even considered them my own little family.

I know it made me juvenile but it was how I felt.

Chapter Three

June 2009

The summer following my first year of college, I turned nineteen and met a little boy named Preston.

Dressed in khaki shorts and a t-shirt, wearing sneakers with my hair in a ponytail, I circulated through the small fair I'd arranged at the local Boys & Girls Club to benefit poor and disabled children within twenty square miles.

My team dressed in similar clothing, sunglasses over their eyes, and I was moved at their efforts not to look dangerous or intimidating.

With gentle rides, games, and assorted entertainment alongside quiet spaces where those with autism could calm and regroup, the day was filled with activities for children who didn't always have a lot in their lives.

Laughter and time to feel like kids for a little while.

It was a test project I wanted to duplicate at their centers all over the country. It provided positive exposure to my parents' holdings but I honestly didn't care about that part.

I stood to the side as a man from the local zoo talked to a group of children and guardians about the miniature monkey he held in his arms when a small hand took mine.

Glancing down, I smiled at a little boy and crouched so I could be at his level. I pushed my shades on top of my head.

"Hello. I'm Ellie."

"P'eston." He held cotton candy in his other hand and offered me some. I pinched off a piece and ate it before showing him how it changed the color of my tongue.

Then he laughed, eyes sparkling, and I was *smitten*.

Throughout the day, I held his hand and took him from exhibit to exhibit, feeding and talking to him as the woman charged with his supervision filled me in on his case.

Preston was HIV positive. Born crack-addicted, he'd sustained severe abuse at the hands of his biological mother until one too many blows rendered him mentally disabled.

The little boy lived in a home located less than *ten miles* from my parents' estate. The facility specialized in kids with severe mental and physical problems.

There were times Preston experienced seizures and had trouble breathing. He was six-years-old and everything that could have gone wrong in his short life certainly had.

Several hours later, he was clearly tired as he swayed on his feet. I picked him up and he came willingly which made my heart expand with happiness. He laid his head on my shoulder and I rubbed his back.

To Padme, I said, "Please get all relevant details about his case. Make sure Miss Daniels has my contact information."

To the social worker, I said firmly, "No matter my family's resources, I'm fully aware I can't save *every* child. However,

I can save *this* one. Keep me informed and I'll be in touch."

At the end of the day, I placed him in the van and buckled him up. "I'll see you soon, Preston. It was so nice to meet you."

"Lee-Lee, I like you."

"I like you, too. Did you have fun?"

He reached out and stroked sticky fingers over my cheek. "I like you, Lee-Lee."

I nodded and kissed his forehead. A few minutes later, I watched as the van pulled away.

Without looking at my assistant, I told her, "Get me a meeting with Mom's attorney, please. I want to see him Monday."

"Ellie…?"

"I know the risks. I can help one little boy. I can do more than give him a day of fun. I can make sure he has a home, medical care, safety, and love."

"I was going to say you're one of the most wonderful people I've ever met in my life." Her slight Indian accent was musical. I glanced at her in surprise. "I'll make the arrangements. If either biological parent is living, you'll have lots of red tape."

I nodded. "Worth it."

Turning to head back to the festivities, I met Hyde's eyes. "I bet cotton candy and balloon animals are new for you."

"I've *never* seen such happy children." He gestured over the field. "This is what you do with your time and resources. That's incredible, Ellie."

Shrugging, I explained, "There's plenty of stupid rich girls in the news for drinking, drugs, and sex tapes. I figure I'll leave them to it. I have better things to do."

I circulated through the crowd with Hyde never more than a foot from me.

Several of the regular vendors and clients of the umbrella corporation sponsored the attractions and one of them was a dunk tank with a laughing young girl who went in and out of the water.

Toward the end of the day, the MC said, "Miss Ellie Fields!" I turned to the stage. "If you go agree to be dunked, you'll receive the following check for the charity of your choice."

They brought out a six-foot check for a hundred thousand dollars. Instantly, I knew where that money would go and took a step toward the tank.

Hyde touched my arm and said quietly, "You'll be too exposed, Ellie."

"The glass is bulletproof. If they hadn't hit six figures I wasn't going to do it." He frowned. "I'll be fine. It's also about a thousand degrees out here and I couldn't enjoy the kiddie water park."

He shadowed me as I walked to the chamber. I waved at the staff for the center as well as several parents and social workers I knew personally who chanted my name.

I handed him my cell phone and took off my sneakers and socks. "If no one hits, have one of the team dunk me. They need to see me soaked." With a wink, I climbed the ladder.

The MC announced, "Miss Fields provided this wonderful day for our local kids and is about to raise additional funds for charities right here in our region. Let's have a little music."

There were a few kids lined up with buckets of balls. It was the fourth girl's third attempt that sent me plummeting into the water with a laughing scream. I came up and slicked my hair back, smiling at the girl through the glass.

"You did it!" She went from shocked to smiling. Hyde helped me out and I almost fell on him from the slippery ladder. "Lord, don't hand me my phone."

Padme wrapped a towel around me but I knew the Texas heat would have me dry in under half an hour.

"One hundred thousand dollars, Miss Fields! Raised for local children's charities. Come on up here!"

I posed for photos and would never tire of seeing Hyde standing behind me in them.

Taking the microphone, I addressed the crowd. "I want to thank everyone for coming out. I'm excited to see what we accomplish over the next five years in our corner of the world. Please make sure you get your goodie bags and enjoy the rest of the day."

Waving as the crowd applauded, I shook the MC's hand and those of the vendors who'd donated the check.

I spent several minutes schmoozing them because it wouldn't be the last time I asked them for substantial amounts of money.

Through it all, Preston consumed my thoughts.

I'd met hundreds of children over the years but he instantly found his way into my heart.

Glancing toward the setting sun, I was lost in thought as Hyde said, "That's the last of it, Ellie."

"Sorry. I was woolgathering as my very precise grandmother used to say."

"Everyone is settled. You're sunburned. Let's get you home and Padme will follow up."

I nodded and allowed him to lead me to the car. As I leaned against the seat, I said tiredly, "It went well. I think the kids really loved it."

"No doubt."

I dozed and woke as we pulled into the driveway. I showered and changed clothes, heading downstairs to join my team at the table with damp hair, in shorts and a tank top.

Opening a notebook beside me made my assistant grin. "Refreshed, revived, and thinking big thoughts."

Chuckling, I nodded. "I want to coordinate an event at the facility where Preston lives. I talked with his social worker and it's too dangerous to take some of the kids who live there out. Their conditions won't allow it. I'd like to deliver some fun right to their door."

"That's a *great* idea."

I picked at the light meal Si prepared after a day in the sun.

My team contributed to the conversation as I made notes. I appreciated their interactions and ideas.

I liked and respected each of them greatly.

Chapter Four

July 2009

Dressing for the event I put together, I went over my notes. The night would raise funds for residents of a large Dallas apartment complex gutted by fire the prior fall.

Two residents died and gross negligence by the slumlord who owned the place for decades came to light during the investigation.

My father purchased the land, leveled the destruction, and built new, bigger residences in the same space. Better, safer, and constructed of environmentally friendly materials, it made me incredibly proud of him.

We cut the ribbon on the new residences for low income families a few days before and I was charged with raising money to help the tenants with furniture, household goods, clothing, and basics for the families displaced for almost a year.

I took in my appearance with a nod and went out to join my staff. The concert I arranged didn't start for several hours but I wanted to get to the venue extra early.

"Oh, Ellie. How lovely you look!" my assistant exclaimed.

Embarrassed, I shrugged. "It's the local style." I tugged at the t-shirt under my plaid over-shirt and shifted my weight between my booted feet.

Padme laughed. "You *run* everywhere. Sneakers are required."

Every member of my detail wore jeans and either t-shirts or button-down shirts. They wore various boot styles.

All of them would blend in well.

We piled into the limo borrowed from my parents for the extra room and drove into Dallas proper. The arena was already bustling and I wasn't surprised. I booked the stadium but it was the band who agreed to perform that filled it.

Piling out at the staff entrance, I made my way through the winding hallways and knocked on a door.

It swung wide and a big man with tattoos stood there. Hyde stiffened and stepped closer to me.

"It's okay, Hyde. You didn't get a chance to meet Brooke and her group last year. This is Rex Black, Brooke's…um."

The man with laughing black eyes supplied, "You can call me her *boyfriend* despite not looking the part." He leaned forward and kissed my cheek. "Good to see you again, Ellie. How's college?"

"Hectic but rewarding. Is she decent?"

He quirked a black brow. "America's *sweetheart*? Always."

"Is that Ellie? Girl, get in here so I can hug you!"

Rex stepped back with a smile and I introduced the

members of my team. I left them to chat and entered the space where a hyper redhead worked to straighten Brooke Kincaid's hair.

She was one of the most naturally pretty women I'd ever met.

"Hey there, honey. You remember everyone?"

"Of course. It's so great to see you again. I've been watching the band's meteoric rise. Congratulations. I knew you were going to break record sales worldwide with that last album." Bending, I pressed our cheeks together. "You look fantastic. How have you been?"

"Crazy busy but my little group keeps me sane."

Sidney rolled her eyes. "This bitch. She keeps insulting me like that and I'm going to singe off a chunk of her hair."

I laughed happily. Sidney had no filter, unlimited energy, and said *fuck* a lot. I found her awesome. "Thank you for doing this, Brooke. I know you just came off your second tour and hesitated to ask…"

"Don't you give it another thought! We're happy to do it. The studio is a couple miles from where y'all rebuilt those apartments. The bosses pledged a fat check as well. It's the least we can do." The singer glanced past me. "Catch me up on what's happening with you. I noticed your new security and lord, girl…*fine*."

I blushed to the roots of my hair.

Sidney snickered. "He could be your older brother, Brooke." Lowering her voice, she added, "I think Ellie is *aware* of how pretty he is. Can I get you some ice, hon?"

"Don't torture me, Sidney," I murmured softly.

"How will you know I *like* you if I don't? Huh? Tell me that!" She put down the flat iron and skipped around Brooke. Making a sudden strike move in my direction, I barely blocked it before she connected. "Still quick. Good to know. You can't only depend on the smoking hot dude beside you."

"You'll give him a heart attack." Hyde pressed against my back and frowned at the redhead over my shoulder. "Hyde is my…the head of my protection detail."

Stoically, he said, "I'd prefer you *not* hit Miss Fields."

The redhead blinked before looking at me. "Oh *shit*." I started to reassure her. "Did you hear that fucking *accent*? Deadly, pretty, and an *accent*…triple threat. Props, Ellie."

Clearing my throat, I spoke to my bodyguard without looking at him. "Sidney and I sparred last year when the storms wiped out the roads. The band stayed at the estate for a few days. She's self-taught in *everything*."

"Hmm." It was all Hyde said and Sidney's smile was slow.

"I *like* him." She put one hand on her hip. "We should *definitely* spar. My men might not like me getting sweaty with such a hottie but I'm so *curious*."

"No." To cover my immediate response, I told her, "Hyde is…different than what you're used to. I don't want Boyd and Zane to deal with that kind of stress."

She winked at me. "Intriguing."

"Sidney is our resident reflex tester." Rex took up a position behind Brooke. "She randomly checks everyone but Brooke and the kids. We stay on our toes."

Taking in my team positioned against the wall and to Hyde at my side, he added, "Your parents went top shelf."

"My team is amazing and I appreciate that you know that." I crossed my arms. "How's Chicago?"

"We head back this week. This one doesn't stop." Rex stroked his palms over Brooke's shoulders. "Talk her into a vacation for me, will you?"

"I'll try but she's a workaholic. If you can't get her to slow down by Christmas, bring her to the estate for a few days and I'll keep her riding until she passes out."

"An outstanding plan." He grinned. "I think it would be good for you, too. I don't know where you two find the energy."

Brooke tilted her head back and stared at Rex upside down. "I know where I get mine." He dropped a kiss on her lips. "See? I'm charging."

"Guests, pretty girl." She laughed and Rex glanced up. "I think you need to spend time with the girls, Ellie. Let's plan it after the first of the year. Alright?"

I nodded. Hyde brought a chair and nudged me into it while Sidney finished Brooke's hair and makeup.

Padme left to find Jeanette and check the venue. I wanted to know everything was going according to plan.

Once the country music singer was ready, dressed in black leather, boots, and a cowboy hat, she pulled me to the couch to chat.

"Where're the kids?" I thought to ask.

"Mack and Buzz have them until show time." The blonde laughed happily. "The girls had a list of things to do when we were back down south. They say Chicago isn't friendly."

I quirked a brow. "Not as *backwards* so…there's that."

"Preach." We bumped fists.

The days the band spent at Elysian Fields were some of the happiest and least lonely of my whole life.

Brooke, Sidney, and Jeanette were close to me in age and the singer understood what it was like to be in the spotlight but still isolated.

There was a sharp tap and the door swung wide at the same time. Hyde moved in front of me faster than I thought possible.

"Well…*shit.*"

Unsure which of the Bradshaw brothers spoke, their eyes went wide as they were surrounded by Bianca, Fiaaz, and Si.

I jumped off the couch. "They're the other members of Broken Bronco!" I stepped around Hyde.

The twins wolf-whistled when they saw me and I pointed my finger at them.

"Stop it. This is Logan and Decklan Bradshaw, brothers and founding members of the band. Guys, this is my team."

I went through names and wondered why Hyde stood so

close to my back.

"Ellie. Ellie. Ellie. How *pretty* you are, honey," Logan said as he bent to kiss the corner of my mouth.

Decklan kissed the other side. "Let us take you to dinner and flirt shamelessly with your fine self. How's that sound?"

I smiled and put my hands on their cheeks. "I already booked a place for all of us to have dinner, I'm not a groupie, and now isn't the time to sow your oats."

They leaned into the touch and each put a hand on my waist with a sigh. "Would beggin' help?"

"Nope," I replied softly. I moved my hands to their shoulders before dropping them. "How's your mama?"

I watched them catch their balance and ached for what I knew of their pasts.

Decklan said, "You remembered. She's doing real good, Ellie. She appreciated the nurse you sent while she was going through physical therapy. The woman was amazing."

"It's not every day a woman almost gets crushed by a five-hundred-year-old oak tree that falls out of the ground due to flooding. I'm glad she's on the mend. Tell her I said hello."

They took a synchronized step forward, close enough that my breasts almost touched their chests.

Logan smiled slow. "You *sure* you won't come out and play, Ellie? We'd be perfect gentlemen."

"Still no," I replied.

Decklan winked. "You're so damn stimulating."

I arched a brow. "You need more rejection in your lives. It makes you strong." Tilting my head, I added softly, "It helps you appreciate the good things when they come your way."

They stared at me for a long moment before bending to kiss my cheeks and murmur, "Right as always, brilliant Ellie."

"You can do this."

They nodded, stepped back, and announced to the room of people watching our interaction closely, "About ten minutes to mic check. See you out there, Miss Kincaid. Miss Fields."

Touching the brims of their hats, the twins nodded at me and left the room.

Sidney was instantly right beside me. "Let them pet you, Ellie. You were good for them when things went sideways."

Staring at the closed door, I said quietly, "They were trying to beat it. I'm easy to spend time with because I don't act like their fans. There's no pressure to perform." I bumped shoulders with her. "Stop trying to corrupt me."

"Walk on the wild side. I love it. Two is the magic number."

I shook my head with a grin. "I can't even handle one."

The redhead sighed heavily. "If people would let me *work*, they'd be so happy."

"Or in jail. That's another option."

"Details."

***

Spending time with the people Brooke Kincaid surrounded herself with was like a breath of fresh air.

After the wildly successful concert ended, the band returned to the stage twice and sang several encores. They asked fans to give generously at the kiosks set up at the exits and reminded everyone that it was a worthy cause they needed to get behind.

I loved their music. I deeply respected those who sang it.

I rented an entire restaurant after closing so we'd have security and privacy. It was good to see all the couples together and catch up with Brooke's younger siblings.

We laughed all night.

As the sun lightened the sky, I hugged them all tightly.

I told Brooke, "Thank you for doing this. You let me know what you need. Anything. You name it."

"Your friendship, Ellie. You're giving those families a new lease on life. I'm proud to be part of it."

Hugging Rex, he hugged me back extra tight. "Take care of yourself, Ellie. These are the people to help you do that."

"Thank you." I cut my eyes to Brooke and back to him.

"Not yet. I need to know it's right for her," he murmured.

Holding one of his big hands in both of mine, I said, "That was last year. Don't wait too long. Take care of each other."

"Always."

The Bradshaw brothers hugged me hard between them. "Don't be a stranger, Ellie."

They kissed my jaw on either side at the same time and I gave a small gasp. "You're doing so well. Another few months and you'll have your *one year* clean. You can do this. Don't cave now after you've worked so hard."

Sighing heavily, they gave me half smiles and Logan said, "You'd be good for us, Ellie."

"Sobriety and self-control. They're worth fighting for and you're going to love your life being in your control again. You've proven you're strong enough. Don't quit now."

They nodded, hugged me between them, and let me go.

One more kiss for Brooke and I let my team hustle me into the limo. Padme sat directly across from me, staring at me intently.

"I don't remember the twins being so...forward last year."

"Substance abuse was the bigger issue then. Physically, they were wrecked. Now that the drugs have worked their way from their systems, the lifestyle they used to lead is probably becoming the greater concern."

Blinking several times, my assistant asked, "Sex addiction?"

"Rampant, completely out of control. It could have derailed their career." I cleared my throat. "It lost them a good woman. Anyone they choose now will pale in comparison. She's the only one they'll ever want and...she's no longer an option."

"Brooke." I nodded. "Wow."

"They have a long road ahead and I'll be their friend. They can beat their demons if they keep their focus. That's what matters. I can't get involved romantically. I might not know much but I know not to accept being a winner by default."

Hyde sat closer to me than usual and the subtle scent of him drifted over me. The warmth of his leg pressed along mine was new and different.

I didn't mind. Not even a little. Hyde could never be *too* close for my comfort.

Chapter Five

August 2009

Since the children's fair at the Boys and Girls Club, I worked steadily through the bureaucratic nonsense required to become Preston's guardian.

My ultimate goal was to adopt him and I was glad my parents were fully behind my decision.

I spent as much time with him as I could, as much as I was allowed, and arranged events with every resident to have more opportunities.

While I waited to clear the way, I made sure his facility received personal attention from our organization.

We upgraded the building and grounds, brought in additional staff that specialized in physical and emotional therapies, and did an overhaul on their amenities to improve the lives of the children in their care.

No matter what happened, the property was practically in our back yard. They needed our help and I wanted to make sure they'd always have it. Seeing the mental and physical state of their charges made it imperative.

Two weeks before I was due to leave for California, I considered withdrawing and transferring to a Texas school.

I wanted to be on hand when I was approved to take Preston home with me. I consulted with his doctor and social worker about everything I'd need to have available for his condition.

Mom interviewed medically trained nannies who could help in an emergency.

On my way to the stables one morning, I was deep in thought when my phone rang. I fished it from my back pocket.

"Ellie Fields."

"Miss Fields." It was Preston's social worker. "I'm sorry to have to call you like this but…Preston died last night."

Gripping the phone, I ground out, "No. It's a *lie.*"

"I'm so sorry, Miss Fields. He died in his sleep. Initial results seem to point to an undetected blood clot. The doctor believes it's been there since his final beating two years ago."

I held myself up on the fence around my house. "I don't understand! It can't be true. I saw him yesterday!"

"His monitor went off and they went to him immediately but he was already gone. They tried for several minutes to revive him but the paramedics called time of death when they arrived. I know it doesn't help but he was smiling and holding that little stuffed turtle you gave him at the zoo."

As the reality hit me, I told her through my tears, "I'll handle his arrangements."

The woman stammered nervously, "H-his mother said she

didn't care what we did with his body."

Crying harder, I lost my composure completely. "I fucking *care*! I'll take him. He deserves to be remembered. Make it *happen*, Miss Daniels!"

Hanging up on the flustered social worker, I returned to the house with a worried Fiaaz and Bianca at my sides.

Slamming into the house, I released a bloodcurdling scream that brought every member of my staff running. Hyde's gun was in his hand.

I know I didn't make any sense in my hysterics. I screamed at my assistant, "You make them *give him* to me, Padme. He's not going in some fucking pauper's grave! You tell my parents to steal his body if necessary."

Then I ran upstairs, slammed my door, and sobbed until I lost consciousness.

Throat raw, eyes swollen, it was my mother's voice that brought me awake. She was stretched out on her side, holding my hand.

"Mom. He *died*, Mom. My little Preston…"

"I know, honey. I'm so, so sorry." I cried for a long time and she held me hard.

My parents didn't judge me. My team didn't judge me.

I walked around for days unable to stop endless tears for the little boy I wanted so badly. Preston's death hit me hard and I had him interred on the estate.

In his coffin, I placed the stuffed animal along with two dozen photos, a flashlight, and a bag of cotton candy. I know I probably seemed like a stupid kid.

"I love you and I'll miss you. I'll miss your *laugh*." I caught myself on a sob. "I wanted to make your life better, a bit more bearable, to fill it with love and happiness. I'm so sorry I didn't get the chance, Preston. I'm sorry."

At my side, Hyde wrapped his arm around my shoulders and whispered, "You *did* make it better, Ellie. The way he thought about time was different than how you perceive it. The time you spent with him, the moments you shared, those overwrote the horrible things that happened to him. It's why he was smiling at the end. He was thinking about you."

Through painful tears, I told him, "Th-thank you, Hyde. I-I hope you're right. I failed."

"No, Ellie. You gave him more joy in *weeks* than he'd had all his life. Remember how happy he was when he was with you. He loved you and he felt your love."

I nodded and let him lead me out of the mausoleum and back to my house. The entire team followed us. My parents walked among them and I could hear my mother crying.

It made me love her so much more.

A few days later, hurting in my heart, I returned to school in California and settled into our well-established routine.

My loneliness crushed me.

* * *

Steeped in my own grief, when one of my few friends suffered a loss that almost killed her, I went to her side. She returned to her childhood home to heal a heart in tatters.

Our sadness, our loss, was different.

She was broken as a woman and I mourned the loss of a little boy I already considered my *son* in my private thoughts.

Holding hands, crying together, started the healing process for me. I'd always be thankful for her strength in her moment of darkest pain. I hope I helped her in return.

I stayed at the farm she grew up on with her brother and sisters for a week. I made a promise to myself to check on her often. We hugged for a long time before I got in the SUV with Hyde beside me.

Padme asked from the front seat, "Are you okay, Ellie?"

Swallowing hard, I stared out the window at southeastern Oklahoma and whispered, "She almost died. Her h-heart broke so badly, she almost starved herself to death."

"She's strong and she's surrounded by people devoted to her healing," Hyde murmured beside me. "They'll keep her safe."

I nodded. "But the loss will still be there." I twisted my fingers together tightly. "The pain…losing what she wanted most in the world. It can be survived but it will never fully heal."

Hyde consumed so many of my thoughts. If I lost him, especially to violence, I wondered if I would survive it.

As my bodyguard untangled my white-knuckled fingers and gently pressed tissue into my palm, I knew I couldn't lose him.

"Everything will be alright, Ellie."

I nodded but I didn't fully believe him.

* * *

Almost a year after my attack on campus, I attended the sentencing of the men responsible. The full weight of my parents' wealth and influence was brought to bear when the remaining five were charged.

While awaiting trial, two of the seven men died. One in a horrific car crash and another from drug overdose.

The unspoken deal was if the men pled guilty to the crime they committed, my parents wouldn't make it their life's work to destroy them.

My folks were apoplectic at the thought of me being subjected to a public proceeding, complete with police photos of my partially unclothed body.

I never stepped into a courtroom. I gave my deposition and it was played at their plea hearing.

They were convinced that doing the right thing – *belatedly* – was the correct course of action. Each received the maximum sentence but since I hadn't sustained severe injuries or technically been raped, they'd be eligible for parole before my graduation.

For me, it was over.

Chapter Six

December 2009

I'll never forget the first Christmas I spent with my team.

We celebrated together Christmas Eve and I insisted on a game of Dirty Santa. No gifts could be more expensive than twenty dollars and Hyde grinned all the way through the local discount store as I picked up silly things for stocking stuffers.

We drank the niche wines I was already accumulating despite being nineteen and we hung out in the kitchen together as Si and I made ridiculous amounts of food.

To keep the others occupied, he placed trays of sugar cookies on the island and instructed the team to decorate them from the dozens of little bowls he laid out. The results were funny but still delicious.

Naturally, I got them other gifts.

I waited until everyone went to bed and slipped handwritten cards telling them how much I appreciated their presence and their protection under their doors.

Inside were Super Bowl tickets and spa weekend gift certificates so each of them could scream at a sporting event I wasn't sure they even liked and have themselves pampered.

Climbing under my blankets, I talked to Preston.

"I always thought nothing happened after death despite my upbringing. I thought it was just over. Meeting you, I hope I'm wrong, Preston. You didn't get long enough. You deserved a long and happy life. Merry Christmas, honey."

The following morning, I showered and dressed quietly. I didn't want to wake anyone. Security from the house would escort me to my parents so we could have an early breakfast before their annual holiday gala.

Opening my bedroom door, I was shocked to see a neat stack of perfect presents on the floor with my name on them.

On top was a card signed by each member of my team. The things they said made me cry long before I sat cross-legged on the floor and opened their gifts.

They gave me several books from favorite authors I hadn't realized were out along with a first edition of two Sherlock Holmes' books I'd been searching for through collectors.

One of them gave me a slim dive watch since I broke my old one and forgot to replace it. A delicate amethyst necklace and earring set in fine silver.

Engraved chopsticks with a note from Si congratulating me on learning to roll sushi.

The last box I opened was from Hyde. Inside was a fine platinum charm bracelet and a note to, "Fill it with experiences that make you smile. Here's one to start you off, Ellie."

I opened the tiny locket and smiled through happy tears at a photo of me with Preston at the zoo.

Glancing up, I grinned at them in their doorways. "Thank you all so much."

"Merry Christmas, Ellie. Thank you for your fantastic gifts. You'll be going with us."

I frowned. "Those are for you guys. I can hang out with my parents. You never take time off."

Hyde approached and bent to help me to my feet. "Watching over you doesn't seem like work. You're going with us." Then he took the charm bracelet out of my hand and attached it around my wrist. "Perfect."

Picking up all my gifts, he placed them on my bed and smiled. "You never forget to make your bed."

"Habit."

"I know it well. Let's get you to your parents."

"I wanted to let everyone sleep in. It's Christmas. You can't work on *Christmas*, Hyde. This whole week, I'll stay up at the main house. I want all of you to have downtime."

"Hmm." He crossed his arms and walked to stand directly in front of me. "Let's talk about this downtime."

"Hyde…"

"Ellie. We've worked together for a decade. The people in this house are my closest friends. They need only ask for time off and I'll make sure you're covered. They haven't asked because you're easy on all of us. You don't even fight reporters and I read that was an American socialite rite of passage."

I laughed. "Pretty much. I can't be bothered."

He winked. "You'd break more than their cameras. The point is, you're a good person. We like hanging out with you whether you need guarding at any particular moment or not." Turning me into the hall, he pulled my door closed behind us. "I'll let you know if there's the slightest ripple of unhappiness."

Inhaling carefully, I nodded. "I'd really like all of you with me for Christmas. You're going to love breakfast."

Each of the team hugged me. It was the most physical contact I'd had from other people at one time ever and I soaked it up. I blushed all the way to the house.

Mom greeted me at the door with kisses all over my face.

Dad walked swiftly from his office to grab me up like a sack of potatoes and spun me around, shouting, "Merry Christmas, my little Ellie elf."

He didn't put me down but carried me through the house to the dining room, bouncing me like he had when I was a kid.

"You gotta stop doing this, Dad. I'm way too big."

"Nonsense. I'll stop when I break a hip."

"That's comforting. Thanks for that." He shook me one more time and put me on my feet with a smacking kiss to my cheek. "I think I'm dizzy."

"Mimosas help with that!" Mom shouted with glee and I realized she'd already had a couple. "You can all crash here tonight if you want to drink." To my team, she added, "You're the closest people to our Ellie and don't think I'm not grateful. I sleep so much better knowing all of you are on the case."

Dad added, "We got you a little something that's small now but growing fast." He took envelopes from his back pocket and handed them to my team, squinting at the names he'd written on the front. "Forgot my glasses."

I should have known my parents wouldn't forget gifts for the people who protected me. They were wonderful about rewarding staff throughout the organization and on the estate.

The envelopes held options in a technology company they purchased the year before that was developing several new devices for the deaf and blind.

Products that would change the world.

Hyde's eyes widened and he looked at my father. "You pay us well for the privilege of guarding your daughter. This isn't necessary, Mr. Fields."

Mom lifted her mimosa. "I disagree!" Realizing how loud she was, she gave a giggle and started again in a whisper. "Our Ellie has never looked so relaxed. That's worth more than you realize. Merry Christmas to each of you and thanks."

I hugged my parents tightly. "I love you guys."

"We love *you*, sweetheart. We're going to make you eat until we have to roll you upstairs to get ready for the party tonight."

By the time we were done with the annual breakfast feast, I truly worried I wouldn't fit in my gown.

Si disappeared into the kitchen to talk with Cook. For years, I'd been asking the woman who ruled over that domain her name.

In a crisp British accent, she always responded, "It is tradition not to use a given name. You will call me Cook."

I always had.

Until Si charmed the woman's name from her and whispered to me later, "Her name is Gladys. Her secret ingredient in your favorite cake is a small spoonful of homemade mayonnaise. I'll continue recon and report."

I laughed for ten minutes.

"Food coma. Oh my god, I can barely keep my eyes open. I'm going to take a disgusting nap like a little kid."

"Do it, Ellie. I bet you still don't sleep enough and we're keeping you up to all hours tonight. Party starts at seven but come down whenever you feel like facing the masses."

I hugged them both and made my way to the suite I'd lived in most of my life. Hyde and Padme saw me to the door.

"I'll wake you in time to get ready, Ellie."

"Thanks. I can't believe how exhausted I am. Way too many carbs." I grinned. "Nap time. Crash for a few hours in the other rooms." I gestured tiredly. "There are…plenty."

* * *

Dropping to sleep the moment I laid my head on the pillow, I startled awake in the late afternoon and raced to my door, throwing it open.

Hyde looked at me. "Are you alright, Ellie?"

"You stood here the whole time?"

"Of course. Are you rested? Padme was going to give you another hour. You have plenty of time."

I blinked up at him. "Hyde. We're in the main house. You don't have to do that. I've always been safe here."

"Yes." He didn't say anything else.

Leaning against the door jamb, I crossed my arms. "I have to think you had the shittiest assignments on the planet. They must have been horribly dangerous, dirty, and awful."

Smiling, he asked, "Why would you think that?"

"You're standing here. Even my parents' personal security doesn't stand outside the door when they're asleep. They have a wonderful seating area down the hall where they can crash and eat, play video games."

Matching my posture on the opposite side of the door, he stared at me for a long time in silence.

"You don't have to work so much, Hyde. I'm okay. I doubt I've ever been safer actually."

"Sleep is when you're most vulnerable. I stand here as much for myself as for you. Your last name, your resources are not what make me glad to do it. It's your actions as a human being. You want to change the world and I believe you're capable of it so I'll stand here, guarding you while your guard is down."

Softly, I said, "Thank you, Hyde."

"You're welcome, Ellie." He straightened. "Padme will be here to help in a while. Do you need anything?"

"I think I'll take a soak. She can come in when she gets here. No rush."

"I'll tell her."

I turned to go back inside and paused to look at him over my shoulder. "I think you're the first person to ever consistently speak to me like an adult. It means a lot to me."

"A woman who puts abused children and displaced families ahead of trips to Vegas to party with friends earns my respect, Ellie. I know your life suffocates you sometimes. Let me know what you need to help with that."

Nodding, I watched him pull my door closed.

I ran a tub and sank into the hot water with a sigh. My thoughts turned to my bodyguard.

It wasn't a new development.

I touched myself with his face in my mind as I so often did in the dark of the night. I sighed his name to the steamy bathroom and imagined his hands touching me.

Until Hyde entered my life, I never wanted a man to touch me.

A quiet, almost desperate, orgasm crashed over my body and I stayed in the water, thinking about the man who inspired it.

It was hard to stand up and walk to my shower, harder still to face my assistant and the object of my quiet obsession without blushing.

Padme kept up a light conversation as she styled my hair and applied makeup. My responses were minimal.

Hyde stood outside my open door and I found myself staring at the part of him I could see in the mirror.

"Ellie?" Padme said gently.

"Yes?" I blushed again, worried she might have figured out what stole my attention.

"Let's get you in your gown."

Dressed in finery for the annual holiday party, I descended the stairs of my childhood home with my team.

For hours, I danced and laughed and talked with the guests invited by my parents to celebrate. Their old friends and colleagues, who'd been a constant fixture in my life.

I kept Hyde in my peripheral vision.

When our eyes met, he smiled and I couldn't help but return it. By the end of the night, my cheeks hurt from smiling.

It was the best Christmas in my memory.

Having so many people I cared about together was better than any physical gift could be. It was the first time I felt as though I was truly healing from Preston's loss.

It was also the night I admitted to myself that I'd fallen deeply in love with Hyde.

No matter how inappropriate, no matter how misplaced…

I loved him.

Chapter Seven

June 2011

During a small break from school, my parents insisted on a family vacation to the Maldives.

I dreaded the idea.

Setting down my fork as I looked at my parents over the smaller and far more comfortable breakfast table, I said quietly, "I'm terrible on vacation. You know that."

"That's because you read the entire time and are nervous to explore." Mom gestured to my team. "Now you have your own posse to explore unfamiliar places."

"Never say *posse* again, Mom. I'm serious. Don't." She laughed. I looked at Hyde and Padme and realized they were looking at me. "It's not a vacation if you're still working."

Directly across from me, Hyde leaned forward and crossed his arms on the table. For a long minute, he didn't speak.

Then he said quietly, "You take no time off. You don't go anywhere that isn't for the charitable organization. The workload you manage for school is outrageous. You need a *vacation*, Ellie. Don't worry about anyone but you. We've traveled. The Maldives are beautiful."

I was unable to look away from his intense gaze until…

"I have *just* the bathing suit for you, Ellie!" The words from my mother terrified me instantly. "I'll order it for you."

Turning my head sharply, I hissed, "Absolutely *not*."

She *hmphed*. "You're from Texas. Home of the debutantes. You gotta shake what your mama gave ya."

I closed my eyes and said quietly, "Dad. Make it stop. I'm begging you. Make. It. Stop." He laughed and I heard barely concealed laughter from Padme at my side. "Mom, listen, I'm not sure what pop culture paraphernalia you've been exposed to recently but you're cut off."

Mom winked. "Pimp my something or club my house or I don't know. When your father was away, I was flipping channels. Some of those shows are train wrecks and I can't look away, Ellie!"

"Take the cable out of your room and don't order me a bathing suit. I'm serious. Your judgment is seriously messed up in that regard." I finished my breakfast and gathered my plate a little while later. I asked with a sigh, "When do we leave?"

Clapping her hands, my mom jumped up and ran around to kiss me. "Tomorrow! Let's just go!"

Frowning, I glanced at my dad. "Is Mom drunk?"

He shrugged. "She's been on a female empowerment thing the last few weeks. Forty years and the woman still takes me by surprise. Let's go with it, Ellie."

I grinned and kissed my mom. "Female empowerment,

huh?"

She nodded happily. "You should have seen your father's face when I did this little…"

Screamed. I *literally* screamed. "I don't know where that sentence is going. I don't want to know. We don't have to be one of those edgy modern families. I like the not knowing, Mom. I'm absolutely *awesome* with not knowing."

Hands on her hips, she said, "I was going to say strip…"

I slammed down my plates and took off running. Hyde and my assistant raced behind me.

We piled into the SUV for the drive to our house. As Padme started the car, she started to laugh.

It was painfully contagious.

* * *

The next morning, we left for the Maldives. My parents found the most incredible resort with homes positioned out in the water. Wooden docks connected them.

I loved it but questioned the security.

Dad pointed below us and I could see divers moving through the crystal-clear water beneath the glass floor.

"What…?" I managed.

"Navy SEALs. The military loaned us a few. Wonderful of them."

I didn't understand my dad's excitement. I backed abruptly from the opening in the floor and bumped into Hyde behind me. He settled his hand on my shoulder.

"These guys will be swimming under the house?"

"Yes. Cool, right?"

"What planet do you hail from and what have you done with my father? No, Dad. That's not *cool*. The whole floor is *open*. How do I change and everything?"

"Honey," Mom popped in, "it's just a body, you know. Our security team walks in on the craziest stuff. Last week…"

"No, I *don't* know, as you should realize about me by now." Taking down my ponytail, I put it back up. "The closest I get to naked around other people is running clothes so I won't be changing in front of Navy *fucking* SEALs!"

The whispered hysteria that entered my voice was uncommon and clearly stunned everyone.

My mom walked across the room and hugged me. "I'm teasing. The floors close. You'll have privacy." Leaning back, she held my face. "I blame your aunt Vera for my level of ridiculousness."

Inhaling carefully, I murmured, "Yeah, right."

"I'm sorry, darling." She pulled me down to kiss my forehead. "What a demure young lady you are."

"I think the word you're looking for is *repressed*." I shrugged a shoulder, embarrassed. "What are the plans for today?"

"Swimming. Drinking. A show later. I left a bathing suit in the bathroom for you."

"Still no."

"Break out of your shell. Try it on. You might like it."

I walked into the bathroom, took down the scraps of material, and laughed as I returned to the open main room.

"You've got to be kidding me. There's like three inches of fabric on this thing. This isn't *breaking* out of my shell, Mom. This is *falling* out of it."

"You never let me dress you anymore, Ellie."

"No, I don't. I love you. Call me when you're ready to do vacation stuff."

Grumbling, my mother allowed my father to lead her out.

Handing the bathing suit – *term used loosely* – to Bianca, I said, "This will look *amazing* on you. I'll stick with what works."

"You have a *great* body, Ellie," the blonde said with one hand on her hip. "You should try it."

Shaking my head, I grabbed my bag and headed for the bathroom. "I'll change. You guys pick whatever rooms and stuff you want. Put me anywhere. Please figure out how to *close* the floor."

One of the SEALs chose that moment to give me a thumbs-up and I waved stiltedly. "My life is *beyond* weird."

We spent a week in paradise and I celebrated my twenty-first birthday there. A milestone I'd honestly forgotten.

I ran every day and caught up on my pleasure reading. I swam a lot wearing the boring sport bra and boy short suit I was comfortable in because it covered what needed covering.

I wore sunglasses constantly so I could stare at a shirtless, barefoot Hyde without him knowing.

The freedom to do so was the best part of the trip.

The group photo taken at the outdoor birthday luau my parents threw me with local entertainment was a close second.

My team huddled close and I felt Padme and Hyde's arms circle my waist. It was so wonderful, I imagined my bodyguard's thumb stroked over the exposed skin between my sarong and bathing suit top.

"Closer!" Mom yelled. I wrapped my arms around my staff, ready to pass out from the warm firmness of Hyde's skin under my palm and forearm. "That's perfect!"

I was grateful for the firelight and darkness that hid my blush.

* * *

The trip did me a world of good. It cleared my head. It was the first vacation to accomplish it.

One afternoon, I stood at my back fence and watched a member of the stable staff pull up to the corrals on a motorcycle.

I sighed. "That must be nice. Being in the open."

Hyde stood on one side of me and Fiaaz appeared on the other. In his voice flavored with the sounds of the Middle East, he told me, "I have a motorcycle."

Turning to him, I knew my eyes were wide. "What's it like? To not be behind bulletproof glass on the road?"

His expression was thoughtful, then he glanced over my shoulder at Hyde.

Returning his attention to me, Fiaaz asked, "Would you like to find out?"

"How?"

"I'll teach you to ride. There's a closed track a few miles from here. It wouldn't be difficult to secure the perimeter."

I glanced over my shoulder at Hyde and he smiled at me. "I'd love to do that."

"Then we'll make it happen," he answered without hesitation.

They did everything they promised and I was grateful for the chance to learn something I never imagined would be possible for me. They often gave me what I thought was out of reach.

Chapter Eight

August 2012

My primary reason for wanting to attend college in California was the proximity to several of our charities and the advantage of talking to some of our most prolific donors face to face.

I graduated with my four-year degree in under three years and was in the middle of my graduate studies.

During a short break, I was booked back to back at charity galas up and down the West Coast. My parents would attend several but in this area of my life, I was both knowledgeable and confident.

I didn't need my parents to take millions in donations from men and women I looked directly in the eye and asked for it.

Preparing me for formal functions was frustrating and time-consuming. The fittings alone were enough to send me into lethargy and irritability for an entire day.

One gala I was scheduled to attend required the use of a chartered plane since my father had his in Europe.

At the insistence of our host, we'd be guests on their estate and I was certain my mother had something to do with the arrangement.

She *loved* the Delkin siblings as much as she'd loved their mother, Hope. Friends since college, the two moms quietly plotted for me to end up in a romantic love match with one of the brothers. Hope's death shook her to the core.

It didn't stop my mother's plans. Since I was sixteen, she slyly planted the seeds in my mind which ensured a very specific reaction on my part.

It absolutely wasn't going to happen.

As the limousine came to a stop in front of their grand front entrance, Harper Delkin himself was there to greet me. With stunning silver eyes and black hair swept back from his face, the oldest Delkin sibling assisted me from the interior.

"Elliana. You grow more beautiful every time I see you."

He bent to kiss my cheek and I couldn't hold back my chuckle. "I have to ask if that crap really works on the socialite set."

"Oh yes. Almost without fail." He winked. "You've managed to remain a stubborn holdout to my charms."

"Spoiler alert…it's destined to continue."

Placing his hand over his heart, he laughed warmly and turned us toward the house.

I smiled at the blonde man who waited there. "Elijah, it's always so nice to see you."

"Miss Fields. The feeling is mutual."

Harper's lifelong friend and personal bodyguard gave an elegant bow. "You have a new team since last we had the pleasure of your company." He took in my group with a careful eye. "I commend your parents for demanding the best."

"High praise indeed." I formally introduced everyone but knew it wasn't their first meeting. I thought Elijah was one of the people who recommended Hyde's crew to my parents. "Mom told you the details?"

Sparkling green eyes held my gaze intently. "She did. I was unhappy. Your former team was sent *here* to be retrained." He paused and crossed his hands at his back. "I made them cry. They're better at what they do now."

"Poor things. College campuses are distracting places."

"No one in your immediate orbit should have difficulty remaining completely focused on *you*...and your protection."

I blinked. Glancing back and forth between men I'd known all my life, I grinned. "My *goodness*. The press is more obvious at twenty-two than it was at eighteen."

Elijah gave me a rare smile that reached his lovely green eyes. "It's more appropriate at twenty-two than it was at eighteen and your parents aren't with you this trip."

The laughter bubbled up in my chest. "Even though my mother would *faint* with pleasure, I must firmly decline all offers outside your friendship and the positively *painful* donation I'll be taking with me when I leave."

"You break my heart, Elliana. Is it because I'm *old?*" Harper said the word with a funny face and it made me snort.

"Your *heart* isn't engaged, Harper." I considered my words carefully. "It isn't the difference in our ages. Unlike the lovely but outright silly socialites you draw like moths to flame, I have my own agenda. How boring it would be for you when I didn't hang on your every word."

"Hmm." Harper wrapped his arm around my waist and led me inside. "You're fucking *right* of course and that's annoying."

"I imagine. You'll have a stunner on your arm three hours from now so I don't feel bad for you."

Harper sighed dramatically. "Elliana…you're so unique."

"Yes. I'm aware. I'm certain it keeps Mom up at night."

Half an hour later, we were settled in a suite of rooms on the second floor. I loved the bright beauty of the Delkin home. Padme came in to lay out my gown for the party and forced me off the computer.

"Harper Delkin, huh?" I glanced at my assistant with a frown. "He's *quite* the catch, Ellie."

"Oh god, are you *kidding*? Did Mom tell you to say that? No. Absolutely *not*. Harper has fucked half the women I know on the charity circuit and those are just the confirmed kills. He's funny and brilliant, an incredible philanthropist. He's a *horrible* choice as a romantic interest."

"He's so *pretty* though."

"Yup. Still not my type."

"Elijah also seems…interested."

"You can't have *one* without the *other*, Padme. They're a…package deal, I guess. Not really sure how to put that."

"Like the Bradshaw twins?" I nodded and her dark eyes widened dramatically. "Oh *my*…does that bother you?"

"Not the general idea…but Harper specifically? Yes. He's been out of control since his wife died." I shivered at the memory of that horrific day. "Women have become a habit to him. Nothing more."

I turned to head to the shower and met Hyde's eyes. "Everything alright?"

"Yes."

I passed him and quipped. "Elijah thinks you're the best. I'm *winning* in personal protection. Woot."

I loved seeing him smile.

"You're a riot, Ellie," Padme said behind me.

"Be back in a bit."

The next hour wasn't fun for me since I fought my assistant on everything to do with getting fancy. Finally, she simply did what she wanted and stopped asking my permission.

It was the better option for both of us.

I stepped into my heels and took a deep breath, turning to take in my appearance. A pale purple gown that hugged me more closely than I liked, a complicated up-do, and dramatic makeup made me look like a different person and older than twenty-two. I added jewelry and called it done.

Padme smiled. "You look beautiful, Ellie."

Waving my hand at the compliment, I said, "Get your shoes on. I'm not going down there without you."

I loved having her with me at formal functions to prompt me with names, dates, and so much more. She was an encyclopedia of fascinating information I used like a scalpel to extract dollars from the ultra-rich.

The green sheath hugged her slim body and highlighted her caramel skin beautifully.

Moving toward the door, I smiled at Hyde who was turned out in a gorgeous suit with his dark blonde hair swept back from his forehead.

He stole my breath.

"You look wonderful, Hyde." My voice sounded much stronger than I felt. Inside, I trembled.

He bowed and held the door for me. Fiaaz was downstairs and Bianca waited in the hall. The silver gown and heels she wore wouldn't slow her down if there was an incident.

I announced sincerely, "I have the best-looking team of anyone I know. Every single one of you is gorgeous."

"The same can be said of our queen," Bianca replied with a smile. "Let's show you off, Ellie."

The words made me blush.

On the main level, the party was in full swing and Harper met me at the base of the stairs.

"Aren't you stunning?" The oldest Delkin sibling lifted my hand and kissed the back. "Are you *sure* I can't keep you?"

I shot back with a grin, "Positive. You're *dastardly*."

Elijah laughed at his side.

Harper winked. "Guilty as charged."

Slipping my hand through his arm, he escorted me around the room to meet the few people I didn't know. Elijah remained at Harper's shoulder and Hyde remained at mine.

Many donations, not nearly enough food consumed, and several hours into the gala, I began to tire.

As I decided to suggest a break to Hyde, a former employee of my parents' company approached.

My expression and tone were chilly because the parting had *not* been amicable. My personal interactions with the man were terrible. I hadn't seen him in years but here he stood.

A snake in a suit.

"Milton."

"Miss Fields. What a *pleasure* to see the heir apparent. No mommy and daddy with you tonight?"

Inhaling carefully, I put my shoulders back and looked the man in his beady little eyes. "I'm surprised to see you. I thought your search for investors took you to Japan."

He flushed. "I came as the guest of my *new* partner. We're going to take the ideas your father didn't want and make a fortune. His lack of vision. His loss."

Folding my hands in front of me, I considered walking away. In the end, there was no *way* I was going to allow passive aggressive insults to my dad.

Particularly since they were lies.

"Technology isn't my division. However, I'm apprised of various departments as a safeguard. Dad sank two million dollars into your ideas. I'm uncertain how you got the prototypes to function during your initial meeting but the results couldn't be duplicated by you or anyone else."

I lowered my voice. "How dare you imply it was a lack of *vision* rather than shoddy *workmanship* that was at fault for your failure. I wish you luck in making it happen with a new source of capital."

"It's unsurprising you have so little class. I consider myself lucky we didn't suit."

I chuckled. I couldn't help myself. "Didn't *suit?* Consider yourself *lucky* my father didn't break every bone in your body for manhandling me."

Hyde stiffened at my side and moved close enough for me to feel the heat from his body on my bare arm.

Milton bared his teeth at me. "Naturally, you warp the events to match your narrative as any *child* caught doing something naughty would."

Once a snake, always a snake.

"The aggressive sexual advances of a man in his forties is the last thing I wanted at fifteen. It wasn't *naughty*, Milton. It was a *crime*. You're lying if you pretend otherwise."

Turning, I met Hyde's eyes. His expression was fierce.

Behind me, I heard, "You little *bitch…*"

Hyde reached out, pulled me flush to his body, and turned

us in one fluid motion. His arms held me *hard* as he pressed my face to his chest.

I heard two shots and felt my bodyguard jerk twice.

"Hyde."

He grunted. I listened as he inhaled deeply.

Padme barked, "Down, sir."

Looking around Hyde's shoulder, I took in the image of an unconscious Milton face-down on the floor with Bianca and Fiaaz gripping his arms.

None of it mattered.

"Hyde?" He continued to hold me tightly.

"I'm alright." His voice was strained. "Cracked a rib."

I found Elijah's eyes where he shielded Harper behind him. "M-my...Hyde is hurt." I gestured to Milton. "That's a stupid vendetta and he took advantage of an opportunity." I swallowed the tears in my voice. "Fuck *him*. Help *Hyde*."

Everything moved quickly after Hyde slowly released me.

A few minutes later, I stood with the others in Elijah's office as a medic tended to Hyde's bare back.

I stared at the impact bruises on either side of his spine. I was thankful for the Kevlar vest that prevented his death from almost point-blank range.

The estate medic wrapped his ribs tightly and Hyde looked better instantly. Stepping back, the man placed painkillers in his hand.

Hyde read the label and shook his head. "These are too strong. I need something milder." Checking his bag again, he handed my bodyguard another bottle. "That'll do. Thanks."

It wasn't the first time a member of my team protected me. It seemed someone was always pissed at my parents or the corporation for some imagined slight.

I'd worried about losing Hyde since my friend lost her man to violence but it was the first time I truly understood that he could *die* keeping me safe.

I remembered witnessing the pain of such a loss and it made my stomach hurt, my heart contract in fear.

"Hyde." He looked at me and I asked softly, "Are you alright?" He nodded. "Thank you. I'm sorry."

Shrugging on his shirt, he turned to me and held my shoulder. "Don't apologize."

"I shouldn't have antagonized him."

"You did nothing wrong. Thank you for remaining calm and don't let this ruin the trip for you."

Blinking back tears, I gave him a small nod.

I kissed Elijah and Harper's cheeks. "I'm going to call it a night. Gunshots spoil my party mood. Thank you for h-helping him."

As I pulled back, I thought Elijah saw more than I wanted him to but he simply said, "You're in excellent hands, Ellie."

"We'll see you in the morning, Elliana," Harper added quietly. "All will be well."

He took my hand and squeezed it. "You're a credit to your family."

"You are, too." I tried to smile. "I'll see you tomorrow."

We took the back stairs to the upper floors and were back in our suite of rooms in less than a minute.

Padme helped take down my hair and remove the makeup as everyone went to change.

Dressed in yoga pants and a t-shirt, I sat in the dim alcove separated from the rest of the space. I stared out at the moonlit grounds, lost in thought.

"An action movie is in order, Ellie." I looked over my shoulder and smiled at Hyde in sleep pants and a t-shirt. "Don't dwell on tonight. Let's take your mind off things."

"That would be great." I joined my team and it was the best way to end the day and assure me that everyone was fine.

The distraction helped me relax but it didn't stop the vivid nightmares I had for *weeks* about losing Hyde.

Still so complicated to be me.

Chapter Nine

January 2014

Completing my graduate studies felt *amazing*. The relief to be finished at last was huge.

Mom and Dad insisted on taking me to Manhattan to celebrate. Si, Bianca, and Fiaaz planned to do some security upgrades while we were gone so only Padme and Hyde made the trip.

I loved the apartment we used whenever we were in the city. The building owner waited in the lobby when we arrived.

Hudson Winters turned to us with a smile and I always found it fascinating how similar he was physically to Harper Delkin.

My father was his mentor in college and he featured in many of my first memories. My mother captured him in numerous photos over the years, starting with my second birthday party.

"Mr. and Mrs. Fields, Elliana. It's good to have you back in New York. Carlo assures me the apartment is prepared and Leonard did an additional security sweep."

"Hudson. How many *times* do I have to tell you to call me Samuel? Hmm?" They shook hands firmly. "I think knowing you twenty years gives us enough familiarity."

Black eyes sparkled. "Samuel. Understood. It's a hard habit to break, sir." He looked at my mother with a gentle smile and took her hand in both of his. "How lovely you remain year after year. Time doesn't *touch* you."

My mom *blushed* and waved her other hand at him. "You stop that flattery right *now*, Hudson. Gracious!"

He bent to kiss her cheek and she fluttered adorably.

Grinning, he turned to me, hugging me as he planted a kiss at my temple. The man gave *incredible* hugs.

"Congratulations are in order. Well done on completing everything so quickly and competently, Elliana."

"Thanks. The last few months felt like *years*."

He leaned back and held my shoulders. "I disagree. It seems only yesterday that you were happily screaming on your first pony as your parents struggled not to panic."

"They still *do* that." I reached up to touch the faintest trace of silver at his temple. "I *love* this." Grinning, I added, "You and Harper remain twins."

"Don't force me to color it, Elliana."

I laughed. "Don't you *dare*." Hudson turned, keeping one arm around my shoulders. I put my hand on Hyde's upper arm. "You remember m-my bodyguard, Hyde."

I rushed on to cover the slip of emotion in my voice. "We didn't bring the full entourage this trip. With Mom and Dad's staff, it approached rock band proportions."

Hudson stared into my eyes for a long moment. "I think you have exactly who you need with you." Hudson held out his hand and took Hyde's measure as they shook. "Leonard would appreciate a discussion while you're here."

Hyde's smile was slow. "We have history. I'll assure him of Miss Fields' safety personally."

Releasing his hand with a nod, Hudson turned to my assistant.

Avoiding looking directly at Hyde, I said, "And you know…"

"Padme." Even I could hear the sensuality in the way Hudson said it and my eyes went wide. He bent to kiss her cheek and her warm skin tinted with a blush. "A *pleasure* to see you again. Stunning as always and you smell fantastic."

"*Hudson.*"

It was all she said but the breathlessness told me my assistant and the real estate mogul had an *intimate* history with one another.

My curiosity started to eat me alive instantly. I stared back and forth between them and wanted to *know*.

With a second kiss on her opposite cheek, Hudson straightened. "Allow me to take you all to dinner. We must celebrate Elliana's milestone properly."

"Outstanding. You have the best taste in food and it isn't *miniature*." My poor father hated the trend of tiny, colorful portions that abounded at most functions we attended.

"A steak as big as your head. Check."

"Will Natalia join us?" I asked hopefully. "It's been forever since I've seen her. You don't get to Dallas *nearly* enough."

Hudson's oldest friend was brilliant and sarcastic.

He smiled. "Do you think she'd miss it?" I shook my head. "She can't wait to see you." Gesturing to the elevators, he announced, "Relax for a few hours and let Carlo know if you need anything."

I loved being back in New York.

Hyde being with me made it so much better. As much as the city called to me, I was usually nervous about seeing the sights.

No matter where we were, he *always* made me feel safe.

* * *

Mom and Dad decided on a nap the moment we entered our suite. He disappeared upstairs after hugging me violently.

Taking my shoulders, Mom ordered, "Go, Ellie. Enjoy yourself. Hyde and Padme are here and you've never been so comfortable with a team while we've been in the city. It's the perfect time to see everything."

"You'll call me when you need me to come back?"

"Darling, Natalia is quite the night owl. You have *hours* to yourself. I'll call you when we wake up."

Turning to Hyde, I asked carefully, "Are you up for some sightseeing?"

"Absolutely." He gave a soft whistle and Padme poked her

head from the bedroom she used when we visited Manhattan. "Ellie and I are leaving. Keep your phone on."

"You got it, boss. Have fun, Ellie! I'll lay out your clothes for tonight." She gave me a little wave and I returned it while crushing down the butterflies in my stomach.

Hyde was taking me out alone?

Pressing the button in the elevator, he smiled at me. "The wonderful thing about a city the size of New York is that you're both exposed and hidden at the same time." I nodded. "What would you like to see first?"

"I…can we walk?"

"If that's what you want."

"I-I was never allowed to walk."

"Then let's tear up some miles."

He winked and I felt like I might swallow my tongue. It was stuck to the roof of my mouth.

In the lobby, Carlo smiled. "Do you need anything, Miss Fields?"

Resting my hands on his elevated counter, I grinned. "When Hudson hired you, I wasn't allowed to go out without a dozen people in tow. I followed you around the building, talking up a storm. You were *so* patient. You need to call me Ellie."

"I remember our many conversations fondly." I heard the sincerity in his voice.

"Today, I'm going to explore the city for the first time."

Grinning, he replied, "You're going to love it, Ellie."

"I'm so excited, I can hardly stand it."

Turning, I slid my left hand through Hyde's arm without thinking. It was something I only did in social situations.

Blushing, I looked up and stammered, "I'm sorry, I…"

He removed my hand and took up a position on my other side. Lifting my right hand, he returned it to the crook of his arm.

His smile was warm. "I need this arm free."

I blinked. "Gun hand. R-right."

I pretended it was something we did all the time and we walked to the exit together. Like a couple.

The doorman smiled at me and I think I smiled back.

Then I was walking down the bustling streets of New York City on the arm of the first and only man to ever make my heart race.

It was magnificent.

* * *

We wandered the shops, bought coffee, and I soaked up the fact that we were alone, free in a way that was *never* possible, in a city of millions.

My happiness was almost overwhelming.

Hyde was fully capable of keeping me safe without the rest of my team. I never doubted it for a moment, then or now.

It was that *he* trusted *me* to react correctly if things went wrong. He believed in *my* ability to help him help me.

His trust, on my first day exploring a city I'd always loved from a distance, made me want him even more.

I worked up the courage to ask him questions about past assignments and he answered them honestly, even when the answers weren't pretty.

"Your life before…it was very different. I, this job, must be boring in comparison," I told him.

Hyde was quiet for a few seconds. Then, he said, "A few weeks before we were contacted about guarding you, we had a mission that went wrong."

"How bad?"

"As bad as it could go."

"Someone betrayed you?"

His eyes landed on my face. "How did you know?"

"All of you work as a single unit. Coordinated, flawless. If something happened, it was probably a new person you didn't normally have with you."

"You're right." He pressed his other hand over mine where it rested on his arm. "There were several women abducted from a small village. Our job was to get them back. Intel from a person we trusted made it seem fairly simple."

He went quiet and I murmured, "You don't have to talk about it, Hyde."

"No. I need to tell you." At the alcove of a closed diner,

he stopped and gently maneuvered me inside, shielding me from the street. "The intel was a trap to get us to the location. The women were dead before we ever left our base. During the ambush, we lost a long-time member of our team. Fiaaz and Si were badly injured."

"I'm sorry. I'm so sorry."

"It took *weeks* to clean up the mess and for Si to be stable enough to travel." He met my eyes and smiled. "We'd been back three days when we got the call about you."

He glanced over my head, using the glass door behind me to surveil the street. Then he locked gazes with me again.

"The first week we evaluated your team, we waited for you to show evidence of being spoiled, selfish, even cruel." He shook his head. "Instead, you were studious, generous, and kind."

I swallowed around the lump in my throat.

"For too long, we raced from one horrific scene to another. We were tired to our bones, cynical. You're the best decision I ever made, Ellie. Guarding you isn't boring. You remind me daily that there's more than death, pain, and suffering in the world. There's hope."

"Thank you, Hyde."

"You're welcome." He picked up my hand and held it between both of his. "What would you like to do now, Ellie?"

Balancing my emotions, I said, "I thought maybe we could go to the top of the Empire State Building. I've always wanted to see the city from there."

"We can do that but I meant now that school is over. You worked hard for years. What are your plans?"

"Oh. Well, I'll work for the company. It's what I've trained to do since I was a girl."

He said gently, "I didn't ask what you were *trained* to do. I asked what you'd *like* to do."

The question shook my foundation. Before I could censor my answer, I murmured, "Write my books. Maybe…travel a little bit. I have a bucket list."

"A bucket list?"

"A list of places I'd love to visit before I die."

He stilled. "Why would you think about death at such an early age, Ellie?"

"I guess…" I sighed. "There's always been protection around me. A lot of it. I understand why, of course. I don't resent it. I don't wish you – my team – away."

I swallowed carefully. "It's a constant reminder that I could die. My life feels precarious sometimes."

"When did you make your list?" His voice was quiet.

There was no *way* I could look him in the eye. "When I overheard my parents discussing my entry on an international sex trafficking site. I realized their money doesn't insulate me. It makes me a more desirable target." I shrugged. "They don't know I know about it."

"That's why you decided to go out of state for college."

"They live in non-stop fear for me. Since the day I was

born. My natural reserve makes them think I'm weak. They love me, they respect me, but they don't think I'm strong. I needed to show them I could be or the fear would eventually kill them."

Hyde nodded, his eyes bright as they focused on me. "Then the trouble at your school."

"Yes." I smiled carefully. "My team is better now."

He returned my hand to his arm and we walked in the direction of one of the most popular tourist destinations on the planet.

"Padme mentioned you write but refuses to share details. She won't tell us your pen name." He laughed. "We've all tried to coax it from her."

My blush was positively *sweltering*. "They're silly fiction. They let me live a different life."

"What sort of life?"

I snorted. "That was good but not good enough. I'm not giving up the genre."

"Fair enough. Pretzel?"

"Oh, yes!"

After an hour of distractions, we made it to the Empire State Building but the viewing deck was already closed.

"We'll come back tomorrow," he told me.

"Really?"

"You have to see the view. It's incredible."

"I'd like that."

"Good. You still have to try the pizza here."

"Alright. Have you been here often?"

"I kept an apartment nearby for a long time."

"Tell me about a day you spent here before I met you."

And Hyde did.

Chapter Ten

Later, I laughed at dinner until I could barely breathe.

Natalia and Hudson were two of my favorite people in the world and more like honorary aunt and uncle than friends.

It felt odd to have Hyde standing several feet away while I sat. A few times, I glanced over my shoulder to make sure he was still there.

The habit didn't escape Natalia's notice.

Her blue-black hair swayed forward and highlighted her dramatic blue eyes. In a whisper that didn't carry, she asked, "Darling, anything to share?"

"I-I...what?"

"I love that you have *zero* ability to deceive. Tell me about the man." My eyes went wide. "Between us. Always."

"I can't...I don't...uh."

Tilting her head, she stared at me for a long moment. "Elliana, we must find time to chat privately. Perhaps you have questions."

I gave an almost imperceptible nod. "I'd like that."

"Ellie!" My mother was such a giddy drunk. "Tell Hudson

about the admirer who scaled the penthouse like a *toad*."

"Suction cups. He climbed using suction cups. The team placed bets on whether he'd make it. They watched him the entire way. I found his exhibition…odd."

Padme rolled her eyes. "He was from an old family on the West Coast. Caught sight of our Ellie at a function and swore it was love at first sight." She lifted her glass and winked at me. "She handled him perfectly."

"I was under the stress of finals. I didn't have time for such a ridiculous demonstration."

Mom giggled. "Honey, you *make* time for suitors."

"No, thank you. Padme pulled his background by the time he fell over the railing onto the balcony. His family lost most of their holdings in the crash." I sat back and sipped my wine. "It was my dowry of *forty goats* he desired. Not me."

"You sell yourself short, Elliana," Dad said.

"Not at all. If a single cell in my body had reacted to the unfortunate thing, perhaps I'd have invited him to stay for dinner. I *wasn't* interested and I *refuse* to fake it in my own home."

"Well *said*, darling," Natalia told me. "Never fake it. Therein lies madness."

Hudson said nothing but watched me closely from Natalia's other side.

Suddenly, she sat back and asked my mother, "Shall we introduce Elliana to *Trois* or preserve her innocence a bit longer?"

My sweet, inebriated mom clapped. "Dancing would be *just* the thing! Samuel, you can spin me around the room."

I frowned. "What's *Trois*?"

Padme nudged me. "Heaven for women. Completely risqué but classy, beautiful, and fun."

"Please tell me it isn't a strip club. I don't need a male stripper spinning his junk in my face to enjoy my evening."

Behind me, Hyde couldn't completely hide his laugh. Around the table, no one else even tried.

When my assistant could speak, she explained. "Nothing like that. Natalia owns the place and it's divine."

My mom added, "People in the public eye can be themselves. It's the ultimate in exclusivity and privacy."

"A club where no one knows me?" Natalia nodded with a smile I couldn't interpret. "Why *Trois*? Three…I don't get it."

"You will, Elliana. You will."

An hour later, we entered the elegantly restored mansion Hudson deeded to his best friend for her members-only establishment.

Drinks were ordered and Hyde took up a position behind the small sofa I chose. I was immediately enthralled by the people and the atmosphere.

Natalia sat in the chair beside me. "Many of the men and women you see here at *Trois* practice a ménage lifestyle."

"What's ménage?" She quietly explained and I observed the gathering with a fresh perspective. Meeting her eyes, I asked quietly, "Like Harper and Elijah or the Bradshaw twins?"

She nodded. "All of whom are members." My eyes were as big as saucers. "This place and a few others like it around the world provide a sanctuary for those who live…outside the norm."

"You guarantee their privacy."

"My precautions are intense. Hudson designed the protocols and a friend helped me implement them." She smiled. "It's not only for those in the lifestyle. It offers a haven for people like Hudson, your parents, and you."

"I could join?"

"Oh yes, darling. It's why I wanted you to see the place. Here, you can be yourself out of the public eye."

After several minutes of watching me, she asked, "It doesn't bother you?" Electric blue eyes waited for me when I dragged my attention from the dance floor. "The thought of ménage?"

"I…no. I didn't, I mean, I know people who live as three rather than two." I thought for a moment. "Actually, I know more than I realized. How strange."

"Perhaps you gravitate to them without thought."

"Pure chance but…interesting." I laughed nervously. "I imagine the participants must have powerful personalities."

Sitting back, Natalia sipped her glass of wine. "What makes you think so?"

Two men danced a laughing brunette back and forth between them. I recognized the men from the charity circuit, known for their beauty as well as their generosity.

"The woman would have to be interesting, confident. Have a keen understanding of her own value." I met Natalia's gaze. "Otherwise, she'd be overwhelmed by the characteristics of two strong men. Even *one* man can present a challenge for some women."

"Observant and intuitive." She gestured around the club. "Most of the women here have a unique quality that draws men interested in or addicted to the lifestyle. It isn't age, experience, or wealth that makes those women desirable, Elliana."

"What is it?"

"Power. Some wield it with delicacy and others with an iron fist but make no mistake, it's the *woman* in control." She sat forward and added, "Even when the men are stronger or dominant, even if she accepts a submissive role, she remains in control. It's the true nature of womanhood."

I frowned. "I'm not very powerful."

"You have more than most women of my acquaintance, darling. Far more than *you* realize." She winked a brilliant blue eye. "I can't wait for you to discover it."

My mother dropped to the seat beside me. "Ellie, you need to dance. You *love* to dance."

"I'm happy people watching," I answered.

"Nonsense! You're young, beautiful, and accomplished." Over her shoulder, she gestured drunkenly. "Hyde, she trusts you implicitly. Dance with Ellie so she doesn't have to dance with her father."

Shockingly embarrassed, I hissed, "Mother, I swear to god…"

"I can imagine nothing I'd rather do." Hyde stood beside me with his hand extended. "Ellie."

Numbly, I placed my hand in his and he helped me to my feet. He led me out on the dimly lit hardwood and took me in his arms as the first strains of *Endless Love* drifted around the room. I was grateful for the low lights since my face was flaming.

He pulled me close and murmured, "Breathe, Ellie. Trust me."

"Always," I answered honestly. As he started to move, I couldn't hide my surprise. "I didn't know you could *dance*, Hyde." His chuckle made my hand tighten on his.

"If it's a task that involves the human body, I make it my *mission* to excel at it." Realizing how it sounded, his eyes landed on mine. "Jesus…"

I laughed so hard, I felt dizzy. "I know what you mean."

"You're the same. Things come easily to you."

"Except relating to people my age, all musical instruments, and flower arranging…to Mom's bitter disappointment."

"Overrated skills. Young people are typically self-absorbed and annoying. You're the exception. Musical talent is a dime a dozen. Flower arranging can be done by florists who *live* for the task."

He winked. "You know several martial art forms, ride a horse like the goddess Diana, and have outstanding aim."

"Th-thanks."

As we moved around the room, I found myself closer to Hyde's body and didn't know if I'd done it unconsciously.

"Am I…too close?"

"No." It was all he said but he tightened his hold at my back.

The song ended and I thought he'd lead me back to the seating area but he didn't.

Kiss Me started playing and I wanted to whimper in need. It was one of my favorite songs and it always made me think of Hyde and everything he represented in my life.

Safety. Respect. Desire. Love.

"Hyde," I whispered.

"Yes, Ellie?" His face was pressed to my hair and I never wanted him to let me go.

"Thank you."

"For what?"

"Th-the way you are with me." I was a soft-spoken person by nature but with Hyde, it was legitimate shyness. "Helping me see the world in ways I never could before and understanding that being me can be confusing sometimes."

"The person you are is spectacular, Elliana. There's *nothing* I'd change about you as an employer, a friend, a woman."

It was the most beautiful thing anyone had ever said to me and that it came from *him* moved me beyond my ability to hide it. Tears instantly formed in my eyes and I was embarrassed.

I started to pull away but he held me close. "Your gentle nature is one of the most magnificent things about you. Stay, Ellie."

Releasing my hand, he stroked his fingers over my hair. I rested my face on his chest and held his waist.

I simultaneously felt absolute safety and utter confusion.

By the time the song faded away, I could breathe and didn't feel as though I was on the verge of an emotional scene.

Hyde bowed over my hand, kissed the back, and led me back to my seat beside Natalia. Her smile of greeting was slow.

"Lunch together before you leave, darling."

"Yes." I inhaled carefully. "I think that would be good."

* * *

We stayed in New York for ten days and I saw every landmark I could fit in. Some days my parents or Padme joined us but mostly, it was Hyde and me.

I had my conversation with Natalia the day before we left and I started forming a plan in my mind.

Over the following year, I gradually built my courage to enact a scene that could either give me everything I desired or make things hellishly awkward with Hyde.

It was the second possibility that held me back.

I didn't give up. I worked hard, trained hard, and fantasized about the life I could have with my bodyguard, my secret obsession, the man I loved.

In the end, none of my plans really mattered.

Chapter Eleven

Early June 2014

Struggling to open my eyes, I felt excruciating pain all over my body. I hurt so badly that I couldn't identify where I might be injured and I didn't know the source.

What's my name?

One thing at a time. My name is Elliana. Elliana Fields. Yes. My family calls me Ellie.

Where am I?

It smelled musty, like damp earth and rust. There were other smells I didn't recognize.

My vision was blurry and it seemed too dark but that didn't seem right. I started to panic and walked myself back as I tried to compartmentalize the pain.

What's the last thing you remember?

I think I was…running. Yes. Running my usual trail around the municipal airfield and community park not far from where I live. I like the change of scenery from…

My parents' home. *Elysian Fields.*

I was running and stopped at the halfway point of my

second lap to refill my water bottle at the drinking fountain.

Then what? Then what, Ellie?

Running again and the sound of two small planes taking off. One was a crop duster, the other a mini jet.

There was a little dog. It charged for the main entrance as a girl in pigtails tried to catch his leash. The Shih Tzu would've surely been hit. The girl went on and on about me saving little Biscuit's *life* like a *hero*.

Laughing. Running again.

I passed Little League practice where boys worked on sliding home. About the same age Preston would be.

Preston. The memory of losing him flooded into my mind and it felt strangely fresh. I reined it in, diverted my mind.

What happened to you, Ellie?

I entered the woods that surrounded the park on three sides. They offered shade and cooler temperatures. I always stayed on the path.

A shadow behind me and to the left made me remove an earbud.

Turning…

No matter how I strained, there was nothing after a flash of terrible pain. Nothing but darkness.

Moving the fingers of one hand, I felt dirt under me. My eyesight was off. I couldn't tell if it was day or night.

I tried to lift my arm but searing pain made me gasp. It

echoed off metal. I assumed the bone was broken.

So many pieces of me felt broken.

Carefully, I attempted moving the other arm. There was pain but I could. I slowly raised it to my head and my face was wet. I was filthy and the skin was badly swollen around my cheeks and eyes.

A huge lump along the side of my head behind my ear seeped something warm and sticky and I knew it was blood.

"Hello?" My voice sounded as if I choked on glass.

There was a foul taste in my mouth. Something completely alien to me but I *recognized it anyway* and I froze.

Hysteria threatened at the edge of my mind.

I knew what happened to my body even if my mind didn't remember the details. The realization caused my focus to clear with a snap and I took in the world around me.

I heard faint sounds of metal bats hitting baseballs. Further away, the sound of a dog barking.

I was still in the municipal park.

Deep in the wooded sections of the park are large steel buildings that hold sprinkler pumps, electrical boxes for the field lights, and landscaping equipment used to maintain the grounds.

I was certain I was in one of those buildings. Landscaping, I thought. The smell of dirt and wood mulch was powerful.

Running my hand over my torso, I confirmed my nudity and a shudder of revulsion wracked my frame. The resulting pain made me whimper like a wounded animal.

"Hyde?" I whispered, suddenly wondering if the person who attacked me was watching from the shadows. "Hyde?"

No answer. Dread filled me. Only one thing would keep him from being with me.

"Hyde?" Tears slipped over my cheeks. "*No, no, no*…please be okay. Please be okay."

Swallowing, which was the absolute *reverse* action my body *screamed* I needed to do, I took as much air into my lungs as I could and shouted, "Help!"

It wasn't loud but the steel walls helped magnify my voice. Resting a few seconds, I gathered my strength and tried again. And again. And again.

After what felt like forever, I heard a boy's voice say, "Mom. Hey, Mom? Did you hear that?"

I shouted again, desperate now. I was tired and furious that I was too weak to help myself. To help Hyde.

"Mom, someone's calling for help!"

"Ricky, are you *sure*? I didn't hear anything. You shouldn't be playing around these buildings, honey. It's dangerous."

I put everything I had left into a scream for help that translated to sheer agony all over me.

The mother of my savior worked to open the heavy door of the building while telling her son to stay back. The scraping of the metal on concrete was beautiful and horrible.

I saw a lightening on the other side of my eyelids so I

thought it was still daylight.

She gasped, "Oh, my sweet Jesus." I heard her footsteps receding. She yelled, "Ricky, run and get your dad right now. Tell him to call 911. Run *fast*, son. As fast as you can. Go!"

The woman crouched by my side and took the hand of the arm that wasn't broken. She held it carefully. "My name is Jamie Vasquez. I'm going to lay my jacket over your body. I can't move you but I'll stay with you until help comes."

The woman had a slight Hispanic accent and I felt fabric settle over my breasts and upper thighs.

"Can you tell me your name, honey?"

"I-I'm Ellie."

I had nothing left but I managed, "They have to find Hyde. He's hurt. He could be dying. *Find Hyde*. Tell them. Tell them to find him. They have to help him."

The woman said, "I'll tell them. I swear I'll tell them…"

I heard the pounding of many feet running on the path. My team racing to my rescue.

Darkness reached for me and I was so fucking *thankful* to slide into it before anyone arrived and I was forced to see their faces when they discovered what happened to me.

I couldn't bear it. I couldn't.

I fell gladly into the nothingness.

Chapter Twelve

Mid-July 2014

After my attack, there were two things I was grateful for more than any others initially.

One, that my parents basically owned a small town less than an hour's drive from Dallas where they built an *incredible* hospital equipped with cutting edge medical technology.

Two, that they were powerful enough to silence the local populace about what happened.

Within an hour of finding me, they threw money at park personnel, first responders, the Vasquez family, and hospital staff to ensure details of my attack remained within a small, trackable circle.

They wanted me at home, under their watchful eyes and loving attention but I refused to leave the hospital until the casts came off. I needed physical therapy to put me back on my feet.

After everything, I couldn't bear being dependent.

When the hospital administrator explained my condition was stable and further recuperation from home was possible, I smiled and shook my head.

"I'll be recuperating *here*, thank you very much. I've scared enough years off my parents' lives."

I spent most of my days in silence, by myself, thinking about the level of hatred and rage that festered after my first attack while I was at college.

The men who jumped me the first time nursed a grudge for five years while they planned the second attempt.

Five years.

Now twenty-three, I'd put the original assault out of my mind. It didn't give me nightmares, didn't instill a fear of men, and didn't change the way I lived my life.

Being a creature of habit made me an easy target.

I ran six days a week. Four of them, I used the path around our estate. For the two others, I liked a change of scenery.

The community park was my preferred secondary location for a silly reason. I liked to watch the normal people. Friends playing Frisbee, couples sharing a romantic picnic, families celebrating a child's birthday party with a barbecue and games.

Running the park, I felt like everyone else.

Whenever I was home, my routine never changed. Tuesdays and Thursdays, Hyde and Padme drove me to the park. She stayed in the SUV and my bodyguard ran with me.

He always gave me space so I could think. Since most of my thoughts were about him, I appreciated not having the sight of his barely clothed body to distract me.

My attackers learned my schedule.

The three surviving members of the recently paroled group found me an easy target on a trail I ran a thousand times. Two of their fellow criminals didn't survive prison.

Apparently, I ruined their lives by pressing charges and seeing them prosecuted to the full extent of the law.

Such men never take responsibility for their actions. Filled with fury, time in prison accomplished nothing other than successfully making them more violent and misogynistic than they were before their incarceration.

The justice system was necessary but not always effective. This time, there would be no courts. There would be no trial. There would be no prison time.

At this moment, there was a small army of mercenaries searching for the men who hit me in the head with a rock, dragged me into the park storage shed, beat me so badly my own mother didn't recognize me, and spent almost an hour raping me separately and together.

I can think about it, talk about it, because so far, I don't remember anything. Despite my physical injuries, emotionally, it feels as if it happened to someone else.

They fractured my skull in their attempt to subdue me without a fight. I didn't sustain permanent brain damage but the headaches made me want to claw out the inside of my head.

Ripped and torn ligaments in the broken limbs and along my shoulders and back would take longer to mend than my bones. There was internal bruising, cracked ribs, a fractured pelvis, a dislocated hip, and deep cuts to my upper back and abdomen to deal with as well.

I was bruised from head to toe, hurt *everywhere*, and felt as though I'd gone through a wood chipper.

I would heal.

Once I get to the blackness on that wooded path, I remember nothing until waking on the dirt floor and calling for help. The injuries I carry don't make sense to me.

I was unconscious through all of it.

When I was brought in by paramedics, a member of my team stayed with me every moment. Even during surgery, one of them scrubbed and stood armed inside the door.

Over the days that followed, a battered Hyde said not one word to anyone but checked the ID of every doctor, nurse, or orderly who so much as peeked into my room in the ICU.

Despite his own condition, he refused to leave his post.

Eventually I was moved to a private room when I stabilized. Two armed men from the estate were stationed outside my door but Hyde stood beside my bed.

We didn't speak when I was awake, and I could barely keep my eyes open most of the time.

I'd never seen such rage written on someone's face.

My attackers took Hyde out first with a tranquilizer dart. Given his size, it hadn't kept him out long but when he regained consciousness, he was bound and gagged ten feet from my body in the landscaping shed.

They hit me too hard. I'm grateful for their ineptitude

because I have no memory of the horror I endured.

Hyde was not so lucky.

He was forced to witness every degrading deed done to me as I remained unconscious. The three men beat him savagely. Killing time in hopes I'd wake up.

When I didn't, they proceeded with their plans. After they finished with me, they left me to die and took turns beating Hyde again. Payback for their first encounter with him.

I guess they figured they'd have gotten away with what they did to me if Hyde hadn't interfered and stopped them.

During his time in that shed, the head of my protection detail sustained internal injuries, broken ribs, a dislocated jaw, and a severe concussion when they hit him with a shovel.

The fools *thought* they killed him. It would take more than a shovel to kill Hyde.

It was when we didn't reappear and Hyde didn't respond to a security check from Padme that she started searching and called the rest of the team.

The 911 call brought my security detail from the opposite side of the park from where they initially looked for us. I assumed it was where my attackers discarded the tracking devices we always wore on our shoes.

The police and paramedics didn't see Hyde at first. It was the park landscaping supervisor who noted the various tools scattered around and a blood trail in the dirt.

My bodyguard's bound and gagged body was tied to a

tractor and covered with a heavy tarp.

Jamie Vasquez told me that the moment they cut him loose, Hyde collapsed beside me and refused all treatment until I was safely in the ambulance.

Si found where the men who attacked me made their escape through the woods to an access road where they got on a bus, traveled into the city, and disappeared.

Knowing Hyde witnessed what happened to me was another reason I stayed in the hospital instead of going home. I felt dirty, wrong in my skin, and unable to face him.

It was likely many of the estate employees would know the circumstances of my hospitalization and I couldn't bear to look people in the eyes with the knowledge between us.

Not yet.

I'd seen each of my personal staff briefly but found it hard to speak with the overwhelming humiliation I couldn't shake.

The first time I was coherent enough to register Hyde's presence, the injuries he sustained because of me crushed my heart. A few days after I was moved from ICU to a normal room, he disappeared.

I hadn't seen him since.

I wondered if he'd return. The thought that I might never see him again hurt me more than I could admit to anyone.

Every day, my thoughts stayed on Hyde. It was hard not to dwell on his absence when he'd been such a significant part of my daily life for so long.

Once I was pulled a bit from the drug haze, I spent my time reading and handwriting notes for my third book.

The days of recovery passed slowly but I avoided trying to piece together what happened to me.

Most days, I felt as though I was still bleeding on the inside but didn't understand why.

Chapter Thirteen

Seven weeks after the attack, my doctor entered the room and closed the door on the two heavily armed men flanking it.

They were the daytime detail and tried to stop her but she had a spine of steel. "I don't care *who* the fuck you are. This is a private conversation between doctor and patient. Back off."

Dr. Theresa Spellman was flown in from Boston to oversee my case. My parents offered her a new lab to make me her priority until I was cleared medically.

It wasn't our first meeting. We worked together on multiple charities and were kindred spirits in our efforts to ease the suffering of the sick and the poor.

Right now, her normally lovely latte skin was pale and the skin was drawn tight around her eyes and mouth.

I gave her a smile. It was small but genuine. "Tell me, Theresa. Best to get it out. Do I have an STD that's going to haunt me for the rest of my life?"

Clearing her throat carefully, she said, "No, no disease of any kind, thankfully. You're still anemic from the blood loss you suffered but otherwise, your progress is proceeding perfectly. Thankfully, you were healthy before your attack."

She was quiet for several seconds.

I whispered, "I can see how upset you are. Tell me, Theresa."

Folding her hands in front of her, she closed her eyes and took a deep breath. "I've waited to talk to you because I can't imagine all the shit you're dealing with and my main priority has been stabilizing your overall condition."

I watched her swallow hard and held my breath.

"I can't wait any longer." She met my gaze directly. "You're pregnant, Ellie."

The statement hung in the suddenly heavy air and the *enormity* of her words reached me like a sharp slap.

My heart slammed against my sternum.

Theresa's voice was intentionally calm. "I can end this pregnancy and no one, not even your parents, will *ever* know. I'll take it with me to the grave."

I turned my head and stared through the window for a long time. The heat vapor coming off the roof below my floor held me mesmerized as I processed the appalling news.

Part of me recoiled in horror, in bone-deep disgust.

To know the seed of one of my *rapists* had taken in my womb made me want to vomit. That I'd been a virgin before my attack was brutal.

They'd taken *so much* from me.

Another part thought about all the children in violent homes or waiting to be adopted. Kids who came from flawed circumstances through no fault of their own.

They hadn't asked to be born drug-dependent or physically disabled or at the wrong time in someone's life. Countless unwanted children dumped in the system or left to suffer.

Some with the same violent beginning as the child inside me.

I was pro-choice and I always would be. Still, I saw the emptiness of my life stretching out in front of me and wondered if this was the one gentle take-away from my ordeal.

With my eyes closed, I examined the person I was, the human being I tried to be. My decision would affect the rest of my life and could result in unbelievable pain for my parents.

In the end, it was Preston who made up my mind.

I met Theresa's gaze with as much certainty as I could. "My parents tried for years to have children. I have no extended family in my generation, few friends, no love life. Someday, Mom and Dad will be g-gone. I'll be alone."

Even saying the words caused me pain.

"I'll never have the opportunity for a relationship or children in a normal situation. The legacy from my parents, the love they've given me, I can give that to a baby no one else would want. I can have my own small family."

I could feel the truth of it.

Theresa sat on the edge of my bed and took my un-casted hand in hers. "If you change your mind within the next few weeks, you need only tell me, Ellie."

I nodded and squeezed her hand as tears poured down my face. I rested my head against the pillow and cried myself to sleep.

When I woke up a long time later Theresa was gone. My door was open and I could see the edge of the black tactical gear my guards wore on either side of the entry.

A frail elderly woman sat beside my bed in her wheelchair and I smiled at her in welcome.

My request to be placed in the geriatric wing initially confused everyone. I explained that I didn't want to be placed near children or other women.

They didn't need to be touched by the violence of my situation or frightened by the armed men stationed outside my door.

I love older people. No matter what happens in the modern world, they can tell you first-hand stories about famine, war, and civil unrest that manages to put things in perspective.

Not that the elderly friends I've made are depressing. Far from it. They lived through it all and have stories about the first television, what drive-ins were like in a '58 Chevy convertible with your boyfriend, and how granola saved them from food poisoning during Woodstock.

It's distracting. *Nice.*

"Hello, Mrs. Franklin."

"Hello, dear. You look better. How are you feeling?"

Her fingers were warped from arthritis and her skin was pale and paper-thin. She reached out to hold my hand.

"I'm fine. How's your hip? And Mr. Franklin?"

With a delicate snort, the old woman's eyes twinkled. "My hip is on the mend. I hate not being able to get around at more than a crawl. My Richard spends all his time here. Says I'll run off with a young orderly if he doesn't keep an eye out."

She waved her hand dramatically. "I'd divorce him for his raging jealous streak but we love each other too much. Besides, if that nurse from the night shift doesn't stop flirting with my darling, she'll learn about my temper."

I had to laugh. A movement by the door drew my attention and I smiled at my parents.

"Hello. You remember Mrs. Franklin?"

Mom swept in to take the elderly woman's hand and inquire after all manner of things.

Her questions told me my parents had checked out every person currently residing or working on this floor of the hospital.

My father approached the bed and sat beside me. "How are you feeling, sweetheart?"

He took my hand and I traced my fingers over the back of his. I love his hands. They're large and warm, more calloused than people would expect for a man of means.

"I'm good, Dad." I grinned, waiting for their usual push.

"Are you here to try to talk me into coming home again?"

A gentle smile touched his face. "No, Ellie. We're *taking* you home. There isn't going to be a discussion about it."

Chapter Fourteen

From the corner of my eye, I watched my mother touch cheeks with Mrs. Franklin and hold the door wide as she left.

Closing and locking it behind the elderly woman, she turned to me with a resolute expression on her face.

I frowned. "I-I think I should finish recovering here…" Watching their faces, my voice trailed off as understanding hit. "You know."

The day I was moved to a private room, an iPod speaker system was placed beside the bed. They wanted me to have music, they said. I never questioned it.

"You bugged the room. I should have known you would."

I closed my eyes with embarrassment and stress flaring all over my body. I felt my mother sit on the other side of my bed.

"Ellie. Look at me, love." The tears started falling before my lids fully lifted. "Your casts come off in three weeks. I found a positively evil physical therapist to work with you and get you back to full mobility. Theresa and her assistant will monitor you from home."

Dependent yet again. I murmured, "Alright."

Dad petted my hair. "Don't cry, please don't cry, Ellie."

"I-I want something of my own. Others might consider this child an abomination but I consider it an unexpected bright side. I *need* to keep this baby."

Mom nodded and stroked my hair. "Then keep it you shall. Our *grandchild* will never know a life without all the love we can give."

"Thank you for understanding. I doubt there's a stupider mother-to-be but I'll learn."

Her fingertips on my cheek, Mom whispered, "You've always been incredible with children, honey. You were amazing with Preston. He adored you."

I twisted my fingers in the blanket. "Thinking about him, it's what made up my mind. He was shuffled through a broken system, hurt over and over, but he was so easy to love. This baby might be my only chance to ever be a mother."

The observation upset my mother. "That's not *true*, Ellie…"

"It *is* true. I've known it for a long time."

"You're still so young. Give things time to happen." Dad stroked my cheek. "Why are you alone so much?"

I gave a small shrug. "I hate the not knowing." I knew he understood what I meant. "Being me, I never really know."

Mom opened her mouth to dispute it and I smiled. "No matter how heavily you vet them, you can't know the inner workings of someone's mind. If you could, those men would have disappeared at the bottom of a rock quarry covered in lime."

"Ellie…"

"I pled for mercy then. I asked you to give them a chance. I thought they could *change* and it was painfully naïve of me. I realize that now. I-I punished Hyde as horribly as myself."

Mom stood to pace. Suddenly she turned and said sharply, "Hyde was not *raped*! No one should *ever* experience what you went through! What you're going to go through!"

She gripped her hands together tightly. "Men rarely know what it means to be raped. Physical torture is horrifying. Rape goes deeper, affecting the mind and emotions. Women are expected to *protect* our bodies and sexual assault takes the ability out of our hands. It's the mind that suffers most."

I felt as if my mother understood firsthand. I glanced at my father who stared at her with pain written on his face.

Closing her eyes, she took a deep breath. "I'm *horrified* by what Hyde endured but the brutality done to *you*…"

"Don't, Mom. Don't think about it."

"Hyde would give his life for yours."

"I don't *want* him to give his life for mine, Mom. He…my team are the only friends I have in my daily life. Losing him…them to violence would break me."

I swallowed around the lump in my throat. "Now I'll have the stigma of *this*. Those men took from me in ways I can't fix, I can't undo. I'll always be…*tainted* by it."

The fury I felt, though not shouted, must have bled into my expression. I clenched my jaw and my good hand so tightly, the joints ached.

My father's rage matched my own. Like me, he kept his voice controlled and even. "Hyde and Si have taken out one of the three men, Ellie. They won't rest until the others are dead."

I knew the men were being pursued. It gave me satisfaction to know Hyde was the one tracking them down.

I met Dad's gaze and silently asked him the question I wanted the answer to. It was something I imagined at night when I thought about the violence done to the man I loved.

It should have shamed me. I thought myself civilized, kind, sometimes too influenced by the gentler emotions.

My need for their blood did not shame me.

He answered honestly. "He went hard. Every minute of your time in that building was repaid. He'll never be found."

A smile curved my lips before I caught myself.

My mother took my face in her hands. "Don't you *dare* feel bad about wanting them to scream. I want them to pay for what they did to you, Ellie. I want them begging for mercy they'll never get."

I pressed my hand against hers. "I wish their deaths guaranteed *no one* would know or-or remember."

Without warning, violent sobs consumed me. My parents held me and did what they could to soothe me.

After a long time, I leaned back to give my parents the

closest thing to a smile I could manage.

There was something I needed to know. "Do you think H-Hyde will come back after he finds them?"

My mother stared at me and I had the strangest sensation she saw into my soul and knew the secrets I held there.

"I think, short of death, you'll find it virtually impossible to shake Hyde from your side for the rest of your days. The man is committed to your safety."

I nodded and picked pretend lint from the blanket.

The silence drew out for almost a minute as I wondered why he agreed to dedicate so much time to my protection. I knew his life before me was difficult, filled with loss.

It didn't explain why he gave up a decade of his life to guard me. My parents must have made it *unbelievably* lucrative.

Mom's tone was gentle. "Elliana, if you loved someone, if they loved you, we'd welcome that person with open arms. Without stipulations. Do you know that?"

I took my time answering. "I used to dream about finding a love story like yours. I won't ever have love like that."

Saying it made it truer than I wanted it to be.

Dad said, "Don't give up, Ellie. It's early in the game."

"There are so few people I-I care for, that I trust. Fewer still whose company I can be easy in. When I lost Sensei Pendragon, I felt it deeply. He taught me for so long."

"You've grown close to your team," Mom observed. "Closer than any other staff in your life."

I nodded. "I forget they're staff. I forget they're with me because I'm an assignment, a job. I *try* to forget. I know it sounds pathetic but I don't care."

Lost in thought, I laid back on the pillows. "I have a pretend world where Bianca is my older sister. She's more world-traveled and confident than I am. I can ask her anything without feeling stupid. She's like a Valkyrie."

My mother's hand tightened on mine.

"Si was so patient while he taught me to cook. He laughed no matter how badly I messed up. When I accomplished Crème Brule, he bought me a pastry torch engraved with my name."

Of my many possessions, it was one of my favorites.

"When I wanted to feel what it was like to ride in open air instead of behind bulletproof glass, Fiaaz brought his own bike to a closed track. He put me in tons of safety equipment and spent all day showing me." I laughed. "I caused a lot of damage but he thought it was funny."

"I'm so glad I didn't know about that, Ellie darling." My father looked positively nauseous.

"Padme teaches me about makeup and clothes and hair. Even when I'm a brat about it. She wants me to know so if I ever need to pull off *glamorous* by myself, I can. We watch romantic comedies and eat ice cream like normal friends hanging out."

"That sounds lovely, darling," Mom whispered.

"Sometimes, everyone hangs out together to watch movies. I really like that." I shrugged and pretended my chest didn't hurt. "Hyde…"

Let it go, Ellie…let it go. It will never be the same now.

My mother's touch lifted my face. "What has he shown you?"

"Being *me* doesn't mean I can't do normal things. I wanted to visit a fair. The exhibits, the shows, the food, the rides. It's hard to manage a protection detail in a situation like that. A lot can go wrong. I didn't think they'd let me go."

"They found a way?" my mother prompted.

I nodded. "They put me in disguise and the team disappeared, there but out of sight, so I could enjoy the experience."

It was so noisy with children screaming and the sound of the rides. The air smelled like popcorn and funnel cakes.

"They maintained a perimeter and I played games and walked the exhibits. There was a huge roller coaster set up along one whole end of the fairgrounds, a hundred feet in the air. The cars were open so Hyde went with me."

I looked out the window as I recalled my nervous excitement at the top, the hardness of Hyde's shoulder, and how warm he was against my side.

He whispered, "Hang on, Ellie."

Then the drop and closing my eyes with my hands in the air, wishing it could go on forever.

I never told anyone about the fair. I wanted to share it with my parents, to help them understand how different I felt as a person, as a woman, from everyone around me.

I gave them a half-smile. "Being with Hyde, with all of them, is the closest I've ever been to a regular girl."

Shaking myself from the memories, I inhaled deeply. "I'll never have normal again. Not after this. I'll work and write. With a child to pour my love into, I'll be content."

"I want so much more than *contentment* for you, Ellie." Mom blinked against the tears in her eyes.

"It's more than most people have. It will be enough." Gathering my strength, I nodded. "I'll return home whenever you're ready."

Chapter Fifteen

Early August 2014

It took a few days to get the equipment Theresa needed installed at home and for renovations to be completed.

I said goodbye to my elderly friends and allowed a team of guards to push my wheelchair to the caravan of armored vehicles waiting in the hospital's secured underground parking garage.

The drive to the estate took twenty minutes and I used the time to maneuver a wire hanger into the top of the leg cast that extended from my thigh to my ankle.

It was awkward because my wrist and forearm were broken on that side as well. I finally asked Padme to help.

The relief was sublime.

"Two more weeks, Ellie." Her forced smile hurt my heart. "Then soft casts that can be *removed* at night. I've organized all your emails and correspondence so you don't have to plod through weeks of crap to get to the important stuff."

Bianca was the only other member of my personal team in evidence during transport. Her grin was huge. "Jamie Vasquez and her little boy Ricky sent a three-page letter thanking your parents for the car and Ricky's college fund but insisted it was unnecessary. They're happy to hear you're on the mend."

My parents sat on the opposite side of the limo. Their smiles of relief were enough to convince me that going home was the right thing to do.

Not having me close, especially in my vulnerable condition, was worse on them. I understood that better now.

As we turned onto the long drive leading to the main house, I absorbed the ambiance of the home where I grew up.

It felt like *years* since I'd seen it.

My eyes widened as dozens of staff members came into view beneath the overhang of the main entrance.

I was assisted from the limo and met with cheers. The biggest man I'd ever seen came forward to lift my wheelchair, with me in it, to the landing stretched before the massive double doors.

One by one, the people who watched me grow up came forward to take my hand or kiss my cheek.

Mrs. Safoya, the matron of the inner domain, had been with my parents for forty years. She embraced me carefully, held my face as she kissed my cheeks.

Her husband, combination butler and majordomo, wrapped his arm around my shoulders and pressed a kiss to my hair.

They were a constant presence in my past. Almost like a second set of parents.

They whispered of their relief to have me home. Originally from Poland, their accents were diluted by so many years in the States.

"Cook is making your favorite tonight and blackberry tarts for dessert. A celebration that we have you back again."

I held them as well as I could. "Thank you. I've missed you."

Nodding, they stepped away to hide their tears. I waved to everyone else as Bianca pushed me inside.

A suite of rooms in the rarely used east wing were updated to give me privacy. Far from the room I used as a little girl.

In the elevator, Padme described the changes cheerfully. She wanted to disguise the fact that my freedom had been completely curtailed for the time being.

"The apartment is *lovely*. Once the contractor realized your mother wanted a full kitchen and an entire room removed to expand and upgrade the bathroom, he stopped trying to upsell her. You'll love the view of the rear gardens."

I wasn't sure how to respond. I lived in this house most of my life and loved it…but I doubted I'd relax anytime soon.

She rushed on diligently. "I set up your office, of course. Dr. Spellman has her office and suite across the hall, her assistant next door to her. The lab is *steps away* so you don't have to go back and forth to the hospital."

I gave her a break. "Padme. It's fine…I'm fine. I'll recover and my parents need reassurance that I'm safe. I miss running and riding. I miss…"

I stopped myself just in time.

Padme and Bianca shared a look over my head and I was

glad I hadn't completed my thought.

Entering the apartment, Fiaaz was there to greet me with a bow before taking my good hand and kissing the back.

I suspected he and Bianca were in a relationship but could never bring myself to ask them. They often rode together and groomed the horses Fiaaz stabled on the estate.

Breathtaking Arabians he agreed to breed for my father.

I knew more about Padme and Hyde than the rest of my team but I'd *love* to know every minute of all their lives.

They fascinated me to no end.

"It's good to have you with us again, Ellie." Fiaaz smiled gently. "There are many things I wish to say. For now, I'll simply welcome you back to your life. You were missed."

"Thank you, Fiaaz."

I loved being back with my team despite the obvious absence of Hyde and Si. I tried not to dwell on it.

Padme and Bianca helped settle me in my bedroom. The suite was too large to contemplate or explore.

I took a long nap and had to be awakened for dinner.

Bianca wrapped my casts and assisted me into the enormous shower stall. Once she was certain I was secure on the medical chair placed in the center, she left me alone.

I took my time. It was the first time since the attack that I could bathe myself. I worked to sterilize every inch of my skin with water that was as hot as I could stand.

Turning off the spray, I grabbed a towel from the hook and idly wondered if I could make it from the shower to my wheelchair.

I wrapped myself in the towel and placed both hands on the chair rails when Bianca's voice froze me.

"I *know* you aren't going to try to leave a wet shower unassisted with broken bones. That would be foolish and needlessly prideful. Two character flaws that don't generally afflict you, Ellie. You were waiting for help. Am I right?"

Giving her a bright smile, I lied through my teeth and gritted them as she helped me to the chair and back to my bedroom.

"God, I *hate* this shit."

Meeting my eyes, she murmured, "I know Ellie. I swear I do. You're naturally independent and brave." She crouched beside me. "It isn't weak to know when to ask for help so you don't make an unpleasant situation worse."

I sighed. "I didn't think about how my parents would react if I'd been injured further due to pure stubbornness. I'm sorry."

I meant it.

She helped me into panties and a flowing sundress that came to mid-calf. It seemed my mother ordered clothing that offered support in soft materials that wouldn't irritate.

One of the wounds I sustained was at my shoulder blade. The stitches were dissolved but it still itched like crazy. A bra was an impossible addition to my wardrobe right now.

Padme brushed my hair carefully and pulled it back from my face. "Shall we do a bit of makeup?"

I rolled my eyes. "When do I *ever* want makeup?"

She grinned at me in the mirror. "I have to *try*, Ellie."

My assistant pushed me from my apartment to the elevator with Fiaaz and Bianca walking on either side of the chair. We made the trip to the main living area in silence.

My nerves were shot.

I caught a glimpse of people waiting inside. Friends of my parents that I wasn't in *any* condition to see.

Sudden panic flooded my body and I dropped my good foot on the floor to stop the chair.

It jarred me sharply and I hissed in piercing pain. Breathing too fast, shaking uncontrollably, my mind locked up.

I was terrified.

Chapter Sixteen

Bianca instantly dropped to one knee in front of me and took my hand. "Breathe, Ellie. It's okay."

I was humiliated that my eyes filled with tears. I blinked furiously to keep them from falling.

"These are people you know," Padme offered softly. "They love you but no one will even be allowed to *touch* you if that's what you wish."

I whimpered in fear I didn't understand.

Fiaaz knelt beside Bianca. "Hyde *never* doubts your strength or bravery, Ellie. He likens you to Diana, goddess of the hunt. Powerful, fearless. You can do this."

Swallowing hard, I worked to get my breathing under control. I blotted at the sweat that beaded on my forehead. Gripping the arm of the wheelchair, I lifted my foot from the floor.

"I can do this," I said shakily.

"Yes, you can." My driver patted my white-knuckled hand and rose with Bianca. "Every damn time, Ellie. You're a fighter."

I nodded and felt Padme touch my shoulder. "We won't

leave your side for a moment."

She pushed me into the great room and my mother and father saw me as they turned. They put down their drinks and hurried across the room to me.

I forced a smile. "S-sorry it took so long."

"Ellie, you look lovely."

It was a lie but I murmured, "Thanks, Dad." Avoiding looking at anyone else in the room, I whispered to them, "Thank you for the apartment. It's good to be home."

My mother knelt to hug me and my father struggled to get his emotions under control. They were on the verge of a breakdown and I didn't want that for them.

"I'm safe. I'm home. We won…again. Let's celebrate."

Nodding, they straightened and turned to the room. I stared at my lap for a moment to get my panic under control again.

Fiaaz and Bianca lightly touched my shoulders and I held my head up as people I'd known since I was little gathered around.

The oldest friends of Samuel and Monica Fields ranged from long-time business associates to men and women who attended Oxford with my dad or Yale with my mom.

Most of them attended my christening and I knew almost immediately that they were aware of my brutal attack.

They were more like family.

As the older set greeted me, they told me how good it was

to see me home with family. I was offered yachts, islands, and castles to get away for a while.

A couple made offers of vengeance and Dad assured them it was being handled. Heads nodded with cool calculation.

Older friends drifted away and younger ones approached.

Natalia approached and I *wanted* to tell her how much I loved her newly blonde curls, that I knew what the necklace she wore *meant*, and how happy both of those things made me for two people I loved deeply.

I was frozen. Our last conversation in New York City made my throat clench up. The things I told her, the questions I shyly asked, the hope I had for my future were all I could hear in my head.

Opening my mouth to speak, nothing came and she dropped to her knees beside me.

"I know, darling. I know." She put her cheek against mine and whispered at my ear, "Your heart continues to beat. They'll rot in unmarked graves as you embrace the next phase of your life. You remain the most *powerful* woman I know."

She leaned back enough to look at me and I nodded through my tears. "I love you," I mouthed.

Her cool palm on my cheek, she mouthed it back and stood.

Hudson's hand cupped my skull and I could feel how he trembled. He said nothing but stared into my eyes for a long moment.

Words weren't necessary with a man like him.

Bending, he pressed his forehead against mine, closed his eyes, and we stayed like that as I struggled to breathe.

Pulling back, he kissed my cheeks and the back of my hand. Then he moved away with Natalia.

Harper took my hand between both of his. He couldn't control the emotion in his voice. "If you feel the need to run away, my home is yours. At any time, now or in the future. Whatever you need, Elliana."

"Thank you, Harper," I managed hoarsely.

Elijah crouched at my side. His green eyes stared into mine for a long moment. Then he bent forward to whisper, "Your Hyde found them all, Ellie. He avenged what was done to you. Bathed in their blood and broke their minds before ending their lives."

He stood, lifted my hand, and kissed the back. I sniffed, wiped my eyes, and smiled.

"Thank you, Elijah."

"Sometimes, you need *precise* news to lift your spirits."

"You're so right." I managed a shaky laugh and he winked.

The media portrayal of the uber-rich focused on selfish bastards who lived to spend their money. My parents made it a point to keep such people out of their inner circle.

Their friends were socially aware and generous to a fault. It was a fact I'd always appreciated. I didn't have to fake enjoyment of their company.

I was exhausted by the time Mrs. Safoya announced dinner.

I asked to sit close to my mother with my team nearby. Long accustomed to the presence of my staff at meals, my parents' friends didn't question it. A couple of place cards were moved and I was assisted into a normal chair.

Course after course of my favorite foods were served. When my entree was placed in front of me, I worried for a moment about being able to cut the filet wrapped in delicate filo dough.

I shouldn't have given it a second thought.

Cook had pre-sliced my food with knives so sharp it still looked whole. I glanced up to see the housekeeper looking at me with a smile.

I took small bites of everything but couldn't eat much. I was anxious, off-balance.

I missed Hyde.

My first speed bump occurred an hour into dinner. Over the years, I started accumulating wines from around the world. I had Dad's discriminating palette.

It was unusual to see me eat a meal without a glass of something from my collection.

Dean DeMarco, a college friend of Dad's and fellow wine lover, asked, "You're not partaking of your lovely wines, Elliana. We're enjoying one of our mutual favorites."

"I-I..." The question took me by surprise and I was unsure how to answer. I blushed violently.

Directly behind me came, "Miss Fields is taking too much medication right now to risk combining it with alcohol."

Hyde's voice startled me and sent chills racing over my skin.

Dean's broad smile directed over my head made me want to turn more than anything. "Of course! Ellie looks so vibrant I didn't even *consider* the danger of mixing pills and alcohol. Thankfully, someone did."

That Hyde came to my defense instantly in such a way told me two things that almost made me shake apart.

He'd been there far longer than I realized and he knew I was keeping the child resulting from my rape.

I hadn't seen him in *weeks* and I worried about passing out from instant, debilitating stress.

My body shook and I placed my hands on my thighs to conceal it as much as possible. Beneath the table, Padme and Bianca each placed a hand over mine.

I stared at the candle in front of me, willing myself into shallow meditation that finally allowed me to calm down. With a final pat, my friends pulled away.

"How's the writing going, Ellie? I'm *dying* for more chapters." Thaddeus Kellering was one of my mother's first business partners. He owned a publishing company and begged to be given first looks at my work. "The stories are so fresh and exciting. I'm *hooked* and you left me on a cliffhanger!"

His lovely wife Sarah nodded in agreement. Their estate abutted the northern border of Elysian Fields.

I swallowed carefully and extended my good arm to lift my water goblet with a steady hand. "I finished another six chapters. I can email those to you if you like."

"Loved the first two books of the series. *Loved them.* Sarah stayed up all night reading. I don't even cringe at the romantic elements. They're well-blended into the overall espionage and villainy." Thaddeus said the last with a stereotypical cartoon villain's voice.

I *never* discussed my writing in front of my team…since they were the basis for many of my characters. I swore my personal assistant to secrecy.

Sarah added, "Your hero makes me flat out swoon. Thaddeus started getting jealous but I can't help it! He seems so *real.* I have to know who inspired you!"

Laughing a little shrilly, I took another long drink of water. I worried I'd give way to hysterics any moment. I was careful not to look directly at anyone.

Natalia said from a few seats away, "Ellie's mind is probably *overflowing* with people to draw from. It seems the circle who knew about these books is rather small and I'm not in it. Firm talking-to later, darling."

Another semi-hysterical giggle and I tried to change the subject. "I should be finished in the next month. Padme is transposing my notes." I cleared my throat and made a subject change. "H-how's Cameron?"

"He's getting over a nasty cold so we didn't bring him tonight but he's practically a giant. I won't be able to keep him away for long." Sarah was always happy to discuss their little boy.

Thaddeus was almost twenty years older than his wife and they adored their child. He said seriously, "He asks about you daily, Ellie. To him, you hung the moon. The colt rarely goes a day without being ridden."

"I recognize a fellow equestrian when I meet one. I knew Sarafina's foal would be perfect for his first horse. I'll be glad to ride again. After…when I'm not wearing these."

I held up my casted arm wrapped in fluorescent pink to cover my near slip of the tongue.

"Send him over for a visit, Sarah. Dad put a PS4 in the media room and I owe Cameron a rematch on *Call of Duty*. Two weeks. Tell him to be here or I'll consider him too scared to face me."

Laughing happily, Sarah and Thaddeus agreed they'd present him the instant I was ready.

Glancing down the table, I smiled at Vera Queen, my mother's roommate in college. "How are the mastiffs?"

"Huge and happy, as per usual."

"I'd like a puppy, please. Preferably a girl. I haven't had a dog since I was twelve."

It would be nice to have a dog again. A *big fucking dog* who could swallow someone's head.

Vera clasped her hands in front of her. "I have *just* the girl for you, Ellie. Perfect form and excellent manners." Lifting her glass, she added, "I'll bring her by to meet you."

I looked at my parents. "I need to call it a night. I'm *exhausted*."

"Of course, darling. We'll save tarts." Mom stood with my father. "Excuse us while we walk Ellie to her wing. Enjoy another glass of wine and dessert will be served shortly."

I smiled and said my goodbyes as Fiaaz lifted me carefully into my wheelchair. "Sorry to quit so early."

Everyone murmured assurances that it was fine and rose to kiss me goodbye. Some told me they'd be around for a few days while others mentioned staying in Dallas.

My parents waited in the doorway and Bianca and Fiaaz stepped back to allow them space to walk at my sides.

"I'm sorry, Ellie. You know how our dinners stretch once we all start talking."

"I'm ready to drop."

Padme said quietly, "We're late on your medication, Ellie." At my sharp glance, she added, "I had the original prescriptions changed to *safer* selections but Ellie…they're not as effective. Are you sure you'll be able to handle the pain?"

I kept it simple. "Yes. I'm sure."

When we arrived at my rooms, I didn't see Hyde. I wondered if I dreamed his voice. Then I caught him from the corner of my eye entering his room without a backward glance.

My heart thumped hard.

Mom insisted on helping me get ready for bed so we could chat about the dinner party. When I was wearing a tank top and sleep shorts, she helped me into bed and sat beside me to smooth my hair.

I felt ten-years-old again in a way that wasn't unwelcome.

Si entered the room with a cup of tea and bowed. "Ellie."

"Welcome back, Si."

"You were missed." His smile was gentle. "You lost weight. I'll make it my goal to reverse that."

I chuckled. "I know you will."

"Until tomorrow. Sleep well, Ellie." With another bow, he left.

Mom stabilized my hand so I could drink the tea and when it was done, my parents bent to kiss me goodnight.

I settled down to sleep, listening to the sounds of my household quieting for the night.

New guards were stationed on the roof and grounds.

Si and Fiaaz had rooms across the hall. Bianca's room was next door. Padme and Hyde slept in my suite.

I heard the locks engage through my partially open bedroom door and the tones of my alarm system being activated.

It took me a long time to relax. I should have known recovery would include subconscious mental trauma.

I wasn't sliding headlong into a drug-induced sleep. My bedroom wasn't brightly lit or noisy like the hospital.

It was quiet.

It was dark.

Terror waited to reach out and toy with me.

Chapter Seventeen

Being home brought down a brick in the wall my subconscious erected around my attack.

I had my first nightmare and it was a whopper.

The contents were hazy but terrifying. I woke on the floor of my room with Padme and Hyde crouched over my body.

My assistant had bleeding scratches on her upper chest and Hyde sported a busted lip.

Streams of sweat dripped from my body. I was in *severe* pain. My hair was plastered to my face and upper body.

Padme reached out and pushed the strands away. "Ellie. Please tell me you're awake." I nodded, confused. "Thank God. Oh, thank God."

She sat cross-legged beside me and lifted my head from the floor into her lap. Then my assistant did something I'd never seen in nine years. *She burst into tears.*

A ripple of fear skated down my spine.

My throat was raw when I tried to ask what happened.

I looked at Hyde's face. Every muscle in his body was rigid with tension. He was flushed, shaking, and clearly enraged.

For a moment, I wondered if he was angry at me. Then a piece of my dream flashed before my conscious mind and my body jerked, sending knifing pain through my healing limbs.

"Going t-to be sick. Please."

Hyde stood with me in his arms in seconds, striding for the bathroom. He held me suspended from the floor around my waist as I lost anything still in my stomach.

The pressure on my ribs was agony but the position was necessary since I couldn't bend one leg. His other hand gathered my hair and held it out of my way.

Padme got a damp cloth and wiped my face and mouth. "Alright, Ellie. Okay. Let's get her to the sink, Hyde."

He gently moved me across the room and held me steady as I brushed my teeth and washed my face with one hand.

Leaning heavily on the cool marble, I looked at Hyde's face behind mine. To me, he was the perfect blend of everything I admired in a man.

He was six-two, leanly muscled. His hair was shaggy. It was light brown in the winter, golden blonde in the summer. His eyes changed colors depending on what he wore.

He had to shave twice a day to keep his jaw smooth but I liked it when he only shaved once. He had a dusting of stubble over his jaw and around his mouth.

He had multiple scars and he was serious almost all the time. I rarely saw him smile but when he did, there were dimples in his cheeks.

I'd seen him run, fight, and shoot. He never, ever lied to me and he always made me feel safe.

Everything about him screamed danger but I'd run toward him before *anyone* else if I felt threatened.

He watched me unblinking in the mirror. My heart rate was too high. I felt dizzy and strange.

I said the words I owed him, words I should've said weeks before but didn't know how. "I'm sorry, Hyde. Forgive me."

He opened his mouth to respond but I was already gone.

* * *

I woke the next morning between clean sheets and in clean clothes. I hurt *everywhere*. My forearm throbbed like an open wound and my shoulder felt out of place. Pain shot down my leg and my toes were numb.

I tried to sit up and moaned in agony despite trying to hold it back. Bianca was at the door two seconds later.

"Jesus, Ellie. You *need* the pain meds. Let me get them."

"No! I can do it. Can you help me to the chair? *Fuck!*" My eyes shot to Bianca's. Through gritted teeth, I added, "I'm sorry. It isn't you. I'm sorry."

Bianca helped me sit up. "Ellie, I realize being the resident sweetheart has saturated your entire life but I think you're allowed some pain-induced fury. It's understandable."

Thirty minutes later I was showered and dressed in cotton shorts and a super soft tank top. The shower was an exercise in pain control. I wasn't sure whether the droplets on my skin were water or sweat.

Every movement hurt.

Padme braided my hair in a thick plait down my back. Inhaling carefully, I nodded and the two women took me into the main room. Fiaaz and Si watched Hyde's room nervously.

"What is it? What's wrong?"

Bianca pushed me to the seating area and Fiaaz lifted me to the sofa. I couldn't control the whimper that escaped.

The blonde whispered, "We *need* to give you pain medication, Ellie. You can't sustain this."

"I can't take anything. I won't. I can handle it."

Everyone was on edge and it freaked me out. This group didn't *get* edgy. When people with their training tensed up, bad shit went down.

"Did something happen? Is Hyde…did Hyde *leave?*"

Padme lifted my hand and I realized I'd been digging my short nails into the top of my thigh.

Clearly shocked at the mere *suggestion* Hyde would quit, Fiaaz said carefully, "Elliana, it's important you remain *calm*."

He crouched beside me. "There's a secret we can no longer keep from you because neither of them will stand down. They insist on guarding you around the clock."

"I'm not getting between them again," Si added softly. "This can't continue. The conflict bleeds into everything around them now. It's time to relieve the pressure."

I rubbed my temples, trying to ease the pain and focus. "I…Fiaaz, I-I get headaches. I don't understand. Is Hyde angry with me? Who won't stand down?"

Breathing too hard, the pain stole my brain function. I wanted to understand what was happening.

Bianca smoothed my hair away from my damp face. I was slick with sweat again.

"Ellie, *please* let us get you something for the pain. Please." I shook my head once sharply. "Ssh, Ellie, slow your breathing, love. Slow, yes that's it. Like that. Slow and steady."

She took a cup and saucer from Si. I stared at it in suspicion.

"It's herbal tea, Ellie. It won't hurt you or the baby. We wouldn't let *anything* happen to your child. It's a brew Si made. Take small sips to help with the pain."

I tried to take it but my hand shook too badly. I was angry at myself, tired of being weak and confused.

"Tell me what's going on and I'll *drink* the fucking tea! Where's Hyde? I didn't mean for any of this to happen. I'm so sorry." I didn't want to cry anymore but couldn't stop.

Tears slipped from the corners of Bianca's eyes. I'd never seen her cry. "No, Ellie. *No*. It isn't you. You didn't do anything."

A door opened but I couldn't move my body to look.

Hyde came around the end of the couch and I gasped, wincing at his busted lip. I put my fingers over my lips as fresh tears fell.

The apology was on the tip of my tongue when *another* Hyde appeared at the first's shoulder. Above the collar of his shirt, I could see a bandage covering what looked like a gunshot wound. His arm was in a sling.

I was *incoherent* with confusion. Rubbing my temple hard, I tried to clear my head. Nothing made sense.

"G-gunshot wound? I-I don't remember…"

I took a deep breath and closed my eyes while I gathered my thoughts. Opening them, I lifted my head.

There were two Hydes.

One version had a busted lip. I put it there in the middle of the night. The other's lips were perfect but he had recent gunshot wounds.

I whispered brokenly, "Am I *losing* my mind? Am I even awake?" I shook my head. "How is this possible?"

Padme said quietly, "They're twins, Ellie. Jonas and Jordan Hyde."

Almost a minute passed in silence while everyone stared at me. They waited for me to react, to say something.

What could I possibly say?

I started to laugh hysterically, doubling over as the laughter dissolved into broken sobs that strung my muscles tight.

They called my mother and cleared the room.

Chapter Eighteen

Mom sat on the couch and held me for a long time as I lost my fucking mind.

Eventually, she helped me lay down and pulled my head into her lap so she could play with my hair. Unbraiding the entire length, she began to plait tiny braids absently.

I appreciated that she let me calm down completely before expecting me to speak. It took a while.

"Why didn't you tell me? Why didn't *someone* tell me?"

She considered her words carefully. "When we searched for your security team, we went through underground channels that would curl your hair, Ellie. We wanted the best of the best for our daughter."

Her fingers worked softly, methodically. It was a comforting reminder of my childhood.

"We needed people with enough experience and ruthlessness to protect you but with enough humanity to understand that their charge was a young woman with a gentle soul."

I nodded as my tears fell into her lap. "You found them. Every one of them is lethal yet so kind to me."

"The meeting to secure your staff was done at Salt Flats at midnight. Very cloak and dagger. Your father *loved* it but he'll never admit such a thing."

I tried to smile and failed.

"Hyde's name was mentioned to us by three impeccable sources. His entire career, no one knew he was a twin except those at the highest levels of government. His safety and the safety of his missions relied heavily on that secrecy."

"It's been five *years*, Mom."

"We had to keep you *safe*, Ellie!" She shook her head and I glimpsed the lioness that lived inside her. "I didn't *care* about the conditions. Security averted two kidnapping attempts before you even left for school. An heiress, eighteen, a confirmed virgin…the bounty for you was *astronomical*."

My sharp laugh was self-mocking. "Two descriptions which are no longer accurate. I'm nothing more than wealthy used goods now. That should get me off quite a few sites."

"Ellie, that's so cold."

"My *life* is cold, Mom."

She flinched. I slowly sat up, gritting my teeth against the pain. I rubbed my face to clear the hysteria.

My hair fell around me as I rested my good arm on my good leg and tried to still the raging agony in every cell.

"They've been covering me and changing places for five years. I never even suspected."

I had to know, to face it. "What happened that day, Mom?"

Her eyes went wide. "You don't know?" I shook my head and she frowned. "You haven't asked Padme or one of the others?" This time, I was the one who flinched. "You're *embarrassed* to ask. Why?"

"He...*they* wouldn't have been hurt if it wasn't for me." Mom started to dispute it but I interrupted, "Just tell me."

"One of your attackers shot Jordan three times on the other side of the trees with a silenced 9mm. He lost consciousness in a drainage tunnel. You weren't due back for half an hour."

"We missed the check-in and didn't reappear." I knew the protocols. "Padme radioed without response."

"Yes. Fiaaz and Bianca found Jordan when they got to the park but no one could find you or Jonas. The trackers on your shoes were deactivated. Those animals crushed them and tossed them in the woods."

She swallowed hard. "Thankfully, the shooter had terrible aim. He used the entire magazine to bring Jordan down. They scoured the structures and woods where he was found."

Mom couldn't look at me.

"Jonas was shot with the tranquilizer dart meant for you. They thought they'd already killed him and had no other options. They resorted to hitting you in the head with a rock. Both of you were dragged to the maintenance shed."

"I was probably bleeding too much to remove from the park without someone noticing." My nails gouged my palm. I said numbly, "They're dead now."

"Hyde took Si and hunted them down. They paid them back for what they did to you. Your people wanted to drag out their torture but decided they couldn't split your staff that long."

Her eyes were bright. "They had you for thirty-seven minutes and did as much damage as they could. I told Hyde to make those minutes *count*."

"Why tell me now? They both nearly died…" I rubbed my hand over my heart. The pain there was excruciating and it had nothing to do with my physical injuries. "I'd quit and move on, not reveal my trade secret."

Mom snorted. "Yeah, you'd *quit*. You've never quit anything. I'm surprised you know the word."

She reached out to smooth my hair. "They can't hide their distinctive wounds and neither will stand down. They refuse to leave you but you know them too well."

"Clearly not, Mom."

"Ellie, you know their features, their bodies, probably better than they do." My face flamed hot. "You would have figured it out almost immediately."

"Someone should have *told* me."

"I regret the decision now." She inhaled deeply. "They didn't want to tell you while you were in the hospital but we knew it was only a matter of time."

Mom stood and went into the kitchen. A minute later, she came back with a glass of orange juice. "You're still anemic and your blood sugar is shit. Drink up, baby."

I took it and considered things. So many things made sense now. Others were far more confusing.

I'd been in love with Hyde for so long, my heart refused to let him…*them* go. Even knowing there were two of them.

I was embarrassed, confused, devastated and there wasn't a *damn thing* I could do about it.

Mom and I sat together for an hour in silence. I fought pain that felt like someone was drilling holes in my bones and tried to reconcile my new reality.

I was a wreck. Physically, emotionally, I was lost.

Padme tapped softly on the main door before opening it a bit. "I'm sorry to interrupt. Hayden Delkin is here to see Ellie."

Mom frowned. "Are you up to that, honey?"

I thought about the quietest of the four Delkin siblings and nodded. We'd always gotten along. Maybe he could distract me for a few minutes so I could get my bearings.

My assistant pushed the door wide and stepped aside so Hayden could enter. I glimpsed my team in the hall.

He wasted no time on pleasantries. Crossing the room, the middle Delkin son passed my mother and knelt in front of me in jeans, a t-shirt, and running shoes.

"I couldn't make it last night."

"That's alright," I told him hoarsely.

"You're off pain medication." I nodded. "It isn't safe for the baby?"

"How did you know?" My voice was barely audible. My mother froze beside me.

He didn't answer the question. Taking my good hand, he held it gently. "Focus on something. A stationary object. Let's see if we can get you some control over the pain."

For fifteen minutes, he walked me through a profound form of meditation. Similar to what my sensei taught me for years to relax in stressful situations but it dove far deeper.

I shouldn't have been surprised that it helped me breathe around the agony but I was.

"Bring yourself back slowly. Keep that connection to your heart, your breathing. That's it." He stroked my hand and I took a deep breath. "It's not perfect, Ellie. You're going to suffer until you're fully healed but it will help."

"I can think. I can focus despite the pain."

"Keep practicing. You'll get better at it." He pushed my hair over my shoulder. "You and I are much the same, Ellie. No matter what we do, we never manage to fit in this world."

"I'm trying." Tears welled in my eyes. "God knows I'm trying. I-I'm a mess."

My mother remained still and quiet.

"There's a lot to process and you've been through hell."

"I don't…remember."

"That doesn't matter. The knowledge is enough to torture you if you let it." His silver eyes stayed on mine. "Don't let it. Those animals can't be allowed to ruin the rest of your life."

"D-did you know about H-Hyde?" He nodded slowly. "I feel like such an idiot that I didn't see it. It hurts that no one told me. I understand why they didn't but…it hurts."

"I'm sorry, Ellie. It's alright to feel like an idiot when you miss something you think you should have seen. I've felt like that often enough."

"Why did you come all this way, Hayden? I got the flowers and your beautiful letter." One corner of my mouth lifted. "Handwritten letters are so rare."

"I was out of the country when I heard. I couldn't leave but I wanted to send you something. I knew you'd need help to manage your pain." I nodded in sincere gratitude. "I also wanted to tell you something face to face."

"What?"

"I think you should marry me, Ellie."

A gasp was the only response from my mom. I didn't speak.

"I know you're terrified about what will happen when you have your baby. I don't have Harper's reputation or Harrison's husband." I smiled softly. "My name would protect you in a different way than your parents can. It would be my honor."

His offer didn't surprise me. I squeezed his hand.

"You're an incredible man and if I loved you or you loved me, I'd have no trouble saying yes." I shook my head. "Love isn't possible between us. You'll *always* love her and I-I *can't* love anyone else. It would be an easy path to marry you but it would break us both in the end."

Blinking back tears that filled my eyes, I added in a whisper, "Thank you for asking me...with everything."

Lifting his body, he took me carefully in his arms and held me as I cried brokenly against his shoulder. He rubbed my back and whispered soothingly at my ear.

Eventually, I calmed and he leaned back to kiss my forehead, my cheeks, and my lips softly. "If you change your mind, I'm here. I don't deny your reasons but I think we could work around them."

Giving him a watery smile, I nodded. "Have you eaten?"

"Not yet. Perhaps we can scare up some leftovers?"

I laughed at the memory of Hayden happening upon me when I was lost in the Delkin house as a little girl. I'd gone to the bathroom and got turned around.

On his way to the kitchen for a snack, he invited me along and held my hand. He made us sandwiches and poured glasses of milk. We enjoyed our late-night meal at the big counter together. I made him laugh so hard that he snarfed milk through his nose.

When I was done, he led me back to the room I couldn't find and tugged my pigtails.

For years, I pretended he was the big brother I didn't have.

"I think I can arrange that," I said.

He helped me into my chair and led the way from the apartment to the lower floors.

My team followed in confused silence.

Hayden walked me through another session of meditation when the pain started to swamp me again. Then he brushed a kiss over my lips and took his leave.

Focusing on my mother as the front door closed behind the only man to ever propose to me, I whispered, "Sorry, Mom. I couldn't do it."

I rubbed my temple tiredly. "I need to lay down for a few hours. I can't deal with the rest right now. I need…to process. I don't know what to say yet."

Without a word, Padme and Bianca returned me to my apartment and helped me into bed.

Staring at the design on the tray ceiling above me, I picked a point to focus on and practiced the technique Hayden taught me to ease the pain that kept trying to pull me under.

It calmed me enough to sleep and that was more than I dared to hope for.

The rest would still be there when I woke. Two Hydes would still exist, my heart would still be unable to separate them, and the confusion would still make me feel like an immature child.

All of it would have to wait.

Chapter Nineteen

After a long nap, I woke wondering if the morning was a dream. Then I knew it wasn't.

My heart ached as much as my healing body. I felt foolish, childish, and undervalued.

For five years, I loved Hyde. A man who was larger than life, deadly and beautiful. I dreamed about him at night and fantasized about him during the day.

It was his face in my mind when I touched myself. He was the only man I'd ever loved, desired, craved.

Disciplining myself to hide my feelings, control my reactions, and ignore my desperation made it possible for me to live under the same roof with a man whose voice made me wet, shaky, needy every time I heard it.

Since I was eighteen, I imagined Hyde as the man who took my virginity. I played out the details in my mind and never failed to climax with a power that stole my breath.

Everything was different now.

I felt wrong in my skin, dirty from the touch of three strangers who had no right to touch me.

They stole more than my physical virginity, they stole my

ability to imagine Hyde touching me. They stole my curiosity if he'd *want* to touch me, kiss me, love me.

Dealing with the loss of things I never shared with anyone was nothing compared to realizing Hyde was *two* men and forever out of my reach outside of my personal protection.

Wiping at tears that slipped into my hair, I forced myself to sit up. Breathing deeply for several minutes, I braced my weight on my good leg and held the footboard of my bed with my good arm to maneuver myself into my wheelchair.

I wasn't calling for goddamn help.

After some time to settle the aftershocks of movement and walking myself through the deeper meditation, I rolled into the bathroom to wash my face, brush my teeth, and drag my fingers through my hair.

It took forever using my good limbs.

It was time to minimize my vulnerabilities.

If I could feel stronger, it would go a long way toward reinforcing the walls around my heart.

A ridiculous expectation but I charged ahead anyway.

Picking up my cell, I called Theresa's private number at the mini-lab my parents built down the hall.

She answered on the first ring. "Ellie! How are you feeling?"

I got right to the point. "I want the soft casts. I have no mobility and I hate it."

The doctor was quiet for a moment. "What's going on,

Ellie? You're on track to get them off in two weeks."

"The last x-rays came back great. Even you were amazed at how fast I'm healing."

"That's true but…"

"I'll wear the soft ones longer if you want," I rushed ahead. "I'll even wear them to bed if you tell me to. I won't be able to do my usual stuff like running and riding but it would be great to get in and out of the shower without a production."

"Ellie, are you alright?"

"No." My voice broke and I hated it. "I'm weak and I'm dealing with a lot of shit right now. I need to feel like I'm in control of something. This is a start."

She was quiet for a long time then said, "Alright. I'll take them off. You follow my instructions to the letter."

"I will. I'll be over in ten minutes."

Disconnecting, I made my way into the living area of my suite where my team and my parents sat quietly waiting for me.

Hyde – *both of them* – stood when I entered the room.

"Hey, Dad."

"Princess. You look…determined." I could tell he wasn't sure what to say after the *big reveal* about my bodyguard. I imagine Mom clued him in on Hayden's visit as well. "You okay?"

"I will be." Inhaling carefully, I announced, "I'm on my way to Theresa." I cleared my throat. "The hard casts are coming off today."

Everyone shot to their feet and started talking at once. The Hyde brothers remained still and quiet, their eyes on me.

Padme walked across the room. "You're not scheduled to have them off for two more weeks at the minimum. What are you *doing*, Ellie?"

I held my ground because I needed to get better at it. "Theresa listened to my argument and agreed that I'm healing fast enough to do it now. I'll use the soft casts longer."

"Why? I don't understand." I stared at her but didn't answer. Her eyes widened and she murmured, "You feel *weak*. You're trying to regain control."

Looking past her to my parents, I said, "I need a powered chair. I can't use crutches with this arm."

"Honey," my mother whispered worriedly, "it's too soon to have the casts off. Wait a little and think on it."

"Maybe you're being a little hasty," my father added.

"Amazing." I was hurt and angry. "I can't even make valid decisions about my own recovery without everyone trying to coddle me. No wonder I'm not in the *need to know* camp."

Shaking my head, I went around my assistant toward the door, using my good limbs to get me there.

"This is happening. I don't give a single damn what anyone in this room thinks about it. It's my fucking body and despite how you treat me, I'm a grown-ass adult."

A few feet from the hall, someone took control of the back

of my chair. One of the Hydes walked past me to open the door.

I couldn't look at them. I couldn't talk to them.

The fact that they stepped up to help me accomplish what I needed to do made tears well in my eyes that I fought to keep from falling.

My pain was slowly climbing and I breathed through it. No one was changing my mind.

Entering Theresa's suite with two identical bodyguards was not something the doctor expected. She dropped a tray and stumbled against the counter.

"What…how in the hell?" Her face paled and she stared back and forth between the brothers.

"They're *twins!*" I said cheerfully. "There are *two* of them! Isn't that fascinating?"

The doctor looked at me, looked at the Hydes, then looked at me again. I could see pieces falling into place in her expression.

"Ellie…"

"Theresa. So help me god…do it or I'll call some quack to do it for me but it's happening. Right now."

The tension in the room was palpable. My mother wrung her hands. My father gripped her shoulders firmly. My staff had no idea what to do or say.

"Alright. Alright, Ellie."

While I waited for her to set up, I looked at my parents. "I need the chair. See if someone can get it here in the next two hours."

Mom nodded and took out her phone to send a text.

Dad whispered, "I'm sorry, Ellie."

Keeping my attention fixed on the wall, I replied, "Don't worry about it. It's a shock but nothing I can't roll with because I'm *Ellie*. Sweet, forgiving, and oh-so-polite."

Mom's face was tortured. "Honey…"

"I need to deal with one thing at a time, Mom. Cast removal is what I'm dealing with right now." I rubbed my temple and ignored the sweat on my brow from pain. "Just…let me breathe."

Everyone remained quiet until Theresa was ready. A young man I'd never seen before entered the room. "This is my assistant Adam. I'll need his help to remove the casts."

Nodding, I locked the chair and stood. Pain arced through my body and I froze, holding myself up with my good arm, all my weight on my uninjured leg.

"Ellie, I don't like this," Theresa said softly. "You're not ready."

"I'm ready."

"I can't numb the pain. The tools…"

Gritting my teeth, I straightened and reached for the table. Turning, I managed to get one side up which gave me what I needed to make it all the way.

I was sweating, I was in agony, but I fucking made it.

"Talk to me like I'm your patient. Not your friend, not your fellow board member, not my parents' child. Tell me *medically* why I can't remove these casts."

It seemed the entire room collectively held their breath. After almost a minute, she shook her head.

"Your bones are knitting together faster than any patient I've ever had. Physiologically, your bones are where most patients are further along in their recovery. Outside of the pain of removal due to the other injuries you sustained, there's no medical reason not to do it now."

"Thank you." My father helped lower me and I stared at the ceiling. "Don't worry about the pain. I can take it."

I added in a tone that broadcasted my anger. "It builds character."

Chapter Twenty

With a nod, Theresa and her assistant prepped to cut the plaster cast away. Slipping goggles in place, she turned on the saw. The buzz was loud in the quiet room.

Setting the blade against the cast, she got to work.

The vibration immediately made me clench my jaw so hard my teeth hurt. After thirty seconds, I gripped the edge of the table with a white-knuckled hand and felt sweat pooling between my breasts and soaking my back.

I stared at an odd fleck of paint on the ceiling, murmuring the meditation to myself, working to gain control.

Si, Fiaaz, Bianca, and Padme excused themselves to wait outside. I think Padme may have been crying.

I knew my mother was. She and Dad stood just behind my head. I could hear her soft whimpers as I endured a level of pain I expected but still made me want to scream.

The Hyde brothers didn't move from their place beyond Theresa and Adam. I allowed myself a single look, then turned away. Their stress was clearly written in the tightness around their mouths and eyes.

My own stress was through the roof.

"Ellie, are you alright?" Theresa wasn't, I could tell. She blinked rapidly behind her safety goggles.

"Keep going. I'm okay." The pain was worth it to gain even a small amount of freedom over my life.

For twenty minutes, I pretended I didn't moan like an animal caught in a trap and the tears running from the corners of my eyes didn't exist.

Mom wiped them away but I said nothing. I was afraid if I opened my mouth to speak, I'd start screaming and never stop.

The cast came away and I whimpered in relief. She cleaned my leg thoroughly before attaching the soft cast and boot.

Bianca tapped softly on the door before opening it and pushing an automated wheelchair inside. "Are you okay, Ellie?"

I nodded but didn't verbally respond. I was busy meditating for everything I was worth to calm the residual vibrations of excruciating pain shooting through my leg.

"Th-that was the worst of it, Ellie. Your arm won't take as long. Are you sure you want me to keep going?"

I nodded sharply.

She smoothed her palm over my wet hair and got to work. The sound of the saw instantly caused my body to tense, my heart rate to climb.

As the blade made its way to the place where my forearm was broken, my mind couldn't take another second.

A hard gasp, a small scream, and I passed out from the pain.

My mother's face was the first one I saw when I opened my eyes. Her hands cupped my cheeks and she pressed her forehead to mine.

"I'm so *upset* with you, Ellie. This wasn't *necessary*, damn it. We should have stopped you."

"Mom." She lifted her face to stare into my eyes. "I love you and I'm so grateful for you." My smile was tired. "But you'll never stop me from doing what I need to do again."

Raking her fingers through my hair, she whispered, "I'm starting to see that, honey."

"The pain was worth it for independence." I inhaled deeply and took stock. "I hurt but I'll be able to move. That's critical right now."

My parents helped me sit up and I was dizzy.

"I need a minute." I breathed through the nausea. When I could speak without throwing up, I asked for a sheet to throw over my new chair. "I'm soaked with sweat."

I made small talk with Theresa and her assistant to avoid interacting with my parents or my team.

Adam was cute enough but my jaded mind considered him too young to take seriously. He flirted like a man who didn't get out much. I listened to his blathering with half my brain, a polite but distant smile on my face.

My true thoughts were focused on the puzzle of Hyde.

More than anything, I felt like an idiot, like I was too stupid to figure out the person living in my house, protecting me day and night was not *one* person but *two*.

I wondered how I'd been so blind.

I wasn't angry as much as I was achingly sad and disappointed. I considered Hyde my friend above and beyond the fact that I loved him. I let myself think I was more than a job.

Not being trusted with something so elemental meant I was wrong. I'd be lying if I didn't admit how much that hurt.

Donning the cheerful persona I reserved for the world outside my inner circle, I shined it on everyone in the room.

Chatting, laughing to hide how *destroyed* I felt.

I maintained a brittle smile while Adam flirted, Padme answered my questions about the foundation, and Mom filled me in on upcoming events.

She was as anxious to fill the silence and gloss over the awkwardness as I was. "We have a few things on the calendar next year, Ellie. When you're back on your feet, we should go shopping. Spend astronomical amounts of money on clothes, shoes, and ridiculous accessories."

"Sure. Whatever you want, Mom."

My security team exchanged glances with my mother and I realized I'd gone too far in being biddable and polite.

I hated shopping. *Loathed it*, in fact.

I refused to shop anywhere but online and there was a woman on retainer who came to the house for formal gown fittings.

My team frowned at me.

My parents frowned at me.

My doctor frowned at me.

Adam smiled like a half-wit. I sighed and wondered why I couldn't find the young man attractive.

On an analytical level, I recognized he was physically attractive but even considering sitting together to watch a movie *annoyed* me.

I pictured him taller and buffer with a gun in his hand. Slightly better but he looked uncomfortable holding it.

I'm pathetic.

When everything was done on my arm, I sighed in relief. "Much better. Lighter, not so rigid. I can actually scratch when an itch gets too bad." I tested my mobility. "Thanks."

Theresa managed, "You're welcome, Ellie. Please don't make me regret it."

Adam came around to help me off the table and into my new chair. He gave my waist a squeeze before letting me go and I growled under my breath.

I barely restrained myself from hitting him in the face.

Hyde tensed, Padme hissed, and I plastered a grim smile that was all teeth on my face.

Adam didn't notice. He thought I found him *awesome*.

Theresa outlined what I could do with the new casts in place. "I'll order a couple more so we can change them out."

Nodding, I tested the new chair to get the hang of it.

"What about your pain medication, Ellie? Are the milder versions working?"

I looked her directly in the eye and lied. "I'm fine. They're great. I'll keep you posted. Thanks again."

When I was free to go, Hyde opened the door and I made my way to my apartment. "I'm gross and need to shower. Food is becoming a pretty desperate situation, too."

"I'll make sure everything is ready for dinner when you come down. Have a shake in the meantime."

My parents came around the front of the chair when I was in my suite. "Honey, I'm sorry about...everything."

"I know. I'll get over it. I'll see you downstairs."

Bianca went to the bathroom with me. The new casts didn't make wet surfaces any less dangerous right now. She unstrapped the boot and casts to help me undress.

"Ellie. Are you alright?"

The way she asked told me she was concerned about more than my bones.

I stilled. "No, but I will be. I need time to adjust."

"I'm sorry no one told you. Truly."

With a shrug, I let her help me to the chair in the large shower stall. "It doesn't matter now."

Sighing, she stepped back. "I'll leave you to it."

When she was gone, I sat under the water for a long time. It felt amazing to have it all over me again.

There was pain but I could use my limbs again and that was a huge step forward. One of many toward physical healing.

I had no clue what I was going to do about my heart.

Chapter Twenty-One

After my shower, I dressed in shorts and a tank top. I pulled the soft casts back on and was glad I had the ability.

I ignored the pain and tried not to hold my breath as I finished pulling myself together.

Before facing everyone, I decided to stretch out on my bed for a few minutes to get my emotions under control.

My body shut down from the stressful day. I never made it to dinner.

In the middle of the night, I woke on the floor of my bedroom again. Covered in sweat, my last scream trailed away as I opened my eyes and blinked in pain and confusion.

Padme held my head as tears slipped over her cheeks. "Hey," she said brokenly. "It's okay, Ellie. It's okay."

My throat was raw when I swallowed. I tried to sit up but the pain cranked high and sharp. I couldn't keep from crying out.

Strong arms slipped under my body and lifted me off the floor. A low whine escaped as my bones and muscles adjusted.

As one of the Hydes straightened, the other wiped my face with a cool cloth. I was placed carefully on my bed and Padme covered me with a light blanket.

Most of my bedding was gone.

She bent over me. "Are you alright?"

"No. I guess not," I told her honestly. "I…leave a light on. I'll figure it out in the morning. I'm sorry I woke everyone."

My assistant was emotional as she gathered the wild tangles of my hair and quickly plaited a braid.

"Can I get you some tea, Ellie?" I shook my head. She brushed her fingers over my cheek and left the room.

The Hydes turned to follow and I whispered, "Thank you."

I thought one made a small keening sound and the other said, "You're welcome, Ellie."

For an hour, I tried to go back to sleep but finally gave up.

I exercised extreme caution as I figured out how to get in the shower on my own. I scrubbed my hair and body quickly, rinsed, and dried with far less production than with the other casts.

Slipping on what was quickly becoming my uniform, I brushed and braided my hair before I put the soft casts back on. I was shocked at how long it was getting.

Taking a deep breath, I left my room. I didn't think anyone else was up but I made a pot of coffee and rolled my chair to the small desk in the solarium.

Turning on my laptop, I stared at the blinking cursor of my

third book. It was almost done but I didn't want to work on it.

I opened a new document and started typing. I was slower than usual but the thinner soft cast made it possible to use my fingers on that hand.

The sun was fully up when Padme appeared in my peripheral vision with a cup of coffee on a tray. There were two others and I frowned in confusion.

Looking over my shoulder, I realized the Hydes were fully dressed, armed, and standing in absolute silence on either side of the solarium entrance.

One of them still had his arm in a sling but I noted it wasn't his gun hand. The thought made me smile to myself.

His...their presence was like so many other days in so many other places. Only there were two of them now.

Unlike security people in my past, Hyde allowed me quiet to work, always careful not to distract me.

I took the cup from Padme and said quietly, "Thanks. Did I wake you?" She shook her head. "Can you do me a favor?"

"Of course. Anything."

"Do some research on sleep aids. I sleep too much during the day but...not so much at night. Get with Theresa to determine interactions and safety. I've got so many residual drugs in my system. I don't want anything that's not one hundred percent safe for...for me."

Clearing my throat, I added, "In the meantime, we need to

get some chamomile and maybe an air diffuser." I met her eyes. "Don't mention any of this to my parents. Alright?"

"You have my word, Ellie."

She took coffee to the Hydes. As was his…their habit, they drank it cooled so it could be consumed quickly. Replacing the cups on the tray, she took it to the kitchen.

I stared through the bulletproof glass at the grounds of my childhood home. I didn't know how much time passed before Padme returned to my side.

"Melatonin. It's safe but Theresa is going to check interaction with all the drugs they gave you in the hospital. Some take a while to leave your system." She put a list on my desk. "I ordered this stuff. A courier is bringing it out later today."

"Thanks." I gave her a smile that I felt. It had been a while. "Still quicker than an oiled piglet."

She laughed and blinked against tears that filled her eyes as she remembered the rodeo we sponsored for some local kids.

A baby pig escaped the pen and Padme was the only one able to catch it.

"It's good to have you home, Ellie. I know it's hard right now but it's going to get better."

"I know. Give me time to…adjust."

"All of us can do that. Let me know if you need anything." She inclined her head and headed back into the suite.

I turned back to my laptop and wrote non-stop for another

hour. My mom visited and I closed the file with a sigh.

Putting a smile on my face, I turned to greet her. "Hey. Sorry I missed dinner."

"You needed the rest."

I nodded. "You look like you need to talk to me. One of your *big* talks."

"I think you need to reconsider Hayden's offer." My smile dropped off my face. "Hear me out, honey."

My voice low, I said, "I will *not*." Backing from under my desk, I faced her. Barely audible, I begged, "Don't do this. Please don't do this, Mom."

"There was a lot of stress yesterday. You were hurting, upset. Maybe it could work. You've always gotten along with Hayden. The entire family *loves* you and with the ba…"

I slammed my good hand on the desk. The bang ricocheted off the glass room and I shouted, "*Stop!*"

She visibly jumped.

In all my life, I never raised my voice at my mother. That she pushed me in such a way stripped away my ability to be polite.

I swallowed the anger and kept my voice calm. "When Grandmother tried to arrange your marriage with the Winters heir, when she told you what a great match it would be and insisted that it was the *best thing*…what did you do?"

Twisting her hands tightly together, she murmured, "Told her to never speak to me again if she thought I was too stupid to pick my own husband."

"I love you unconditionally. I know you love me so much that you can't always think clearly."

I shook my head. "Hayden is a good man but I don't love him and he doesn't love me. His proposal was the equivalent of *falling on his sword*. I won't let him do that and I won't let you try to convince me it's the *best thing*."

"I-I'm sorry, Ellie."

"I never thought you underestimated me so much." The lump in my throat was agony. "I am not *weak*! When will you *see* that?"

Moving past her at the highest speed the wheelchair had, Padme opened the door with a look of clear confusion on her face. I made it into the hall and to the elevator.

As the doors started to close, the Hydes joined me.

My freedom, my choices, were all an illusion. Nothing more than a fucking illusion meant to soothe me, to keep me calm. I lowered my head with a sigh.

"It's going to be alright, Ellie."

I didn't know which Hyde spoke. How could I? *We hadn't been introduced*. The thought filled me with aching sadness.

I shook my head and gripped the arm of the chair as the door opened on the first floor.

Beyond the library doorway, I was surprised to see my mom's best friend Vera with a beautiful mastiff puppy sitting perfectly still at her feet.

I entered the room and held out my hand. The dog approached my chair and laid her big head on my lap.

"Hey there, pretty girl."

I heard the way my voice shook and fought to keep from crying in front of my godmother.

I was tired, hurting, and embarrassed. I didn't know what to say or do about anything.

Feeling out of control, I focused on the sweet dog. I ran my palm over her silky head and she gave a pleased huff. From the corner of my eye, I saw when my mom and Padme entered the room.

Vera knelt in front of me and I struggled for something fake and cheerful to say. I didn't have it in me.

Staring into her eyes, every pathetic defense I had started to crumble. Shaking, blinking back tears, I couldn't speak.

Without looking away from my face, she said firmly, "Give us a few minutes alone please."

The team and my mother withdrew to the hall instantly. The moment I heard the door close, I buried my face in my hands.

"Sweet Ellie. Get it out before you *choke* on it, honey."

The older redhead with bright hazel eyes gathered me in her arms and said nothing as I cried for everything I'd never have and my inability to change any of it.

When I had nothing left, she pulled back and wiped my face with tissues from the side table.

Pulling a chair closer, she held my hand in both of hers. The puppy returned her head to my lap. She stared up at me with no expectations.

Nothing but unconditional puppy love.

Needing to calm my emotions, I said, "Thank you for bringing her, Vera. I think she'll help. What should I name her?"

"Her official name with the AKC is Lady Godiva of Elysian Fields. I've been calling her Diva."

"You knew?"

She stroked her palm over my head as she had when I was little. "Animals are wonderful for healing. They expect nothing and give so much in return. I thought when she was born that her gentle nature would match yours perfectly."

Reaching down, she scratched Diva behind the ear. "She's taken to her training wonderfully and isn't rough."

Glancing up and meeting my eyes, she added quietly, "She won't give you any trouble with a little one in the house."

I stared at her, struggling to explain. I should have known it wasn't necessary.

"I've loved you as one of my own since you were born and my best friend broke down in pure happiness. You know my children were almost fully grown then and you held off the empty nest syndrome for me."

"You're part of so many wonderful memories, Vera."

"Over the years, I've watched Monica's fear for you grow. Your attack strikes at the heart of what your parents love most in the world. They'd give up money, possessions, or position to keep you safe and happy. I know love and fear can suffocate, honey. I know."

I whispered, "I'm angry, tired, and ungrateful."

"You're *human*, Ellie. You're also a young woman who's lived much like Rapunzel. Sheltered from the world even as you long to experience what you see from your tower." She took my chin in her hand. "You'll be an *excellent* mother."

Tears filled her eyes. "I'm sorry for all you're going through but so proud of how you're handling it." She smoothed my hair with both hands. "Tell me what else is happening. You look like your heart is broken."

"Don't talk about it with Mom."

She shook her head and I remembered how many talks we had over the years that she kept in confidence.

"Vera. I love someone with all of myself and it was foolish *before* but now it's *completely* out of my reach."

I told her everything.

For the second time in five years, I confessed my love for a man I wasn't supposed to love.

A man who protected me, witnessed the absolute degradation of my body, and insisted on continuing to guard my life.

A man I recently discovered was *two* men.

"It hurts. In so many ways, it hurts. I'm not sure how to act, what to say, how to be around him…*them*. I feel like a stupid teenager and I hoped that by *now* I'd feel more confident as a woman. Despite…all that happened, I know *nothing.*"

Taking my hands, she said quietly, "The one thing I want to tell you is that women far older than you get confused, Ellie. That isn't exclusive to the young."

"I wish I could be more like you and Mom."

"Honey, your mother was a basket case when she met your father. You see the *results* but the beginning was nowhere near as seamless and beautiful."

Eyes wide, I whispered, "Really?"

"Your mother was almost as sheltered as you've been. She didn't know anything about men and was one of the most awkward females I ever met. We became friends because I had to save her from herself."

I couldn't help it, I laughed shakily.

"Not kidding. The first time she introduced herself to Samuel, she spilled an entire glass of wine on him. Poor thing looked like a crime scene."

I put my hand over my mouth.

"What I'm saying is looking at them *now* doesn't tell you about the speed bumps at the start."

Taking a deep breath, I nodded.

"Trust your instincts, Ellie. Don't judge what you feel in terms of age or status or how many people are involved. Anything else, *everything else*, will fall into place. Don't stop believing in your own happy ending."

A genuine smile crossed my face and I nodded as she kissed

my cheeks. "Thank you, Vera."

"You're welcome, darling. Anything else of interest? Other than all the crazy bullshit you're wading through?"

"I yelled at Mom after she suggested I marry one of the Delkin brothers who proposed yesterday to protect my reputation and give my baby a legitimate father."

Bright hazel eyes blinked several times as she processed that. "Lord. I need to visit more. I'll straighten that shit out. Wipe your face, let's eat, and I'll take you through Diva's training."

When I was presentable, she stood and gave a sharp whistle. The double doors opened and my mother and my team entered, watching me carefully.

Vera glanced back and forth between the Hyde brothers several times.

It's funny how your perception changes when you learn additional information. Now that I knew there were two of them, I didn't understand how I missed it for so long.

One hand stroking the dog's back, I announced, "This is Diva. The newest member of my fa…my team. I'll make sure she isn't a bother."

The Hyde men approached and knelt on either side of the large puppy. As one, they reached out to pet and scratch her until she was practically melting.

The way their hands moved over her soft fur hypnotized me.

Jealous of a dog.

Chapter Twenty-Two

"Strong yet gentle. A perfect match for her owner."

Again, I couldn't tell which of the men spoke but the words affected me deeply. I stared at my lap as one of them stepped behind my chair to push me manually.

I knew it was Jonas because he had the full use of both arms. He bent to say at my ear, "Freedom can be arranged, Ellie. Whatever you need, we'll make it happen. Don't take off without us. Alright?"

I nodded.

Straightening, he pushed me to the dining room. His twin walked beside me and Diva trotted happily on the other side with an occasional exuberant puppy bounce.

As we gathered around the table for lunch, the Hydes took places on either side of me after placing me carefully in a padded chair.

I tried to hide my shock.

Even when I thought Hyde was one man, he never sat *beside* me during meals at my parents' home. My face felt warm but I ignored it.

If I stared at my water glass and allowed my eyes to lose

focus, I could see them both in my peripheral vision. Part of me – the young and foolish part – imagined Hyde was mine.

Both of them.

Diva rested her head on top of my good foot under the table. For a little while, my unusual life felt almost normal.

I shook off the daydream and ate as much as I could of the baby greens and salmon placed in front of me. Si brought me a cup of tea and I drank it.

I dealt with the gradually building pain and pretended it didn't cause sweat to break out on my body.

Interacting with my mother was almost impossible. The strain from our earlier argument hung over me in a way that was unfamiliar.

After half an hour of trying to sit calmly and pretend everything was fine, I reached for my water glass with a shaking hand.

I knocked it over.

Hyde caught it before it did more than splash the tablecloth and I returned my hand to my lap.

Inhaling deeply, I closed my eyes and breathed through the shooting pain from my hip to my shin.

"I-I need to lie down. I'm sorry."

The Hydes instantly stood and pulled out my chair. Sliding his arms under my thighs caused me to gasp in agony.

My voice shaking, I whispered, "Do it fast."

A second later, I was lowered carefully to the wheelchair. Leaning heavily on the arm, I tried to smile as if everything was fine. "Vera, thank you for bringing the puppy. Can you, will you text me her basic commands?"

My godmother stood and walked around the table to sit in my vacated chair. She took my hand. "Stop acting like you're not allowed to be pissed off at the fucking pain or I'm going to annoy you until you scream this place down. Is there *nothing* you can take to manage it, Ellie?"

"I…nothing safe. No." Sitting up straight, I whispered, "It sneaks up on me."

"No, honey. You fake it for *our* benefit. You've barely been able to sit up." She stroked my hair away from my face. "For the next week, don't leave your suite. Get Si to make those dumplings you love, sleep as much as you need, and breathe."

Turning to look at my mother, Vera added, "Come stay with me for a few days while Sam is traveling, Monica."

"But…" my mother began.

"Pack your shit and let's get out of her hair. Ellie is wounded and vulnerable. Your hovering doesn't help. *Let her fight it.* She's goddamn strong enough if you give her the room."

Sighing heavily, my mother walked around the table to me. "I love you, Elliana."

"I know, Mom. I love you, too."

"I *know* you're strong, honey. Seeing you like this…knowing how much you hurt, I want to *fix* it but," she smiled with tears in her eyes, "I can't. I feel powerless."

"I'll beat it. I'll get to the other side but I won't make choices about the rest of my life based on pain, fear, and confusion I feel now. Now is temporary…and I'll survive it." Gritting my teeth, I reached for her hand. "I know you mean well."

She bent to kiss me and I inhaled carefully. "I need to rest. Stay with Vera and I'll see you in a few days. Swim, drink margaritas, and talk dirty. It'll be good for you."

Sitting beside my godmother, my mom watched as Hyde removed my shaking hand from the controls and pushed me from the room.

The moment we were out of sight of the dining area, I crumpled in my seat with a soft moan.

Padme murmured, "Too much. You need rest."

In my bedroom, my assistant pulled back the blankets and Hyde lifted me from the wheelchair carefully. The moment I was lying down, I turned my head with a whimper to keep from looking at anyone.

"I'll sleep. It will be better in a while." I think I said the words to convince myself as much as my team. "Th-thank you."

Too tired to fight sleep, I heard Hyde whistle for Diva. She stretched out beside me on the bed and I smiled.

Her body was sleek and warm. I focused on the feel of her fur under my hand. I said tearfully, "Good girl. Good girl."

"We'll be right outside, Ellie."

I think I hummed a response. I listened to the soft cadence of Diva's breathing until my eyes closed and I found temporary relief.

My dreams took me back to the first time my thoughts about Hyde changed from a girl's crush to a woman's desire.

* * *

When I moved into the penthouse in LA after my first attack, it was something of a culture shock.

I'd lived around trained men all my life but none of them slept across the hall from me every night.

Having a man like Hyde sleep near me was…distracting.

I was young and ignorant when it came to the opposite sex. My *body* wanted him, my *mind* had no idea how to make that happen. Not that I'd have the necessary confidence to act even if I *did* know anything about sex or relationships.

A few weeks into the new living arrangement, I heard the bathroom shower in the main hall as I headed back to my room with a glass of milk.

When I passed, I realized the door was open slightly. Reflected in the large mirror over the sink was Hyde's back and muscular ass beneath the water.

My hand tightened on the glass I held and I stopped. Thankful for the clear enclosure, I watched the play of muscle as he washed his hair.

It was *wrong* to watch him when he wasn't aware and I *knew* I should look away.

I tensed to take a step but froze again as he leaned against the shower wall on his forearm and stroked his hand down his abs to fist his cock. Every cell in my body sparked to life and I realized only an outside force could have moved me.

I was incapable on my own.

I'd never seen anything so sensual, so raw, and I was spellbound. For several minutes, I watched him stroke the shaft with long pulls and saw when he neared orgasm.

I watched his body tense, his legs lock, his motions speed up as semen spattered to the floor of the shower. His head dropped back on his shoulders and his rough exhale echoed through the small room.

My own breathing was too fast and my heart felt like it could slam through my chest at any moment.

As he straightened, I slid along the wall to my bedroom, ashamed and afraid of being caught doing something so invasive of another person's privacy.

Beneath the covers, those thoughts abandoned me and I touched myself everywhere, remembering.

* * *

Coming awake after all that happened, the dream dissipated and left me aching for touch.

I thought back on that night and the ripple effect it had on my life. The next day, I started writing my first book.

The initial plot was about a gorgeous but deadly mercenary with a soft spot for a woman who ran a dog rescue organization.

Filled with action, near-death experiences, and sex scenes I researched to get right, I didn't think it was very good.

I didn't write it for other people to read at first but to relieve my own stress. It was my secret pleasure to fantasize about my beautiful bodyguard in ways that wouldn't happen in real life.

It sold more copies than I believed possible and I never revealed myself to readers…or to my own staff.

Sighing heavily, I gently petted my dog until I drifted back to sleep. I didn't bother wiping away my tears for all that was lost and all that would never be.

Chapter Twenty-Three

September 2014

It felt disloyal not to miss my parents over the next week but it gave me a much-needed chance to get the pain under control.

Between meditation, holistic creams that Bianca rubbed gently into healing ligaments and tendons, and a little more sleep, I felt as if I could think again.

Not perfect but certainly better.

Every day, I slept too much during the day and usually woke before dawn to nightmares my team had to help me recover from but I decided not to fight it.

I stopped trying to go back to sleep and started my day.

As slow as I was typing, I was surprised at how much I was getting done. It was a quiet story, painful in so many ways, and often made me cry as I purged it from my mind.

Forgetting Hyde's presence because he could remain still and silent for so long, I had more than a few breakdowns in front of him without thinking.

The writing was good for me, almost therapeutic, and the tears seemed to ease much of my anxiety the rest of the day.

During my sessions, Padme would appear silently with tissues, tea, or snacks. Several times during the day, she attached Diva's leash and took her for a walk.

Fiaaz exercised my beautiful Sarafina regularly. He rode her beneath my window so I could watch my mare respond to the training she learned as a colt.

A woman named Addison Hauser trained all our horses and didn't charge *nearly* enough for her skills as far as I was concerned. She specialized in Native American techniques using the legs to guide rather than yanking on the reins or using crops. It was better for the horses and the riders.

I missed riding but seeing the care my driver and fellow equestrian took with her made me feel immensely better.

Si cooked my favorite meals and legitimately worked to fatten me up after all the weight I lost in the hospital. If I ate more of something than usual, he cheerfully pressed second helpings on me.

It was good to have the men and women I trusted gathered at meals together and it made me miss my own home.

Conversation was stilted, awkward even, but we pushed through it. The Hydes assumed places on either side of my chair and the rest of my staff worked to keep me distracted from a situation I was clearly struggling to adapt to.

For the most part, I tried to behave as if nothing had changed, nothing of importance had occurred.

It ate me alive on the inside.

My security detail were the only friends I had in my daily life and I wanted to care for them as they'd always cared for me.

I might be a *job* to them but to me, they were *family*.

* * *

Each morning, I had evaluations with Theresa. She checked my mobility and vitals.

During my appointments, Padme and Bianca kept her hapless assistant from getting too close. Adam didn't always respect boundaries and every member of my detail disliked him.

I tried to be polite but he annoyed me.

The doctor monitored my pregnancy diligently and confirmed that my blood work remained excellent.

More than a month after returning home, I finally ditched the soft casts. My bones were healed but the damage to joints, muscles, and soft tissues required more time.

The pain was no longer an enemy to defeat but a dogged companion I made peace with through meditation.

As I rebuilt the strength in my left side, I used a cane. I was glad to be upright again, even if I moved too slow for my liking.

Breakfast was eaten downstairs with my parents whenever they were home and any guests they had visiting.

The argument with my mother gradually faded into a new sense of mutual respect. She stopped questioning my choices and made appointments through Padme to visit with me around my physical therapy routine.

Hyde was my constant shadow and I appreciated when other members of my team were around as a sort of buffer between us.

The biggest adjustment was having *double* the visual distraction, writing inspiration, and overall protectiveness that had always been a hallmark of my personal bodyguard.

It took me years to adapt to *one* Hyde.

Then there was the love I felt for the two men my mind understood to be *separate* but my heart judged as *equal*.

I didn't know which of them saved me on that path in college, who comforted me after Preston's death, who took two bullets meant for me during a gala, or who rode the rollercoaster at my side.

I wasn't certain which Hyde brother was with me as I wandered the streets of New York or who danced with me at *Trois* the night I knew I couldn't keep pretending my love for him could stay in a box.

Many of the most important moments in my life included Hyde and it didn't matter that there were two of them because one of them had always been with me.

At my side as a steady source of strength.

I knew it was Jordan who was shot and almost *died* as he was airlifted to another hospital in Dallas. I knew it was Jonas who was *tortured* mentally and physically during my attack.

Only that horrific day had names to attach. The ugliness, the brutality that could have resulted in all our deaths.

It made me angry not to know who was with me in the moments I cherished, that I thought about often, that made me smile.

In each of *those* memories, there was only *Hyde*.

That was the wall I hit repeatedly and I didn't know how to bust through it. Once again, I was awkward and shy around men who *knew* me…but I was no longer sure I knew *them*.

* * *

I embraced physical therapy with a vengeance, determined to get my independence back. I endured hours with the therapist until I wanted to kill myself from the pain.

I was scheduled for two hours but insisted on four. The sooner I was back on my feet, the better, but there were times I could barely sit up in my chair.

Theresa insisted on massages after each PT session but the man hired to deliver them was caught trying to take a photo of my naked body.

Padme dragged him from the room by his hair as she cursed at him in what I thought was German.

Her reaction was *nothing* compared to the Hydes.

The house staff descended on the scene, alerted by the man's hysterical screams. It took several men to pull the massage therapist from the Hydes' grip. They shoved him toward the exit as others piled on the twins to restrain them.

Scrambling off the table and wrapping myself in a sheet, I made my way as quickly as I could to the door.

I watched in disbelief as Fiaaz, Si, and four of the house security team tried to restrain my bodyguards while the creep was forcefully removed. The brothers were *enraged*.

"Let them *up*," I said the moment I took in the scene. Fiaaz and Si stepped back immediately but the members of the house detail hesitated. "I said *release them*. Now."

The house staff loosened their grip and the Hydes immediately bound to their feet. The twins took a single step toward the front of the house where the therapist could still be heard crying and yelling.

"Stop." The single word from me was all it took for them to freeze. They pivoted on their heels to face me. "He's gone and he didn't get what he came for. That idiot doesn't matter. Are you both alright?"

In an unconsciously coordinated movement, they raked their hands through their blonde hair and walked to me. They stood shoulder to shoulder and I frowned.

Glancing down, I realized they were blocking me from view of the men assigned to the estate. The opening of the sheet revealed a sliver of my skin from hip to toe.

Gathering the fabric more snugly to me, I murmured, "Are you alright?" They nodded but didn't speak. "I'll get dressed."

"Wait." Bianca came down the hall at a casual jog. "I made sure the twerp was scared shitless before the house team bodily threw him in his car. You need a massage. Your physical therapy is brutal."

"It's okay…"

"Get in there, toga girl. You wouldn't *believe* how many times I've posed as a masseuse," she said with a wink. "I've already seen your naked ass a hundred times so hustle."

Chuckling with a small blush, I nodded. The brothers gave

me a final look before taking up positions on either side of the door. Padme closed it with a whistle.

"Stupid little shit. You get his plate?" Bianca nodded. "We can't kill too many people. Where will we hide the bodies? That was damn close."

My mind reflected on the way the Hydes looked in defense mode.

Sigh worthy.

Soft music, aromatherapy, and Bianca's skilled hands put me out like a light.

* * *

Twice a week, I met with my parents in their joint office on the first floor. Padme joined us and Hyde stood inside the door while they reviewed business matters with me.

I fell comfortably back into my position as the president of my parents' charitable organization. My assistant from our Dallas headquarters drove out regularly to go over important papers and get my signature on dozens of documents.

After one such meeting that lasted well after dark, I practically stumbled back to my apartment. I'd been going for eighteen hours and with physical therapy, I was wiped out.

I tripped getting out of the elevator and Hyde caught me carefully. He carried me into my room and deposited me in my bed fully clothed.

"You're going too hard, Ellie. Let's slow it down for a few

days." Jonas took off my sneakers and Jordan pulled the blankets to my chin. "Rest. Come, Diva."

My dog settled beside me, I petted her once, and dropped off the edge of the world.

* * *

The next day, my team arranged for me to take the entire day off. As motivation, Thaddeus and Sarah's son was delivered to the house.

Cameron and I held a video game marathon and tried to outdo each other on the funniest YouTube videos we could find.

We watched ridiculous movies while Cook loaded us up on snacks and ice cream.

Hyde stayed on either side of the door to ensure a day of relaxation.

Cameron was easy to be around. He had no expectations more than a companion to play with. He could make me laugh until I was in tears.

In return, I made him laugh until he spewed soda out of his nose. It was great. It was a break from my life.

My charmed and painfully lonely life.

That night, I shyly thanked my team for a much-needed day of fun and no thinking. I took a long soak and turned in early.

I felt better but it didn't stop the nightmares that were steadily getting worse. It was usually Padme who woke me and Hyde who prevented me from hurting myself.

That I continued to consider *two* men with *one* name was probably a sign of mental deterioration.

It was impossible to tell them apart again once Jordan no longer needed the sling for his arm.

Everyone was careful not to touch me more than necessary but helped me when I woke the other inhabitants of my space screaming from the horror I faced when I closed my eyes.

The physical therapy became a demon I used to exhaust my brain for a dreamless sleep.

It didn't work but I pushed anyway.

A member of my team went to Theresa about the safety of the baby, which I *stupidly* hadn't considered might be at risk.

She was stunned to learn the level of therapy I was putting my body through and promptly cut back my exercises and the amount of time I could work out.

It was firmly *suggested* I use the indoor pool and swim laps to avoid too much strain on my body.

So, I swam.

Lap after lap after lap, until I could barely lift my arms. One of the Hyde brothers swam every single lap with me.

The other usually had to help me from the pool. On a day I had to be fully lifted from the water to the bench that ran beside it, he whispered, "Be gentle with yourself, Ellie."

Other than an embarrassed nod, I couldn't respond.

The days passed and I insulated myself as much as I could

despite being around people twenty-four hours a day.

My pregnancy wasn't acknowledged openly but it was obvious everyone on the estate *knew* by the way they watched out for me. I never talked *about* the baby if it could be avoided but I talked *to* my baby about many positive things every day.

I made purchases and piled the boxes up in the connected room I planned to use as a nursery when it was time.

At the beginning of October, I pulled on a pair of my favorite jeans and couldn't snap them.

Overnight, I had a belly. I was a bit more than four months along. Wearing nothing but a bra and panties, I turned to the side to see my profile in the full-length mirror.

There it was.

A gentle rounding that wasn't evident the day before. My breasts seemed heavier.

I called my mom and she crashed into my room like the Gestapo ten minutes later. The Hydes stood behind her with weapons drawn, uncertain what was happening.

I sat on my bed in yoga pants and a bulky t-shirt. "Alright, Mom…now what?"

My mom hugged me and said, "I'll take care of *everything*."

She spent a long time staring at my reflection with tears in her eyes. She practically *glowed* with happiness.

I love how much she loves me.

Chapter Twenty-Four

October 2014

A few days later, I sat in the small back garden off the kitchen, reading in the shade. The stretchy leggings and flowy tank top were gifts from my mom. They were so soft, it didn't feel like I was wearing anything.

My sandals were…somewhere.

Hyde stood behind me despite my suggestion that they sit and be comfortable. Padme sat beside me working on her iPad.

It was peaceful and quiet with a gentle breeze blowing through the low-walled hideaway no one ever used but Cook.

Of the many gardens the estate offered, this one was like a hideaway only I knew about.

Since I was little, it was my favorite place to read.

I felt the strangest crawling sensation and jumped off the chair, totally freaked out. My book on the ground, arms patting myself frantically, my staff tried to figure out what was wrong.

Padme assumed a bug was crawling on me and walked

around me, brushing at my clothes.

Then it happened again and I was *speechless*. I suddenly realized what it was the second time and went still.

My assistant's eyes went from my face to my belly and back again. "Did you feel the baby move for the first time?"

I couldn't *answer*, couldn't *think*.

In that moment, I fully understood there was a *baby* in there. A small human being incubating in my belly that was *depending* on me to love and protect it.

I tried to speak but words wouldn't come.

Padme sent a text to my mom. The Hydes stood behind me and I couldn't bring myself to look at their faces. I wasn't sure what I'd see there.

I was *showing*. The baby was *moving*.

Everyone was going to know now. People would talk about it. I wasn't ashamed of the baby, I was ashamed of the method by which I'd become pregnant.

Though Hyde didn't know how I felt, I found it difficult to face the man – *men* – I was in love with carrying the product of my gang-rape.

Strangely, I felt as if I'd done something wrong, betrayed them somehow. On a logical level, I knew my thoughts were stupid and irrational but I couldn't seem to help it.

Exiting the kitchen, Mom approached me slowly. I was probably broadcasting my inner chaos.

"It's alright, Ellie. It's going to happen all the time now."

As if on cue, it did and I fidgeted. "Don't be afraid, honey."

My dad appeared from the other side of the garden. Standing side by side, my parents put their hands gently on my stomach.

I flinched. "I-I'm sorry."

"No one here will *ever* hurt you, Ellie. No one." Dad kissed my hair. A moment later, the baby moved again. "There it was! Did you *feel* that, Monica?"

He sounded so happy. Mom nodded and her beaming smile went a long way to lifting some of the weight from my heart.

"Ellie," Padme said gently, "are you alright? You're pale and trembling."

"I-I don't know *anything*. I'm going to *fail*." Then to my utter humiliation, I hyperventilated and passed out.

I didn't need to ask who managed to catch me before I splattered my pregnant body on the cobblestones.

Hyde always caught me.

* * *

I woke up being carried down the hall to my apartment, Hyde's face above me. I knew I was shaking badly.

He looked down. "I'd *never* hurt you, Ellie."

"I know. I *know* that, Hyde."

"Jonas. I'm Jonas."

It was the first time one of the brothers said their name to me and it made my heart hurt even as I appreciated what felt like a clue to a mystery I hadn't known to solve.

I didn't know what to say and swallowed hard.

As we approached my apartment, his twin held the door. I started to speak and closed my lips in confusion.

"I'm Jordan, Ellie."

I swallowed hard and nodded.

As we entered my suite, Bianca jumped up from the sofa and opened my bedroom door. Hyde…Jonas laid me gently on my bed and Bianca fussed over me.

Ten minutes later, the Hydes stood on either side of my door inside the room as Theresa walked in pushing a portable ultrasound machine. My parents followed in her wake.

"I hear the little one's moving around. Let's see if we can determine the gender of your tiny tenant."

I focused on my stomach, afraid to meet the eyes of anyone in the room. Theresa lifted my shirt to under my breasts and smeared goo on my slightly rounded abdomen.

A wide wand was run over me and after thirty seconds, the doctor smiled. She leaned over to raise the volume of the machine and a clear heartbeat *thumped* through the room.

I gasped and my mother took my hand. I gripped the linens under me in a white-knuckled fist.

"So far so good. Excellent size, normal growth. Look at that! You're turning for me. What a good baby. It's a *girl*, definitely a girl, Ellie."

"A little girl?" I whispered and Theresa nodded. "A daughter. Th-that's…better."

My parents understood. The chance a little boy would grow up to look like his biological father was too much to think about without screaming.

Theresa took several measurements. "Ellie, I'd like to do an amniocentesis to make sure there are no other issues from medications but all signs indicate a healthy pregnancy."

I told her to go ahead and she had Adam hold the ultrasound wand while she inserted a long needle into my belly. I watched the vial fill with the murky water surrounding the baby.

"This will help me determine if there are any abnormalities. I honestly don't foresee anything but better safe than sorry."

When it was done, Adam rushed to wipe my stomach which made me fist my hands on my bed.

"Adam, let Theresa do that."

"Oh, I don't mind! Almost done!"

"*Adam!*" I shrieked. Each of the Hyde brothers took one of his hands and lifted them carefully but firmly away from my skin. "Please don't *touch* me."

Seeing his stricken expression, I tried to soften my words through gritted teeth. "I d-don't like to be touched."

Jonas and Jordan moved him further from the bed and released him. A light seemed to go on in the man's expression.

"Oh, yes…I'm sorry, Ellie. That was thoughtless of me."

Theresa cleaned me up and asked if I had any questions. I assured her I didn't because I wanted Adam out of my personal space. Within a few minutes, she and her medical assistant were gone and my parents sat side by side on the bed.

My mom picked up my hand. "Are you alright?"

"I-I almost struck him. I wanted to *hurt* him. I barely stopped myself." I pressed the heels of my palms to my eyes.

"You're under a lot of stress, Ellie," Dad said gently. "Theresa can bring in a female assistant. She'll understand."

"No. It would give weakness power. I can handle it."

"If you change your mind, tell me." Shaking his head, Dad added, "A man who makes you uncomfortable doesn't belong around you, honey."

Mom brushed my hair away from my face. "I bought you some books. I think they'll help you understand what you're going through and explain what's coming."

Dad grinned. "You're due in March. We'll have everything ready." Tilting his head, he asked, "Do you want a nanny?"

"I'm not sure about a nanny yet. I need to get the room next door ready. There are *things* I'm supposed to do."

Mom laughed. "That room is filled with a ridiculous amount of stuff already. I'll have a decorator come in. Do you have a theme in mind?"

"Something happy, cheerful. No wall-to-wall pink."

They sat talking for a long time about everything and nothing. It took my mind off the stress and uncertainty rocketing through my system.

It was pleasant and relaxing.

Jonas and Jordan stood still and quiet by the door. Looking at my parents, I could still sort of watch them. I felt better with them there.

I wondered how to tell them apart.

Chapter Twenty-Five

Late November 2014

The next two months passed without incident.

I kept up the swimming and Mom brought in an instructor who taught me yoga and tai chi that was safe for the baby.

I focused on my writing and worked behind the scenes with our charities.

Occasionally, random aches took me by surprise but Theresa reminded me I was still healing *and* carrying a baby.

"Your body is serving you *well*, all things considered."

I didn't want the outside world to know I was pregnant so I didn't leave the house. I wouldn't have my child carry the stigma of her conception for the rest of her life.

My folks brought in a team of attorneys who created confidential documents regarding the artificial insemination I'd supposedly had done.

The birth certificate would list *father unknown* but when my daughter asked one day, I'd tell her how badly I wanted a child and couldn't wait to find the perfect dad for her.

Should anyone in the media ever uncover the deeply buried

story of my attack, they'd receive the same explanation.

She was *now* and *always* my child, my little girl.

Thanksgiving at Elysian Fields saw the arrival of all my parents' closest friends. Men and women I loved, who loved me.

Everyone raged over my progress and hugged me as tight as my expanding belly allowed.

Hudson and Natalia visited for two days but explained they couldn't stay away from New York too long because of a friend who was recovering from a hit-and-run.

I was awed at the engagement ring on Natalia's finger and stared at it unblinking for almost a minute.

"I'm excited, stunned, happy beyond belief, and so many other emotions that I can't adequately express myself."

For half an hour, I grilled the old friends, now a new couple about the circumstances that brought them together at last.

They told me of their ingénue and I was madly curious.

"You'd *love* our Brie. When you're past all the chaos, I need to bring you out for a long visit." She added in a whisper, "I'm terrified of children but Brie is a *natural*. We have a lot to catch up on. Now I'm going to let Hudson interrogate you privately."

"Uh…"

"I've already received the third degree, as did Leo. It's your *turn*, Ellie. Chin up, darling!"

Hudson took in my pair of identical bodyguards standing a

mere foot behind me. "I have many questions," he said stoically.

I laughed. "I can *imagine*."

Glaring at them over my shoulder, he ordered, "I wish to speak to Ellie. Stop hovering. Give us ten feet." When the Hydes hesitated, he growled, "I'm capable of guarding her for two minutes in this fortified castle."

With a sound of obvious displeasure, I watched the Hydes walk away to stand beside Hudson's long-time bodyguard.

"Leonard was unaware of this little development. That displeases me."

"Don't blame Leo. They lived with me for five *years* and I didn't know either." His expression was intense. "It's okay, Hudson. I trust him…them implicitly."

"Hmm. You appear to be telling the truth. Should that change, I expect a call."

"Of course." I leaned up to kiss his cheek and he bent to meet me. At his ear, I said, "Life is endlessly full of surprises. I'm so proud you made her yours at *last*, Hudson."

"Thank you." Leaning back, he petted my hair. "You feel alright?" I nodded. "After the dust settles, stay in the building for a few weeks and let us spoil you."

He hugged me with a gentle smile I doubted most people had the chance to see on his face. Then he glared at the Hydes and they reappeared at my back.

"A steady hand on the reins, Ellie. I'll stop monopolizing

your attention but plan a visit. We're greedy for your time. Natalia is correct. You'd get along well with Brie."

Laughing, I hugged him again and let my dad pull me away to introduce me to several new members of corporate staff that worked in my division.

As I feared and expected, several of my mother's friends asked to speak to me away from the party. Hyde escorted us to the library and started to leave so we could talk privately.

Unthinking, I grabbed the hand of the brother closest to me. Dropping it instantly, they stared at me before taking up positions inside the room on either side of the door.

As conflicted as I was about my bodyguard, his presence always reminded me that I was strong.

I needed that reminder now.

The much older women belonging to Mom's inner circle asked pointed, often uncomfortable, questions about the child I carried in my body.

My skin was hot, I shook, and my voice trembled…but I answered them honestly. In the process, I cleared an emotional hurdle I dreaded for months.

"It's…the circumstances aren't ideal. Of course, they're not." I placed my palms over my belly. "A silver lining. That's what she is. I want her to feel loved and welcomed."

Sarah took my hand. "I had four miscarriages before Cameron was born. I'd do the same in your place, Ellie. No question."

"Thank you," I whispered.

"Is it, the baby, healthy?" Nelinda was a younger neighbor of Mom's when they were little. They shared several joint business ventures and she was a woman I admired. Unlike Mom and so many of her friends, Nelinda was quiet and studious like me. "Are you worried about her…genetically?"

"So far, so good. I'm as certain as any expectant mother. There are never guarantees."

Never married with no children, she whispered, "I was always too afraid for any of it. I'm glad you're not like that, Ellie. You're brave and beautiful." She patted my hand. "If you need anything, you let me know."

I nodded, relieved.

Lydia was married to my father's best friend. My parents were matron of honor and best man at their wedding. She was genteel but louder than some people could handle.

"Girl, get yourself a husband and put all the whispers to bed! No need for you to go through this alone. A sweet man will add another layer of protection, and say this little baby is his. Just the ticket. I can make you a list of eligible men whose family fortunes could benefit from such an alliance."

The suggestion didn't surprise me. These women were two generations ahead of me and the world was *very* different when they were my age.

It was a shock that my mom answered the question for me.

"Ellie has a delicate heart that deserves a husband who loves her deeply, madly. Until she has such a man in her life, she'll be a single mother." She smiled at me. "I have no doubt she'll excel at this as she does everything else."

I nodded at her and there were so many emotions in my heart.

"I don't understand why you'd *do* this, Elliana!" My great-aunt Margaret was a good woman but I *never* doubted she'd be the strongest critic of my choice. "To let the product of those *beasts* grow in your body…to raise that *constant* memory!"

Taking her frail hand in mine, I kept my voice calm. "She didn't hurt me, Aunt Maggie." I perched on the table beside her wheelchair. "She's as innocent as I am in all of this."

Eyes that were so like Mom's and mine teared up. "You need to forget…*forget*. A-a baby will never let you."

"I can't forget but I can take something beautiful from it." I placed her hand on my stomach and my daughter moved as if on cue. "A child to love, who'll love me."

"I remember the first time you moved in Monica's belly." Maggie smiled softly. "She cried for an hour in happiness."

For almost a minute, we sat in silence. She lifted her other hand and placed both on my belly to better feel the way my baby adjusted for comfort.

"I'm scared for you, Elliana."

"I know. I have moments where I'm scared for me, too. I have Mom and Dad, my team, and this baby. I'll do the best I can."

Smoothing her palms over me, she nodded and folded her

hands in her lap. "I expect to see her on my birthday."

Grinning, I replied, "I've never missed a birthday, Aunt Maggie. Katie won't either."

Her eyes widened. "You're naming her after Mother?" I nodded and tears slipped over her soft cheeks. Sniffing, she added, "Every birthday, Elliana. However many I have left."

"You have my word."

The other women had questions but I felt as if the worst ones were behind me. Mom and Vera were there for moral support but let me navigate the situation on my own.

They wouldn't always be there and all of us knew that.

I stood and faced half a dozen women over fifty who'd known my mother most of her life and me for all of mine.

"I know this situation is…painful and confusing. I need your help to protect my daughter. All my life, you've been fixtures of strength and steadiness for me to emulate. I hope you can extend your love and protection."

Inhaling deeply, I added, "Without conditions. No matter how she came to be, she's *my* child, *my* daughter, and I want you to see her that way. To see her as an extension of *me*, n-not the rest of it."

There were hugs and whispered assurances. So many tears as these women processed the changes in my world.

In the end, they gave their word and offered their substantial power to protect my child and her future.

As I knew they would.

One by one, they filed from the room until it was only my mother who remained.

I lowered to the sofa and she perched beside me and smoothed her fingers over my cheek.

"Well done, Ellie." Her voice was quiet. "Would you like a few minutes to get your balance?"

"Mm hmm." I didn't trust myself to speak.

Leaning close, she kissed my forehead and left the room. I sat staring at the rows of books my parents painstakingly collected.

I did what I could to steady my breathing and my thoughts. Half an hour later, Padme tapped softly on the door and Hyde opened it.

"Dinner shortly, Ellie. Shall I make excuses?"

Standing, I shook my head. I wiped my fingertips over my face and smoothed my hair. Straightening my dress, I approached the door the Hydes held wide for me.

I didn't look at them but murmured, "Thank you for staying."

Together, they replied, "Of course, Ellie."

We assembled in the formal dining room that was rarely used in the center of the house. Guests took their seats and I was glad to see my team seated around me.

My closest friends, the people who probably knew me better than my parents. I gave thanks for their presence, their gentleness, their constancy.

For the Hyde brothers on either side of me, I gave thanks that they survived an event that could have taken them from me.

Before I even knew there were two.

No matter the strain that lingered between us, I loved them still. I would love them always.

Chapter Twenty-Six

December 2014

The holidays were something my parents took seriously. All month, friends and relatives arrived for visits.

Some of them weren't part of our inner group of trusted people so I kept my head up and answered questions with prepared statements.

After a while, I didn't even have to think about them.

On Christmas Eve, the long-time staff at the estate presented me with gifts for my daughter culled from my own childhood. I imagined they dug through the many storage trunks of keepsakes in the attic.

The results were spectacular. A quilt of memories, sewn by hand, created from my old Halloween costumes, ballet outfits, and formal gowns. A shadow box containing awards, ribbons I'd won, and photos of special moments in my life.

The thoughtfulness of gifts for my unborn daughter made me cry like a fool for twenty minutes. Their kindness left me speechless.

My parents gave me the deed to a small refurbished castle in Ireland. "You'll want time away from here eventually and we thought, with your writing, you might get lots of novel ideas in such a place. Your staff provided valuable input on security. We couldn't leave them out of the loop."

That they considered a home so far from their reach told me they were getting better at allowing me to be an adult.

"The first visit, we'll all go together and explore it." I told them with hard hugs. "Thank you."

From my team, I received two nickel-plated 9mms and a set of small throwing daggers with intricate designs.

Si said, "After the baby arrives, we train."

Excited to learn the art of throwing knives, I smiled and nodded. Another box held a new charm bracelet.

The first one Hyde gave me was lost and never recovered. The locket with a photo of Preston, an intricate horse, and my college charm were duplicated from before the attack.

There were new charms that dangled from the platinum. I touched the tiny Empire State Building, a dancing couple, a jeweled K, and fountain pen while blinking back tears.

"I-it's beautiful. So beautiful."

Padme knelt to attach it to my wrist where it glittered cheerfully. "You never took it off so it was odd for it to be missing. Another piece returned to its proper place."

I nodded through tears.

After hours of food and conversation, I was exhausted. Bianca, Fiaaz, and Si hugged me tightly before heading to their own rooms. Padme and the Hydes escorted me into mine.

In my bedroom, I found another gift. An intricately carved mahogany chest. The words *Katherine Elliana Fields* were engraved and embossed on the glossy surface.

The chest was breathtaking.

Opening the top, I removed a card bearing Hyde's masculine script. "*For Katie. Fill this hope chest with the amazing moments waiting in your future. Merry Christmas! J&J Hyde.*"

I stared at it for a long time, absently running my fingertips over the design. Jonas and Jordan gave me a *hope chest* for my daughter. Something intentionally infused with happiness and positive thoughts.

For her future.

I set it beside my bed so it was the first and last thing I saw every day. From my nightstand, I removed the first ultrasound pictures and the antique baby rattle Vera gave me.

Lined with cedar, it held a satin lavender cachet. Smiling, I set Katie's first memories inside it and closed the lid.

Leaving my hand on the warm wood, I said aloud, "Thank you...both of you...very much. It's perfect. I wouldn't have thought of a hope chest."

"You're welcome, Ellie."

"Merry Christmas, Ellie."

My door clicked softly shut. I didn't even have the courage to face them.

I wanted things to be easy between us again. To watch movies together and laugh over observations of other people.

To be able to look them in the eye again without blushing. An accomplishment that took me more than a year when Hyde first came to work for me.

Most people would envy the world in which I lived. I never took the charmed life I was born into for granted.

However, I envied the ease of everyday people all over the world who could talk without blushing, express emotion without shaking, and go after what they wanted without fear.

In so many ways, mine was a life of ease.

In others, I felt frozen.

* * *

After the first of the year, my nightmares worsened without explanation. I was glad that I didn't recall most of the details but hated the nausea, the fear, I felt when my team helped pull me from it.

Exhausted, I attempted to go back to sleep but soon knew it was a lost cause yet again.

Sighing, I threw back my covers and sat up.

Carefully making my bed, I took my time showering and getting dressed for the day.

I sat quietly to meditate for fifteen minutes. I found it helped to shake off the last of the nightmares.

Orange juice and a snack sounded like just the thing.

Opening my door, I tripped over a sleeping Hyde. Seven months pregnant and something of a klutz on the best of days, I would have hit the floor without his quick reflexes.

Strong arms caught my weight and settled me on my feet. He stood and put his hands on my shoulders.

"Are you alright, Ellie?" His voice was raspy from sleep. Looking down, I noted the blanket, pillow, and two pistols on the floor outside my door.

"Yes. I…why are you sleeping on the floor, Hyde?"

"I'm Jordan, Ellie. I have a small scar here on my jaw."

I stared at it in a mix of confusion and happiness that I had a way to tell them apart. His voice was like warm whiskey and it always had the same effect on me. Butterflies in my stomach and heat *everywhere*.

"Thank you." I swallowed hard. "Why aren't you in bed?"

"We trade off every night."

I tilted my head in confusion. "But…why?"

"Your nights are getting worse. Padme needs help to wake you and it's easier if we're already here."

His words flowed over me and I realized he wore sleep pants and no shirt. I stared at the bullet wounds that were puckered scars now. One in his upper pec, another along his side.

Terrified to ask, I whispered, "Where else were you shot? M-mom said you were shot three times."

Bending, he separated golden blonde hair to show me a

jagged scar along his scalp above his ear.

"That was close. You could have died."

"You could have died as well…but you didn't." He straightened and gave me a gentle smile. "Don't worry about us, Ellie. Let *us* worry about *you*." I considered the words. "Can I get you something?"

"I w-was going to get some orange juice. Would you like some?" He nodded and followed me into the kitchen. "I feel terrible that I'm keeping everyone up all hours of the night."

"You have no reason to apologize."

"I'll be able to take the sleeping pills again soon. If I get a n-nanny in. I-I mean…never mind."

I turned from the fridge and Jonas stood on the other side of the door. I was so startled I dropped the jug and he caught it.

"I was coming around to get glasses. I didn't mean to scare you, Ellie." I couldn't reach the glasses anymore. My extended belly robbed me of several inches of height.

He lined them up on the counter and I poured juice. Jordan watched me from the other side of the bar as he pulled a fresh t-shirt over his head.

"Are you hungry, Ellie?"

"A little."

"You barely touched your dinner last night. How about a croissant and some apple slices with honey?"

Before I could answer, Jonas washed and dried an apple, tossed it to Jordan, who sliced it rapidly while his brother grabbed a ramekin and filled it partially with the raw honey I loved. He took a croissant from the cake plate and set it on the side.

When they put the plate in front of me, I realized it was exactly what I needed.

"Where would you like to eat?" Jonas asked quietly.

"The solarium." I picked up my glass and plate and headed for the room that received the most morning sun.

A Hyde brother walked on either side of me through the French doors to the glass room that glowed. The greenery of the potted plants kept it from being too glaring.

We sat around one of the small tables and the silence drew out between us as I ate my apples. They watched me intently.

Jonas said quietly, "We haven't really talked in months. How are you doing?"

"Good." I cleared my throat. "Trying to stay busy."

Tilting his head, Jordan asked, "Have you adjusted to there being two of us?" I shrugged lightly. "I'm sorry we waited so long to tell you."

Considering my words, I admitted, "I understand why you didn't. It's a secret weapon. Also, a secret weakness."

"You're right on both counts." Jonas paused. "We still should have told you. We discussed it a thousand times."

"W-why didn't you?"

"It was hard for you in the beginning." I knew what Jonas meant and blushed. "You're a gentle yet deceptively strong person, Ellie. Someone new and different to us."

"Confident in many things that leave other people shaking yet strangely uncertain in your own skin." Jordan's mouth lifted in a smile. "We didn't want to overwhelm you."

I thought about how long it took me to adjust initially to my new bodyguard and could see why they'd be nervous about sharing their secret with me.

Sitting back, I took a deep breath. "I understand."

"Do you?" I nodded and watched them exhale slowly. Jonas told me, "I want you to know something, Ellie. In the years we've been in your service, we've always been linked. A necessary habit we adapted in the field."

I blinked. "Listening devices?" They nodded and I mulled over what they were telling me. "Y-you had to know what the other said or did to maintain continuity."

They nodded again.

Jordan explained, "One of us at your side, the other with eyes on you at all times."

Realization hit me and I held my breath. Barely audible, I said, "Both of you were with me the entire time."

Instantly, a wounded part of me righted itself.

No matter which twin was talking to me, guarding me at my side, or dancing with me, the other was there as well.

Year after year, the twins spent their waking hours with me, whether they stood at my side or not.

"Unless you were traveling, sometimes even then, we changed places daily. At first, it was splitting the workload." I stared into Jonas's eyes. "Then it was about having equal time with you."

Sitting back, he drank his juice and rolled the glass between his large palms. The movement was hypnotic.

I met his eyes. I didn't know what to say.

"More on all of this after you have time to process." With a gentle expression, Jordan asked, "Why do you censor what you say about Katie in front of us, Ellie?"

"I-I don't know what you mean." They didn't respond to my denial but even I knew it was weak. "I don't censor…"

"You can do better than that, Ellie," Jonas said before looking past me to the entrance of the solarium. "Think on it," he added under his breath.

"Good morning, everyone," Padme said behind me.

Thank goodness my assistant chose that moment to join us.

The question was one I didn't want to answer. I wasn't even sure I *could* answer it.

How could I explain the shame I felt? The nervousness about keeping the baby conceived during a rape Jonas witnessed? My residual guilt for being the cause of their injuries?

Padme was cheerful and energetic. "Ellie, how are you feeling this morning?"

"I'm g-good. What's on my agenda today?"

I let her claim my attention and eventually we all moved inside to dress and get ready for our day.

Over the next month I avoided alone time with Hyde. I couldn't trust myself around either of my bodyguards.

They were my personal weakness.

Now I knew every cherished memory I replayed often in my own mind involved *both* Hyde brothers. For the first time, I perceived them separately as well as together.

I also thought a lot about my conversation with Natalia on a night that felt like another lifetime ago.

The word ménage drifted through my mind and wouldn't shake loose. My heart didn't care that I was pregnant, it didn't give a damn that two men were involved.

I wanted them, Jonas *and* Jordan, for my own.

Chapter Twenty-Seven

February 2015

During a rare trip to Dallas to meet with corporate lawyers about a charity I wanted to assume, we were waylaid in the underground parking garage by a member of the media.

Jonas moved to step in front of me but I placed my hand on his forearm and whispered, "It's alright."

"Miss Fields! May I ask you a few questions?"

Beside me, Jordan ordered gruffly, "Put your hands against the side of the vehicle."

Looking terrified, the reporter obeyed instantly and my bodyguards gave him a pat down that was almost a deep cavity search. They went through everything in his wallet and gear bag before removing his shoes and belt.

"Oh, god," he murmured as his jeans started to slip over his slender hips. Jordan returned his belt. "Thanks."

"What's your name?"

"Tom Brady." He held up his press pass that looked homemade. "No one ever believes it but that's my name."

Padme held out a fingerprint machine. "Put your thumb

there. You don't check out, you don't get one word with Miss Fields."

Ten minutes later, my team returned Tom's possessions and nodded to me that he was clean.

Padme whispered, "You don't have to do this, Ellie."

Meeting the eyes of the reporter, I said gently, "How did you gain access to our secured garage?"

The man blushed brightly. "Through the lobby. I joined a group headed to lunch."

"Good to know." I tilted my head. "You've been waiting here a long time. How did you know I'd be here?"

He was too thin, about my height, with extremely pale skin and dark hair and eyes. He answered, "I didn't. I've been here every day for *weeks*." As if just noticing my belly, he asked loudly, "Are you p-pregnant?"

Jonas cuffed him lightly on the back of the head. "Watch it."

I held up my palm. "Tell me why you're here, Mr. Brady."

"I came to, I wanted to…ugh." A look of frustration entered his expression. "Sorry, I'm nervous." He inhaled deeply a few times and I thought he was murmuring affirmations. "This is my first story."

"For what outlet?" He looked confused. "Who assigned me as a story?"

"Oh, no one." Now I was confused. "I'm writing a story. For myself. Well, my readers. About you."

"In what capacity, little man?" Padme leaned close to him with her teeth bared.

"Oh geez. Can I, is it okay if I start over?" I nodded and he wiped nervous sweat off his brow. "You're even younger than I remember."

I frowned. "We've met?"

He nodded shyly and a bright blush spread up his neck and face. "I'm Tom Brady," he said cheerfully. "Wait, I told you that already. I bet you meet thousands of kids every year. Geez, you're a dummy, Tom."

The Hydes stared at him as if he had two heads. I could tell they were losing patience.

Jonas barked, "Kid, what the hell are you *doing* here?"

He swallowed hard. "I aged out of foster care when I graduated high school last year."

"You were in foster care?" He nodded. "I tell you what, Tom. If you promise to be on your best behavior, you can sit with one of my bodyguards while I have a scheduled meeting. It could be a couple of hours."

"I don't mind. I've spent about forty hours a week down here for the last month hoping to see you, Miss Fields. I can wait."

"Alright."

We walked together to my floor and Jordan cleared my corner office while Padme ran a scan for bugs. I gestured to the small seating area on the opposite side of the office from my desk.

He immediately sat and folded his hands in his lap.

"Padme, will you have one of the admins bring Tom a drink and something to eat? I didn't see any food in his bag."

"You don't have to do that, Miss Fields."

"You're not to leave this room, Tom. Wait here with Jonas until I return. The bathroom is through that door but say something before you get up. My security doesn't like surprises. Do you understand?"

"Yes, ma'am. I can hold it."

Looking at him strangely, I motioned to Jonas who joined me across the room.

"Be careful with him. I think he frightens easily. Make sure he eats and goes to the bathroom. I'll wrap up the meeting as fast as I can so we can get to the bottom of this."

He nodded and told Padme, "Dig deep if you have the chance. I can't figure out what he wants. He's so *young*."

"I'll be back." With a wave at Tom, I left with Jordan and Padme. "How odd."

My meeting with the lawyers took almost three hours and I was exhausted but exhilarated by the time I shook hands with the two men and one woman who kept our corporations running behind the scenes.

In the elevator, Padme grinned. "You did it. You've been wanting access to that shady bunch's list for two years."

"The charity was using those poor people as a front. Now they'll get the help they need."

Entering my office, Hyde stood and Tom sat perched on the edge of the couch where they were when I left.

"Everything okay?" I asked carefully.

"He hasn't moved. I tried to get him to eat, use the restroom, *anything*...he refused to take advantage of your kindness."

Turning to Padme, I murmured, "Order food. I need to eat and I'm *certain* he does." She nodded and walked away on her phone.

Walking across the room, I used the restroom and washed up before returning to the main room and taking a seat opposite the unusual Tom Brady.

"Before we talk, I need you to use the restroom and drink that bottle of water, Tom. I won't have a conversation until you do that for me."

"Yes, ma'am." He stood and Jonas opened the door. A couple of minutes later, he took his seat again and chugged the bottle of water fast. "Thank you."

"Tell me why you're here, Tom."

Jordan stood at attention behind my chair and Jonas held a similar position behind the young man.

He cleared his throat several times. "I get nervous talking to people in person."

"It's alright. Take your time."

Glancing at Jonas, he asked, "Can I get my file?"

My bodyguard nodded and Tom pulled a manila folder from

his bag. We watched as he pulled out photos of a dozen women and placed them on the coffee table between us along with what looked like stills from traffic cameras.

"When I was ten, you gave a speech at the home where I lived in California. I didn't realize you were so young and that you were with your parents. You were only sixteen then. I thought you were older because you're so smart."

Raking his hand through his shaggy hair, he coughed softly. "We were an at-risk facility. Kids who were expected to end up in jail or drug addicted. I was addicted to meth my mom gave me to keep me quiet. I talked too much."

"I'm sorry."

"Don't be. Your visit changed what I did with myself." Fidgeting, he said, "You talked about violence against women and children. About the unsolved and unreported cases that leave thousands dead or missing every year."

"That was pretty intense for someone your age…"

"I wasn't supposed to be there. I was hiding in the chair storage. You woke me up. I-I…" He looked fearfully at my bodyguards. "I'm not a stalker or anything but…I've done stalkerish things."

"Tell me what you mean."

"I followed you. I wanted to be like you. The men who tried to hurt you a couple of years later, I think they hurt a *lot* of women, Miss Fields. I-I don't think you were the first one."

I glanced at the photos on the table. "You followed them?" He nodded. "You could have been hurt."

He shrugged. "I've been hurt worse than they could have done. Twice, I watched some of them try to take women and I set off an air horn I stole just in case." He pointed at himself. "I'm not strong or anything but I hoped noise would make them run off."

"Did it?"

"Those times but there were other times when I know they got someone I didn't see."

"How do you know that?"

"I'll be eighteen next month, Miss Fields. I'll tell you honestly that what I did was illegal…"

"We don't care about that, Tom. Tell us what happened."

Taking a long sip of the fresh water bottle Jonas placed in his hand, he took a deep breath. "I hacked into the driver's license computers and then the traffic cams."

He pointed at the photos. "These women went to the same school you did or worked there. All of them applied for new licenses and reported their old ones as lost. I started tracking the cameras on campus. They didn't report what happened to them. I doubt they ever told anyone."

"You think they were attacked?"

"The images were fuzzy and it was dark but all of them got new IDs shortly after I found footage of women being jumped, dragged into an SUV, and driven away. I-I think the guys kept the ID's like trophies. I searched for lost IDs by women in certain age ranges then went backwards on the recordings."

I stared at him for a long moment. "It's thin, Tom."

"That's what the police said when I went to them. I showed them the women but couldn't tell them about hacking the database. I tried to get them to understand there was a group of men terrorizing women but they wouldn't *listen*."

He took another long drink and said, "Eight men behaved like a pack of wild dogs and probably destroyed the lives of these women. Maybe others I didn't find, too. No one would listen so I'm writing a story about it."

My heart raced out of control. There was one thing he said that caused a *screaming* inside my mind.

"Tom," I said hoarsely. "What do you mean there were *eight* men? You're sure you saw *eight* in your surveillance?"

Padme entered my peripheral vision as the Hydes stiffened sharply.

"Always eight. They worked in teams to box the women in. When I traced their movements through the traffic cameras, sometimes half would abduct the woman but wherever they took her, there were always four others waiting."

His frustration was clear. "They moved their sites a lot. Those were the places I tried to find."

I stood and paced to the window of my office that overlooked downtown Dallas. I worked to calm my breathing and racing heart as I processed information we never knew.

In all my dealings with the men who attacked me, we only knew of *seven* men.

There was a member of their group unaccounted for.

"We'll find him, Ellie," Jonas said softly.

"Breathe, Ellie."

From behind us, Tom asked, "Did I say something wrong?"

I turned to him. "No, you didn't. As a matter of fact, I'm fascinated that you've pieced all this together at your age." I approached him. "Where do you live, Tom?"

His expression shuttered. "Here and there."

"Do you have a home?"

"I shelter hop. Staying at whatever ones have beds."

"Padme, he needs a place to stay." Turning for the small table on the other side of the room, I added, "Let's eat and talk about your possible employment, Tom."

"My possible…what?" he asked breathlessly.

"Employment. I bet, with the right training, you could become one of the best mercenaries on the planet."

He gestured down at his body. "I doubt that."

Padme laughed. "I'm one of the best. Why not you?"

The brunette's eyes were as big as saucers.

We filled his belly then filled his mind. Not unlike a dozen times in my childhood, I took home a stray.

Chapter Twenty-Eight

Early March 2015

We ended up placing Tom in the estate's security compound so he wouldn't be alone all the time.

The main staff for my parents were older and steady. A good influence on someone so young.

He received one of the single cottages set up like a studio apartment. Unlike most studio apartments, he had top of the line technology at his fingertips.

The pale youth stood in the middle of his new home and turned in circles. "This is my own space?" I nodded with a smile and he said, "I won't let you down, Miss Fields."

"Call me Ellie…and I know you won't."

My mother walked beside me as I returned to the main house after checking on our new protégé.

"You changed another life, honey. He's a sweet boy."

"Tom is changing his own life. He made the choice not to be a statistic."

Every afternoon, he trained with Padme and other members of my team. He soaked up new material like a sponge.

Shy around most people, Tom preferred to work alone with headphones in.

A month into his training, when Padme was certain she pulled every scrap of information available on his past, we brought Tom a little deeper into our circle of trust.

He was informed of the fate of the seven men we knew about and I watched him piece together what we didn't say.

Though he didn't comment on it, I could tell he was deeply upset. Then he was given his first assignment as a member of my personal security team. A job he didn't know he had.

Identify the eighth man.

* * *

On the twelfth day of March, I brushed down my beautiful Sarafina. Though I couldn't ride her, I found it relaxing to groom her the way I used to.

It was a bright, pretty day and the Hydes stood on either side of the door inside her stall.

A shooting pain arced from my low back to my abdomen and I dropped to one knee with a surprised gasp.

I felt my water break and suddenly I was being carried at a near run for the house. Jonas held me tightly while Jordan texted the go message to everyone who needed to know.

In the elevator, I whispered, "I weigh a ton. You can put me down, Jonas."

He looked down but otherwise ignored me. Then he was striding purposefully toward Theresa's lab.

"Wait, I-I need to shower. I'm gross. This is embarrassing." He clenched his jaw. "Jonas. Please." With a soft groan, he walked into my apartment.

Bianca shouted at us the second we cleared the door. "What the hell are you doing *here*? We were on our way to the medical suite!"

"I need to shower, Bianca. Stand watch for a few minutes."

Jonas put me down in the bathroom and held an obvious internal argument about leaving me alone.

"Five minutes and I'll go right to Theresa."

He nodded once briskly and left. I heard him barking orders at Bianca and she burst through the bathroom door to watch over me.

After a small scream, I showered fast.

Wrapping myself in a towel, Padme appeared with my hospital gown and robe. I wasn't to wear anything under it.

One glance at the urgent look on her face and I smiled. "It's weird to see you guys in a *panic*. I'm ready."

"I've gotten seven texts from your mother in the last five minutes. Let's *go*, buttercup!"

Laughing, I opened my bedroom door and squeaked as Jordan literally swept me off my feet. He carried me down the hall with Jonas at his side clearing the way.

He set me down long enough for me to remove my robe then lifted me to the bed. They moved to stand at the door and I raised my brows.

"Um, guys? Can you stand *behind* me maybe? I've heard that's not a view you can ever erase from your memory."

Jaws clenched, they chuckled nervously and took up positions at the top corners of my bed.

They watched Adam like hawks as he hooked me up to an IV and fetal monitor.

Padme stood directly across from him and stared him down like a vicious, but incredibly feminine, mama bear.

Theresa entered clapping her hands. "Let's do this, people! You ready, Ellie?" I nodded.

I was *so* ready to get this over with. I missed being able to see my feet, put on my own pants, and go more than an hour without having to pee.

She put my feet in stirrups and checked dilation beneath a tented sheet. Looking between the Hydes, she asked, "You guys plan on staying?"

They must have nodded because she gave them strange looks.

My parents entered together. They told me later that their driver broke every speed limit getting them back from Dallas.

Theresa grinned at me. "Things are going to move fairly fast, Ellie. You're already eight centimeters dilated. She made up her mind and that was it. Sit tight while we prep."

Everyone fussed over me, trying to keep my mind off the steadily worsening contractions. I was grateful.

Mom braided my hair so it didn't stick to my face. Padme

pulled up labor breathing instructions and some sort of soundtrack to help me keep rhythm.

Bianca handed me crushed ice. "Don't ask me what this is for. Theresa gave it to me. I'm assuming you suck on it or some damn thing."

My father has strong hands and let me squeeze them as hard as I could when the pain would crest.

"You didn't have any signs earlier, Ellie?" Theresa asked with a frown. "No contractions? That's unusual for a first baby."

"Weird aches but it's not like that's new."

She paused and put her hand on her hip. "So…contractions." I shrugged. "I won't ask anything else. I'll have a stroke."

Half an hour later, there was a lull in the noise.

"Theresa, should I push? I *really* want to push."

The doctor pulled a stool between my legs instantly and whispered, "She's *crowning* already. You quick and clever girl. Ellie, we're going to sit you up so you can bear down."

My parents put their arms behind my back and held my hands.

When Adam moved to stand between my spread legs, I kicked him as hard as I could in the face.

Shocked at myself as his eye began to swell, I gritted out, "Contraction. So sorry, Adam!"

He put his hand on my bare knee to tell me it was no

problem. I could see the words forming but I was going to break his fucking wrist if he didn't take his hand off me.

Padme shoved him away with zero politeness and got between us. Bianca took up a position on my other side. They refused to move an inch.

Theresa, focused on the baby getting impatient, missed the byplay. "Ready, Ellie? I want you to push and keep pushing for five seconds."

The next minute was a blur to me as the most awful pressure built and built. "Give me another good one, Ellie."

More pressure and then... *release*.

I laid back with Dad's help and panted frantically. A small cry echoed through the room and you could have heard a pin drop.

"Give Adam a minute to clear her airway, Ellie."

I stared upside down at Jordan and he moved to follow the medical assistant across the room with my baby. I knew he'd gut the man where he stood before he let Adam hurt her.

"One more push, honey. That's it."

I may have passed out. The next thing I remember is Theresa beside me, putting a pink wrapped bundle in my arms which were shaking too hard to support the weight.

Mom helped so I didn't drop her during our first meeting.

"Hello, my little Katherine. How perfect you are. I'm Ellie but *you* can call me Mommy."

There was more hustle and bustle as I was cleaned up.

Hands touched me, touched the baby. My mom cried and so did my dad but he tried to hide it.

My team murmured about the baby, how well I'd done, and how happy everyone was that things went smoothly.

Padme and Bianca kept a block between the annoying assistant and me. He iced his eye to bring down the swelling.

Theresa murmured, "I'm giving her something for pain. Her milk never came in so I don't think she'll breastfeed."

Mom answered, "No, she knows she can't…"

I let myself drift, my eyes felt too heavy. Large hands cupped either side of my face and firm lips on faces with a trace of beard stubble kissed my cheeks at the same time.

Out of my mind with drugs and exhaustion, I imagined it was Jordan and Jonas. To be fair, where they're concerned, I'm *never* in my right mind.

"I *love*…stubble."

Even exhausted, I managed to catch myself and pretend I didn't love them with all of myself.

It was a lie I grew increasingly tired of telling.

* * *

Having a baby was both exhausting and exhilarating.

It's also one of the most frightening experiences I've ever had. I ended up agreeing to hiring a nanny because when

Katie was two weeks old, the shriveled bit of her umbilical cord fell off and I ran *screaming* to Theresa.

For a while it was touch and go on whether I'd have to be sedated.

Mom summed it up. "Except for much older children, close to school age, you've never been around infants. It isn't surprising you'd worry when a little bit of baby falls off."

I swayed on my feet and Jonas put a steady hand on my back.

She rushed on. "Bad choice of words, honey. Getting a nanny will stop your slow descent into madness."

I worried constantly something would happen to my daughter. That I wasn't going to be allowed to keep anything good and clean from that horrible day filled with degradation and pain.

My staff was *enthralled* with her.

Bianca and Padme changed her clothes several times a day. Since I was constantly putting her in new outfits myself, we bought a lot of spares.

Katie didn't cry. I don't mean she rarely cried. *She did not cry*. I set timers to check her diaper so she never sat wet and to remind myself to give her a bottle.

Si and Fiaaz sang silly songs they made up to describe what they were doing. She stared at them with wide eyes and I wondered what she comprehended.

The biggest surprise was how Jordan and Jonas were with her.

They held her constantly and talked as if she could understand them. Since she stared at them in rapt fascination, maybe she did. When I saw them with her, my heart clenched painfully.

Distractedly rubbing the heel of my hand over my sternum, I met Jordan's gaze accidentally. The intensity on his face held me still. I felt like a gazelle faced with a lion.

I quickly dismissed my reaction as juvenile and misplaced.

In the solarium, I sat at my writing desk with Katie in a bassinet beside me. Typing away, I rocked it with my foot.

Sometimes, I'd glance down and forget everything in my desire to pick her up…just because.

Holding her close to me, I'd stand up and stare out at the estate. Swaying gently and murmuring to her, I watched her fall asleep.

Katie was my little girl and worth every moment of pain I experienced to have her with me.

I regretted nothing. I couldn't. She filled up a heart that too often felt empty.

Chapter Twenty-Nine

Late March 2015

Mom was interviewing nannies with Padme and until the right person was found, my parents insisted on taking their granddaughter every afternoon to give me a break.

I used the time to swim and then relaxed outside until I missed her too much to stay away.

The Hyde brothers were my constant companions.

Some days, I visited Sarafina's stable and gave her treats or groomed her. Other days, I strolled the gardens.

I was almost always lost in thought as if I was holding my breath. Waiting for the other shoe to drop.

On a day I chose to sit in the garden, the book I brought remained open and untouched on my lap. I hadn't read a single line in twenty minutes.

Something was *off* and I couldn't place what it was. I thought I might crawl out of my skin from the sudden but inexplicable stress.

"Ellie. What is it?" Jordan asked quietly.

I shook my head because I didn't know, couldn't place, what

it was that had me off-balance and shaking.

I looked around, listened, and then took a deep breath.

The answer hit me hard and I wanted *out* of the gardens and as far away as I could get. I jumped up, my book falling to the paved walkway, and started to run for the house.

"Ellie!"

At the covered back patio, the Hyde brothers pulled me carefully to a stop, surrounded me in protection mode, and held me still.

I couldn't *look* at them. I couldn't *breathe* around my panic.

"What is it? Tell us, Ellie." I didn't know which of them spoke. "You can tell us. It's alright."

"M-mulch and dirt. I can't…"

I turned away, dropped to my knees, and vomited in the bushes along the cobblestones.

Gentle hands stroked my hair, rubbed my back, and whispered soothingly to me. I was mortified as I lost everything in my stomach and couldn't stop the dry heaves.

"It's alright. You're safe, Ellie. You're safe."

The feel of their hands on me, strong and warm but incredibly gentle, began to calm me.

After what felt like forever, the roiling in my stomach eased and I knelt there, unsure what to say or do.

Tissues were placed in my hand and I wiped my mouth before a bottle of water replaced it.

Rinsing and spitting several times, I finally sipped it, allowing it to cool the burn the bile left behind.

"No one will *ever* hurt you again, Ellie."

I managed to murmur, "I'm sorry."

If I didn't get inside and away from the various beds being freshly prepared as they were every spring, I was going to throw up again.

I was bodily lifted to my feet.

"No more apologies, Ellie. Not one. You've done *nothing* that requires such a thing."

They guided me through the house to my suite and waited in my bathroom doorway as I brushed my teeth and washed my face.

Jonas asked, "Do you want to lie down?"

I shook my head. "I'd like to sit in the solarium. I need to be calm before Mom brings Katie back."

Hands crossed over my waist, the brothers led me through the suite and out into the warm and welcoming glass room.

They sat on one of the sofas and gently tugged me down to sit between them. Si appeared with iced green tea laced with honey to soothe my throat.

I sipped it until it was gone and the cup was taken from me. Leaning against the cushions, I closed my eyes and let the world settle for a minute.

In the years since these men took over my protection, I'd rarely sat close to *one* Hyde brother.

Never had I been so close to both at the same time.

When they took my hands, I squeezed as if to soak up their steady strength. I didn't say anything. I couldn't. Other than my parents and some of their friends, I didn't experience much physical contact that wasn't for a specific purpose.

Something so simple, so kind as holding my hands in comfort, had me close to tears and I couldn't let them know how much their touch affected me.

I was afraid they'd take it away.

We sat there for a long time in silence and I dozed off. When I opened my eyes, surprised at how warm I was, I discovered my head on Jordan's shoulder. Jonas was closer to me.

Their sides were sealed to mine and there wasn't another time in my life when I'd felt as safe. Jonas held my hand in both of his. Jordan held my other and smoothed his thumb along the inside of my wrist.

I flicked my gaze to his and he smiled. "You need to eat, Ellie."

"Alright." I cleared my throat. "Everyone tries to feed me an awful lot around here."

Jonas chuckled. "You forget to feed yourself. Come."

They stood with my hands held firmly, pulling me up to stand between them.

Jordan ran his hand over my hair. "Better?" I nodded and I meant it. "Good."

He pulled me into a quick hug before I was turned and hugged by Jonas. Without another word, they led me downstairs where my parents waited with Katie.

The world suddenly seemed to be a much brighter place.

* * *

A few weeks later, Theresa officially released me from medical care. Hugging me tightly, she said, "I'm heading back to Boston. I need to get back to my practice and my family."

"I'll miss you."

"You'll see me often. The new charity will take a lot of hand-holding the first two years but those families are worth all the hours we're going to commit."

"Agreed."

"This has been a trying year for you and it's made me remember what family is supposed to be. I need to reconnect with mine. When you visit, bring the baby."

Tearing up, I whispered, "Thank you for everything. No one could have brought me through all of this as efficiently. I'm grateful for all the time you gave us."

"It was my honor."

The next morning, Theresa left for her Boston home. It was an emotional parting.

Adam left with her to continue his position at her clinic. He hugged me too tightly in the driveway after Theresa was already seated in the limo that would take her to the airport.

"Stay in touch, Ellie." The words were whispered at my ear.

"Sure, Adam. Travel safe." I patted his back distractedly to keep from snapping his neck. Finally, he let me go.

He glared at the Hyde brothers no more than six inches from my shoulders. "Can't Ellie say goodbye to her friends without you guys looming? Good grief."

"No, they cannot. My men guard my back. That's what they do." I added sharply, "Goodbye, Adam."

As if I'd said something sweet, he gave me a huge grin and leaned as if to kiss me. I was bodily *moved* out of his reach.

"It's time for you to go. Theresa has a plane to catch and so do you." I crossed my arms over my chest.

"Goodbye, Ellie."

When he was in the car and it pulled away, I hissed, "What an asshole. I'm starving."

Barely a week later, the rooms dedicated to Theresa and her assistant's lab and living quarters were returned to the bedrooms they once were.

All the equipment was shipped to the doctor for use at her clinic in the heart of Boston. It was her true passion.

I was ready to return home myself.

Chapter Thirty

June 2015

I was heartbroken I wouldn't see Hudson and Natalia exchange their vows but I wouldn't leave Katie and wasn't ready to make such a public appearance where so many people knew me professionally.

Not yet.

There would be too many questions. I refused to be such a distraction on the happiest day of their lives.

My parents attended and I decided to make good use of the time they were gone.

The Hydes accompanied me as I walked across the grounds to my own home on the other side. I wanted to see the condition of the place and consult with a contractor.

I hadn't been inside since my release from the hospital and it felt as if I was seeing it for the first time.

The front entry was wide and brightly lit. The first floor held a kitchen with a smaller dining room, a library, two living areas, two bedrooms with bathrooms, a full gym and sauna, and a large semi-covered patio with a swimming pool and hot tub.

The main rooms were all done in soothing earth tones.

Each member of the team worked with me to decorate their rooms for the most comfort.

Si and Fiaaz had bedrooms on the first floor, closest to the kitchen and garage, to cover the front and back of the house.

Si's room featured low profile furniture I asked him to help me select, with a black and white color scheme, giving the room a decided dojo quality. He meditated every morning so an area beneath one window held plants and thick floor cushions.

Fiaaz preferred heavy furniture with a royal burgundy palate. Heavy mats allowed him to practice body isolations privately instead of using the main gym.

The second floor had five bedrooms, each with their own bathroom.

Padme's room featured vibrant colors and hand-carved furniture. One wall concealed a staircase to her security room behind the kitchen. A private workspace held the basic technology she used regularly.

Bianca's room was cool blues and iridescent creams. It resembled an ice palace but felt strangely comfortable and welcoming. Much like the woman herself.

My combination bedroom, bathroom, and sitting room were done in varying shades of browns and greens. From caramel to espresso, sage to emerald. I used ivory as an accent color and loved the peace I always felt here.

Since I hadn't known there were *two* Hydes, I decorated a

single room in pale blue-green to match his eyes and furnished it with clean lines and masculine accents.

It was right next to mine.

The room directly across the hall was a guest room. I planned to transform the uppermost floor into the nanny's quarters, nursery, and a massive playroom.

I spent an hour walking through the house and re-familiarizing myself with the spaces. I knew I wanted a play space on the first floor for Katie.

Part of my mind noted the rarely used second living area that I could convert into space for Tom when he became a permanent member of my team.

I made notes on my iPad for Padme to help me coordinate and grinned at the puppy who followed me into each room and promptly fell asleep.

The first change would be to give each brother their *own* space. I wanted to duplicate the furniture and freshen the colors.

"You look like you've missed the place." The brothers approached silently as usual.

"I'm ready to move back into my own home. I know I'm still on the estate but…it's different. I took the coward's way out by staying with Mom and Dad so long."

Jonas turned to me. "Don't beat yourself up for wanting family around you. I'm glad you feel strong enough to come home." He swallowed hard but said nothing more.

A few weeks later, the contractors and cleaning crew

declared the house ready, and we moved back in.

Everyone giddily dispersed and I headed upstairs. I watched the Hyde brothers disappear into the bedroom they were accustomed to sharing.

Knocking softly, Jordan opened the door and smiled brightly at Katie in my arms.

I cleared my throat and steadied my voice. "You each have y-your own rooms now. The empty one a-across the hall. I figured…well, anyway."

"You kept both of us beside you?" Jordan noted as Jonas appeared at his shoulder.

"Of course." Katie touched my face and I smiled at her. "The new nanny should be here soon. I'm going to check her diaper and…stuff."

I carried Katie into my room and laid down on the bed with her after I put her in a fresh diaper.

She was starting to smile all the time and I *loved* it.

"You're *such* a happy girl. No one could ask for a better baby. I think you're going to like your room, Katie. I wanted you to have the run of a *huge* floor." She gurgled cheerfully and I stroked my fingers through her soft curls.

"When you're big enough, Grandpa will bring my old wooden horse for you to ride. Don't get me started on your first *real* horse, honey. I'll pick the *sweetest* darling for you and you'll ride with Mommy all over the estate."

Katie laughed and it filled me with pure happiness.

"I love you so much. No little girl will ever be loved like

you. I think your grandparents argue over which of them loves you more, can you *imagine*?"

I leaned to kiss her chubby pink cheek. "You're also an *excellent* listener, Katie."

A sound at the door made me look up. The Hyde brothers stood inside the room, looking gorgeous and huge in a room that wasn't small.

I was sprawled on my stomach talking to a two-month-old and I blushed. "We were having a little chat. Everything alright?"

"Ellie…"

"You'll have to come closer or tell me which is which. I can't see scars from here." Katie laughed and I gave her a proud smile. "You probably have them *all* figured out already. So much smarter than Mommy aren't you, sweetheart?"

When I looked up again, both men were crouched at the side of the bed, barely a foot from me.

"Thank you for giving us our own rooms," Jonas said gently. "You didn't have to do that."

"Of *course*, I did. Either you were trying to share a bed or one of you got the floor. Either way, it's not necessary since there was an empty room. Does everyone have what they need?"

Jordan smiled. "You added flat-screens to all the bedrooms. They're happy to be home but now you don't have any guest rooms."

I snorted. "There are *plenty* at my parents' house and besides, who comes to visit? I would have done that originally…if I'd known. Cramped with no privacy is no way to live. Not in your own home. All fixed."

The brothers stared at me and I had that gazelle feeling again.

A knock across the room broke the spell and Padme jumped up on the bed beside me. "You're our *queen*. I adore the new shoe racks!"

Glancing at the brothers, I winked. "You say *flat-screens*, Padme says *shoe racks*."

They laughed and I was dumbstruck. I'd never understood the expression before. I blinked too fast.

"I love the playroom and new bedroom on the first floor," my assistant said like the saving grace she was. "You were right to ditch that formal space we never used."

"Movies are *better* in the other living room and there's more than enough room for all of us."

"What are your thoughts on Tom?"

"I want him to finish basic training with the house team." I looked at the Hydes. "How's he doing?"

"Exhausted by the end of the day," Jonas answered. "He's small and fast. He'll never be a fighter but that wasn't the point of the training."

Jordan added, "He needs to understand emergency response. He'll never be able to guard you or Katie but he has to know how to protect *himself* when things are moving fast."

"Excellent. Let's keep him in the loop."

Padme grinned. "Have you seen the nursery?"

I shook my head. "Not yet. We should check it out. Katie told me her space *better* be perfect or she's going back to Grandma's." I backed off the bed and picked her up.

Bianca walked toward us down the hall. "Robyn's here."

Robyn was the nanny hired from a pool carefully vetted by my parents and Padme. I was pretty sure she was a ninja Mary Poppins and I was fine with that.

She was pixie cute with brown hair and green eyes. Based on her bio, her adorable looks were deceiving.

"Perfect timing." I greeted her warmly as she approached. "It's good to meet you at last. We're headed up to check out the nursery. Come on up."

I walked upstairs with the big silly puppy beside me.

Nothing I imagined, nothing the contractor suggested, prepared me for the full realization of a child's fantasy space.

Repainted with pastels, a mural on one wall depicted a fairy wood, and colorful lighting globes in assorted sizes suspended from the crossbeams gave the space warmth I could feel.

The carpet was pale green and lush. There were huge overstuffed couches and chairs scattered around.

Diva sniffed everything then went back and sniffed it again.

Enormous windows held glass that could stop a .50 caliber bullet and featured one-sided tint. You could see out but no one could see in, no matter how bright the space was lit up.

There were two large actual bedrooms at the far end, one for Robyn and one for Katie. A big bathroom sat between them.

A built-in cabinet with bulletproof glass doors and recessed lighting held many of the keepsakes from my childhood. On the top shelf in the spotlight was Katie's hope chest, my daughter's name glowing.

"Miss Fields, this space is incredible."

"Robyn, *please* call me Ellie. You'll find we're informal here. You'll be with us a good many years. Mom said you can take over Katie's lessons before she starts school as well as her comportment?"

She nodded, stunned.

"This is Texas. She'll be forced to make her debutante debut. I *hated* it and she will, too. Nonetheless, we do what we must. So! Eighteen years of *Miss Fields* or *Ellie*...what do you think?"

Robyn gave a small laugh. "Most families don't keep a nanny like me for eighteen years."

"My parents wouldn't have hired you unless you were weapons trained and certified as a lethal weapon yourself. That means when Katie no longer needs diaper changes or an after-school snack, you'll become her personal bodyguard."

Her eyes were huge.

"Everywhere she goes, you go. I'll pay you more than you'll ever make anywhere else to keep her safe." I tilted my head and added, "If anyone makes you an offer, I'll beat it."

Katie laughed and I grinned at her. I hated that talk of self-defense was necessary. She was a *baby*.

"Coordinate days off with Padme, whatever you need. If you need vacation time, a member of my team will cover her in your place. She'll train with the men and women who protect me but incorporate self-defense tactics in play as well."

Robyn nodded. "I like the way you think."

"Jonas and Jordan are my personal protection. When it's time for college, they'll train an entire team to accompany my daughter or she won't go. You'll lead that team, Robyn."

"You've really thought this through, Miss…Ellie."

"Obsessed over it, yes." Katie put her little palm on my lips and I kissed her fingers. "Pretty girl."

I was distracted for a moment and suddenly remembered I was in the middle of a conversation. "Sorry. She's so snuggly."

"She's a calm baby."

"A true joy." Cradling her closer to my body, I said, "Remind me of your background."

Her accent was a blend of various cultures and I loved it. "Originally from England, my father was based at the embassy in Jordan. I was a target and had to learn to protect myself. It seemed natural to go into protection as an adult."

"You look about my age. Work for me for the next twenty or thirty years, and never worry one day about your retirement. I won't let you regret it."

Katie was drifting off and it made me smile. "Get settled in and we'll hammer out details over the next couple of days. Let us know if you need anything."

"Come here, little one. You look like you're ready for a nap." Robyn held out her hands and I felt confident handing her my daughter.

I whispered, "Princess, relax and Mommy will see you in a little while. Don't play with everything at once."

I kissed her forehead and headed for the stairs.

On the first floor, I walked into the well-appointed kitchen and grinned at the master of the domain. Grabbing my apron from the hook, I bumped hips with Si.

"What are we cooking?"

He gave me a huge smile and I felt like I was falling back into my own skin.

Chapter Thirty-One

Being back in my own home allowed me to remember the rhythm of my life before the attack and lengthy recovery.

It was both peaceful and exciting.

Everything was the same and yet different in all the ways that mattered. I had my little Katie now and two Hydes. Robyn expanded our family yet again.

Diva had fully abandoned me to shadow whoever was holding my daughter and I didn't mind.

Thankfully, Robyn was a dog lover. Their regular outings into the walled garden with the mastiff usually inspired a member of my team to snap photos and bring them to me.

For the first few days, I worked on reacclimating myself to my office and returning to my usual gym routine.

We were home three days and I was getting in a workout while Katie napped. Padme was stretching me because I was stiffer after my injuries.

"Don't stop. I need to get the range of motion back." I gritted my teeth as she gradually added pressure to the back of my thigh. There was pain but I ignored it. "This sucks."

"We'll keep stretching you and Bianca will give you a

massage when she and Fiaaz get back from Tom's. For now, let's see where you are with endurance."

Si entered from the kitchen and watched us with a frown. "Stand, Ellie."

I did so immediately and faced him. He held out his hands with his palms flat and squinted his eyes.

Dropping his arms, he said, "You're crooked."

"I'm *what?*"

"Your posture and bearing are regal, as you were trained. However, one shoulder is higher than the other. Your hips are no longer aligned properly."

I growled. "Can you *fix* that?"

"Possibly. May I?" He gestured at my hips and I nodded. He stepped to my side and pressed a spot that made me almost buckle. "This area hurts you. You said nothing."

"It's…I mean, I guess I got used to it."

"Your right hip is dislocated. I believe it's a combination of favoring your uninjured side and childbirth." He nodded as if to himself. "I need the massage table."

The Hydes carried it into the center of the room.

"Lie on your back, arms at your sides."

I did as instructed, and the Hydes took up places beside me. I think they could tell I was nervous.

Jonas put his palm on my shoulder. "Si doesn't do massage but he's brilliant at putting bones back where they belong."

I hummed. "Breathe deep, exhale when he tells you to."

"I'll start at your neck," Si explained. "It's going to *sound* terrible but tell me immediately if you *feel* pain. Do you understand?"

"Yes."

Si placed his palms along my jaw. "Breathe deeply. Hold it. And…exhale."

He jerked my neck and it sounded as if an explosion went off in my body. "Um…"

"Your bones will thank me, Ellie." I nodded. "Now roll to your stomach with your arms extended off the side."

Working from my shoulders to my low back, Si used what felt like slow motion punches to crack bones that had endured a lot over the past year.

"I need to touch your hips, Ellie."

"Si, I have absolute trust in you. Do whatever you need to."

Putting his knee on the edge of the table, he rose over me and placed his palms along the joint of my right hip. I felt him pinpoint the connection with two fingers.

Then he used his body weight to push down.

My entire body jerked simultaneously with the bang and I held my breath. He checked my other side, made a smaller adjustment, and returned to the right again.

One last crack and he bounced lightly to the floor. Extending his hand, he helped me sit up.

"Let me check, Ellie." He examined me closely. "I'll repeat once a week until the cartilage firms in the original position."

I put my weight on that side and slowly raised my leg. "Higher than before and no pain." Dropping my foot, I hugged the chef as hard as I could. "Thank you."

"It's my honor, Ellie." He bowed. "I'll see you at dinner."

He left the gym and I tested my range of motion. "Better. So much better."

"Treadmill, Ellie?" Padme asked with a smile.

"No. No, I don't think so." I was *done* with running. It put me at too much of a disadvantage and my men by association. "Let's do some yoga. I don't want to undo Si's work."

Over the next weeks, Si adjusted me several times and I felt physically more like myself than I had in a long time. He continued to pump me full of dietary nutrients to help rebuild calcium and iron losses.

I was confident I could return to my standard training.

During the first several years of having my new team, I sparred regularly with Padme. She was female and closest to me in height. She filled the void left by my childhood sensei.

Occasionally, Si joined us and showed me additional movements more efficient for my build and strength.

The pair were spending the day with Tom so I decided to work out alone during Katie's afternoon nap. In meetings all morning with my parents and corporate assistant at the main house, I needed to *move*.

Taping my feet and hands, I walked into the gym and stretched deeply. Aches and stiffness eased more by the week.

Turning on the gym speaker system and selecting my playlist of gothic classical, I went through a series of ballet forms that were second nature to me. I took *years* of dance and thought it might help get my balance and coordination back.

Warming up my muscles, I smiled as the pounding rhythms of Bach's *Toccata and Fugue* filled the room fifteen minutes later.

When I was seventeen, it was the song I chose for my final ballet recital. My poor mother was *scandalized* at the time. All the other girls chose pretty, lighthearted music while mine was deadly dark and something of a shock to the audience.

Around the room, I moved, falling into a song that never failed to make me feel powerful.

My jumps weren't as high as they once were. My landings were softer, gentler on bones that had been through enough. I didn't dare attempt pointe after so many years.

The sweat poured from my skin as I focused on nothing but the music. As it crested, I leapt, my arms wide, and stuck the landing.

Proud of myself, I jumped when applause came from the door. Beside the Hydes were my parents, Bianca, Fiaaz, and Robyn holding my daughter.

I wondered how long they'd been watching.

Folding my hands in front of me, I said, "Hello."

"As stunning as you always were, honey. I love seeing you dance." Mom walked across the mats and hugged me tight.

"I'm disgusting. All sweaty, Mom."

"Hush." My dad kissed my damp hair and said, "Go shower. We came by to see Katie and heard the music."

I kissed my little girl and went upstairs. I took my time showering and changing into a sundress and sandals. Then I went to the kitchen to help Si with dinner.

I felt incredible. I felt like *me* again.

* * *

My parents didn't stay to eat with us. They had a gala to attend and sadly handed Katie to Robyn as I walked them to the door where their own security waited.

"Come for brunch tomorrow," I said softly.

Nodding, they hugged me tight and I watched them drive away.

I made an announcement over the intercom an hour later that dinner was served.

Sitting at our long table with every member of my team, I made a toast, "To starting fresh." I took a long sip of my wine and sighed in pleasure. "And a well-stocked wine cellar."

Diva casually licked the top of my foot with her big tongue.

After that, the conversation flew. I watched them happily, content to listen and comment now and again. Their decade of history was obvious and I never tired of the stories they told of their pasts.

They trusted one another and I trusted them.

Robyn was the first to turn in, taking the baby upstairs after I snuggled Katie and whispered for her to have sweet dreams. My big silly dog followed them.

Fiaaz and Bianca stood and announced they were going for a drive. I liked the way they looked at each other. Friends, co-workers, and lovers, I was almost certain.

Si and Padme were involved in a quiet discussion at the opposite end of the table. I watched their expressions and the way her eyes seemed to sparkle.

I was always curious about the private lives of my staff.

Was she involved with Si? Their black hair glinted almost blue in the light as they sat with their heads a few inches apart.

I watched them while I sipped my wine. Ten minutes of silence delivered me into a sort of euphoric buzz. It had been almost a year since I drank anything alcoholic.

One glass slapped me smartly.

Pulling my gaze away, I focused on the two men on either side of me. "I zoned out. Sorry."

Jordan and Jonas were angled in my direction, sprawled back in their chairs with their legs stretched out in front of them.

Jeans and t-shirts never looked so good. Their shaggy dark blonde hair was still damp on the ends from the showers they took before dinner.

My shoes had long since been discarded. I didn't remember where I'd kicked them off.

"I'm thinking *Wanted* or maybe *Blade Trinity*. Yeah, that sounds fabulous." I stood and grabbed my plate and other items that were close to my end of the table.

I cleaned my plate and stacked it on the rack before putting away a few things. The Hydes cleaned their plates behind me.

Refilling my wine glass, I headed into the remaining living room filled with comfortable furniture big enough for giants, a massive sixty-inch flat-screen, surround sound, and dim lighting with the flick of a switch.

I flipped through my movie library and chose an action movie. Grabbing a cashmere throw blanket, I threw myself into my favorite corner and got comfortable.

When I was settled, the Hydes took seats on either side of me. Placing their guns on the couch cushions beside them, I laughed at how much my own life resembled an action movie.

Halfway through *Wanted*, despite it being one of my favorites, I started to nod off. They offered to help me upstairs but I told them I wasn't tired.

I wanted to stay where I was. Having them close and relaxed didn't happen often and I wasn't ready for it to end.

I don't remember falling asleep but I must have gone out

hard.

My den was dark except for the screensaver on the television and at first, I wasn't sure where I was.

I was warm and comfortable. It hadn't been a night terror that woke me. It was the unfamiliar sense of complete safety despite the darkness.

As my eyes adjusted to the pale light, I realized my head was on Jordan's lap. His hands were in my hair and curled around my hip. Jonas was sealed to the front of my body, his arms loosely holding me to him.

I had one arm curled under and around Jordan's thigh, the other curled around Jonas's waist.

Even fully dressed, I could feel the heat coming off their bodies. They smelled fantastic, like sunshine with a hint of sandalwood.

As the full impact of where I was and what position I was in with my two closest bodyguards hit me, for an instant, I stiffened, unsure what to do.

They positioned themselves to protect me in the open space of the first floor.

I asked myself what was wrong with enjoying a rare moment of warmth from two human beings I both liked and trusted with everything inside myself?

These men would never hurt me. The hurt I carried around in my heart was a result of my own immaturity and stupidity.

I didn't want to lose the incredible sensations yet.

Long before my attack I was considered an untouchable ice

queen. Too rich and pure for anyone to really get close to…for anyone to love.

I never wanted that. I never meant to exist apart from the rest of the world. I craved touch, contact, and connection.

Life now was different than before. I was no longer pure and I didn't want just *anyone* to touch me.

Most people scared me, most touch felt foreign.

I wanted *these* men to touch me and I desperately wanted to touch them back. I craved contact with them like air.

They were sleeping. Tomorrow, I could pretend I hadn't slept between them.

Until then, I could soak up their warmth, their scent, and pretend – for a little while – that I *wasn't* untouchable. I could pretend I was a different person.

The kind of person, the kind of woman, men like Jordan and Jonas would want for more than an assignment.

I breathed deep and took the scent of them into my lungs. Every inch of me in contact with their bodies rejoiced in it.

I wanted to rub against them like a cat but I contented myself with the experience of the muscled thigh under my cheek, the long masculine fingers in my hair, and the long, hard body pressed against the front of mine.

For several minutes, I stared at Jonas inches from my face. I wanted to touch hair that was gilded from the sun, to run my fingertips over sensual lips, to trace the fine webbing of scars from injuries he sustained for me.

Afraid to wake him and lose the contact, I held back.

I tucked my arm between our bodies and turned my palm so I could press it to his chest. His heart beat steady and strong. Some part of me should have been afraid but I wasn't. I felt drunk on touch.

Allowing my body to relax, I thought there was a slight tightening in my hair and around my waist.

I fell back to sleep breathing them in and I had no nightmares.

***

My house had perfect natural light in all the rooms. Large windows filled with bulletproof glass allowed pre-dawn pink light to slant across the floors and brighten every surface.

I knew what it looked like because I slept in this room many nights over the years. Today, I didn't dare look.

As much as I loved the play of light and color, I found myself unable, unwilling even, to open my eyes.

During the night, my sundress rode above my knees and I could feel Jonas's jeans-clad thigh on the skin of my inner leg. I wasn't ready to give up the most amazing experience of my life. I refused to return to isolation.

A light kiss touched my forehead as a warm hand stroked repeatedly, hypnotically through my hair.

"Ellie, open your eyes."

I didn't *want* to but I forced myself to do it anyway. I stared at Jonas's face.

"Good morning, Ellie."

I knew I should say something but my brain wouldn't cooperate. In the dark of the night, Jonas's face was in shadow. Seeing him inches from me in the light was surreal.

Sleep-ruffled with golden brown hair along his jaw, he was so gorgeous up close that my mind locked up. All I could think about was hugging him tighter. Kissing him.

Jordan said quietly from above me, "You didn't have nightmares, Ellie." It was he who stroked my hair.

"Ellie, we'd never hurt you," Jonas murmured softly. His palm smoothed small circles on my back. The combined effect of their touch was euphoria.

Please don't stop…don't ever stop.

"I know. I know that, Jonas."

He smiled and moved to get up. I didn't realize I tightened my arms around him until he did the same. Jordan's warm hand slid along the side of my neck, his thumb massaging the nape.

I felt my eyes grow heavy, felt a bone-deep peace I wasn't sure I'd ever felt before. I leaned forward and kissed the hollow of Jonas's throat and registered his soft moan an instant before I slipped back to sleep.

When I woke again, the sun was higher in the sky and Padme stood in front of the couch, staring down at the three of us with a smile.

Before I could figure out how to address the completely inappropriate situation, she tucked Katie between my body and Jonas.

"Good morning, Ellie. The little princess had that tiny frown between her eyes that says she isn't altogether happy. We figured some mama time might fix it. Between you, she's snug. Sleep some more. You haven't slept this well in a year."

With a wink and a smile, she turned and left the room.

I glanced at Katie's face, smooth and happy now. Stroking her silken cheek, I watched as she drifted off.

The sound of her soft breathing, the scent of the men surrounding us, and the warmth I hadn't realized would be exactly what I needed combined to pull me under yet again.

The adjustment of my blanket brought me up. Jonas stood with Katie in his arms. He smiled at me, "Sleep, Ellie. It's still early. I'm going to change her and get her a bottle."

Jordan turned and moved his legs, stretching them out beside me and pulling my upper body higher to lie on his chest. My body sealed along Jordan's side, my knee over his, my arm over his waist.

His hand smoothed through my hair and down my back. "Sleep, Ellie."

The strong, steady beat of his heart hypnotized me. I didn't remember the last time I slept so much without medication. I was disoriented but not stressed.

That he played with my hair told me he was awake. I lifted my head to look at him.

"You're achingly beautiful, Ellie."

"Thank you."

He lifted his other hand to trace along my cheek. Even the simplest touches over the years affected me strongly.

I went up on my knees beside his torso.

He picked up my hand and placed it palm down over his heart so I could feel it thump. Neither of us spoke.

Jonas approached from the dining area. "Do you feel rested, Ellie?" I nodded. He picked up my other hand, kissed the back, and wrapping it in both of his. "You must be hungry. Si is making those fruit crepes with fresh cream that you like."

Leaning over the back of the couch, he scooped me up, careful to hold my dress against the back of my legs as he set me on my feet.

In one fluid movement, Jordan bounded over the back and landed beside his brother. He raked my hair back from my temples and dropped all of it down my back. He gave me a gentle kiss on my forehead.

Then they nudged me from the room to get ready for the day. I managed to make it to my room without tripping.

Chapter Thirty-Two

July 2015

When I was dressed, I left my room and smiled at the Hydes on either side of the door. They'd showered as well.

"Ready?" Jonas asked with a smile.

I nodded and they placed their hands at my low back and gestured to the stairs. They escorted me like a thousand days before but the way it felt was brand new.

At breakfast, I chatted with Robyn about her first few days with our team. Katie sat in her reclined baby seat beside me and I kept a hand on her while I ate with one hand.

When she got a case of the hiccups, I picked her up and patted her back until she fell asleep.

"You're so good with her, Ellie," Robyn told me.

I blushed. "I don't know much about kids this small. She makes it easy on me though." Had she been a big crier there's no telling how lost I'd feel on an hourly basis. "Once she hits three or four, I'll be more familiar. Once she can ride, I'll feel like I know what I'm doing."

Robyn crossed her arms on the table. "I've met a lot of wealthy parents over the years, Ellie. Most of them foist their kids off on others like a burden. My own parents were that way. Did someone have to convince you to get a nanny?"

"I wasn't sure, not at first. Then I realized there needed to be one person who wasn't distracted by me or my parents. Someone only looking out for her."

My daughter opened her eyes and smiled when her gaze landed on mine. "You look more like Grandma every day. Get older, a little older, so I don't feel like I'll break you, Katie."

She laughed at me and I sat her on the edge of the table. She reached out to touch my face and I kissed her little hand.

Unintentionally ignoring everyone at the table, I stood and walked outside to my tiled patio. The sun glinted off the pool that resembled a mountain spring.

Kicking off my flip flops, I sat on the side with my feet in the water. I scooped handfuls and dribbled it on her bare toes. She laughed so I did it again. "You're a *water* baby. Yay!"

Pulling my sundress over my head, I carried her down the steps and walked around the warm pool with her. She laughed and smiled, kicking her feet in the water. I smoothed my damp hand over her hair and she kicked more.

I held her, talked to her, and I think she understood everything.

"Elliana Monica Fields, are you swimming in your *bra* and *panties*?" My mother's scandalized voice came from the back gate as she raised her sunglasses.

Diva lifted her head, hmphed, and went back to sleep.

Without looking up, I smiled at Katie. "Grandma forgets this covers more than the bathing suits she swears look good on me." I added in a whisper, "Selective memory." Smiling cheekily, I said, "Hi, Mom. There are fruit crepes inside."

Her delicate sensibilities forgotten, she sighed. "Did Si make the cream with ground vanilla bean?" I nodded seriously. "Sweet *lord*. I'll be right back." Passing the pool, she blew kisses at Katie.

I whispered with my daughter about silly grownups. "I imagine I'll be as silly as Grandma one day. Be patient with me."

From the corner of my eye, I saw my dad approaching the gate with his huge bay stallion.

"Ellie, you look lovely. I saw your mother heading this way." He paused and blushed. "Honey, are you wearing *undergarments* in the pool?"

"Yes, Dad."

He gave a heavy sigh then shrugged. "Better than some of those scraps your mother bought you to wear actually. Tell me you have coffee."

"Of course. Nectar of the gods, Dad."

He tied off the bay and walked around the pool. He motioned me over to the side so he could crouch and give us forehead kisses.

Heading inside, he waved at Katie until he disappeared.

"Dads bluff and bellow but in the end, they're wrapped around your finger. Use your powers for good with Grandpa. He'll be unable to resist you."

Katie thought I was ridiculous and I chatted about all sorts of nonsense while I walked around the pool with her.

"You put her right out, Ellie." Robyn's voice made me look up. She held a thick towel and grinned.

I unbuttoned the cotton dress Katie wore and peeled it from her in the water, throwing it on the edge. When her diaper was removed, I set her in Robyn's hands and watched as she was bundled snuggly.

I powered up on the side and kissed her head before taking another towel from Padme. "I'll change her and put her down for a little while. I'm truly glad to be here, Ellie."

"I'm glad to *have* you, Robyn. Make no mistake."

My parents sat at the patio table and I kissed them both, scooped up my dress, and dashed upstairs to change.

Meeting the eyes of my bodyguards as I left my room in dry clothes with riding boots in my hand, I held my breath when I saw the expressions they wore.

The moment felt explosive.

Slowly, they slid their hands along my waist and moved in front and behind me to hug me between them. It was unlike any hug I'd ever received.

Being pressed against their warm bodies was incredible.

Lowering their heads to either side of mine, they murmured at my ears. At first, I could tell them apart but soon lost track. My eyes drifted closed.

"There's no pressure, no rush. Let us hold you while you sleep. Let us slay your dragons."

Dropping my boots, I lifted a hand to a muscled chest in front of me and lowered the other to the hard thigh behind me.

Anchors to keep me from losing my way as emotion flooded my system and overwhelmed my ability to think.

Hands smoothed over my shoulders, my waist. Strong fingers massaged me through my tank top. They laid soft, open-mouthed kisses along my jaw and down my neck.

My heart pounded and I panted softly.

Strong fingers tipped my head back and firm lips settled over mine. A careful exploration that made me ache.

I gasped softly as the tip of a tongue licked across my lips. A second kiss as another hand turned my face to the side. Lips that were different and the same made another careful study of my own.

Back and forth between them twice more and I was unsure if I could function.

My back touched the wall outside my room and they stood shoulder to shoulder in front of me, leaning with their forearms above my head. I didn't remember lifting my arms to hug them but relished the opportunity.

Jonas asked quietly, "Are you alright, Ellie?"

I nodded as heat climbed from my chest to my face.

"We have to get you downstairs," Jordan murmured with a hint of regret. "We'll talk more later."

My only response was a sigh of longing.

They lifted away but took me with them. Jonas smoothed my hair and Jordan straightened the strap of my tank top.

One in front, one behind, they led me back to the patio. My mother was in heaven, devouring Si's crepes piled with fresh cream. "Ellie! If Si doesn't give Cook the recipe for this manna from heaven, we're going to have words."

She glanced at me before returning for a longer look. Eyes narrowing, she opened her mouth to speak and I rushed out, "You know how he guards his recipes, Mom."

There was a long moment of silence and she remembered to finish chewing. "Darling…" She paused again, looking between me and the Hyde brothers. "Um, don't you have it?"

Grateful she let it go…for now, I answered, "I do but I'm of the *inner circle*. Spar with him. I bet he'd give it to you then."

I winked as she laughed at the image. "I'd likely break a hip."

Snorting, I shook my head. "Yeah *right*. You'd probably kick his butt." Si placed a small bowl of cream beside her and nodded in agreement.

"You're both outrageous. Come."

She pulled me down in the chair beside her and stroked the

back of her hand over my cheek. As usual, I felt like she could see into the heart of me.

"What a lovely woman you are, Ellie. More relaxed than I've seen you in years. Whatever you're doing to accomplish this vibe... *keep doing it.*"

Releasing me, she picked up her fork. Nonchalantly, she mentioned, "Your dad had the stable hands exercise Sarafina this morning. He thought you might be ready to get back in the saddle. Sarah and Thaddeus are driving Cameron over."

"I'd love to go for a short ride. I-I'll grab my boots."

I remembered dropping them in the second-floor hall. The *reason* made me redden brightly. Padme set them beside me with a smile and a wink.

Putting them on, I pulled my hair into a long ponytail.

To Mom and Padme, I said, "Will you let Robyn know I'll be back in a little bit?"

"Of course. Have fun, dear." Mom dug into the second plate of crepes Si put in front of her and I chuckled as I stood.

"Love you, Mom." Using exaggerated sign language while she chewed blissfully, she expressed her love for me in return.

Dad stood on the other side of the gate with his horse. "I wondered where you disappeared to, honey." As I joined him, he wrapped his arm around my shoulders. "Ready to ride?"

"God, yes." We walked side by side to the stables that were positioned between my home and the main house. "Thanks, Dad. Today was the perfect day."

Chuckling, he replied, "The world is your oyster and such simple things please you, princess."

My parents had triple the amount of personal security that I did but it was rare to catch a glimpse of the men and women who guarded them behind the scenes.

Their relationship was strictly professional and I was glad my own staff dynamic was different. However, I knew I likely had many such invisible protectors now myself.

As we neared the stables, Cameron waved madly from the back of a golf cart driven by his dad down the rambling path between our properties.

I waved back with a grin. "That boy is going to be a hit with girls in a few years. Where did the time go?"

My father turned to me and took my hand. "It goes too fast, Ellie. Savor every minute and make no apologies to anyone."

He twined our fingers and I saw tears in his eyes that clenched my heart. "You're the best thing to ever happen to your mother and me, Elliana. I'd give everything I have to keep you safe, to see you happy."

"I know. I love you both so much."

His eyes closed for a moment and he cleared his throat. When he opened them, I could see the serious thoughts in his mind.

"Now that time has passed and you have your precious Katie to love, I want to say I've never been prouder of another human being in my life as I am of you. All of you were just...*gone*. The 911 call from the Vasquez family was the most terrified I've ever been."

"Y-you were *there* when they...found us?" The thought of my dad seeing me like that *destroyed* me.

"You were delirious. You didn't know who was around you. You murmured that you loved us. Then you begged us to find Hyde. To find him and save him. We'd already found them but you didn't hear or understand." He swallowed hard. "That was the worst day of my life, Ellie."

"I'm sorry you were there, Dad. I wish you hadn't seen that."

Scrubbing angrily at a tear that escaped, he said hoarsely, "Look at you now. Healed and the proud mama of a darling daughter. You're my life's *greatest* accomplishment."

"I love you, Dad." He hugged me hard and I said, "You can do *everything* right and something can still go wrong. The only people at fault were those pieces of shit who are dead now."

Leaning back, I cupped his cheek with my palm. "Thank you for always trying so hard to make me happy and keep me safe. I may chafe at the restrictions but I'm grateful."

He kissed my knuckles and wrapped his arm around me as we continued to the stables.

Watching the proud profile I memorized as a toddler, I said, "I was so lucky to get you as my father. I love you more than you'll ever know."

He squeezed me to his side as the golf cart stopped a few feet away.

Cameron jumped off and ran full out to my side. "I've been *waiting*, Ellie. I was afraid you'd never ride with me again. Mom and Dad ride too *slow*."

"Not everyone can be crazy like us, Cameron."

"So *true*," he said with a sigh.

Our saddled horses were led from the stables and Sarafina nudged me happily with her nose.

"I missed you, too." I rubbed her face and kissed her warm cheek. "Let's tear up some dirt, pretty girl."

Thaddeus and Sarah didn't have stables on their estate. We stabled the colt I gifted their son gladly.

Lilith wasn't as wild as my girl but still loved a good run. Cameron scrambled up on her back with a huge grin. "You'll be proud of me, Ellie. I've been *practicing*."

Dropping into my well-used saddle, I was startled when Jonas and Jordan mounted to either side of us. They appeared comfortable on horseback but never rode with me.

Bianca and Fiaaz were always my riding companions.

They each wore a shoulder holster with a matte black pistol prominently displayed. I smiled and guided Sarafina out of the stable yard with a wave to Cameron's parents and my father.

As soon as we hit the open field, I turned my girl loose.

The feel of her pounding steps was like a memory I'd forgotten. I let her have her head and gave her the trust she earned over our many years together.

Cameron laughed beside me and the Hyde brothers were in my peripheral vision. It was perfect.

Half an hour later we topped the ridge to the pond near the rear boundary wall, dismounted, and let the horses drink.

I'd be sore later but it was worth it. I missed riding every day of my recovery and pregnancy.

Cameron was so excited he could barely stand still. He was a happy and intelligent child that was a pleasure to hang out with. He caught me up on his school while I fixed my ponytail.

I wondered what Katie would be like at his age and looked forward to such outings with her.

As we laughingly mounted to head back, Jordan stilled beside me. I knew that look.

"Jonas, movement on boundary wall." He added sharply, "Ellie, Cameron, *move*! Straight to the stables."

Without hesitation, I turned toward home. "Cameron, stay low. We're moving fast. Stay *low*, understand?"

He nodded. The boy came about and nudged Lilith's sides sharply with his knees. I angled Sarafina to block as much of his small body as I could.

We tore away from the pond and built speed fast.

Chapter Thirty-Three

Jordan rode beside me, one hand holding a cellphone that he barked orders into. I didn't see Jonas.

We entered the stable yard and the grooms took the reins to guide us all the way into the covered stalls before pulling us out of our saddles.

Jordan pushed us firmly into the panic room every building on the estate held. This one was big enough for the horses.

The door was locked down behind us. Neither of us would be allowed to leave the building until we received an all-clear from the basement command center at the main house.

I distracted Cameron with grooming the horses.

When they were unsaddled and brushed, we gave them apples and filled their feed bags. I opened the faucet for the large bucket and when Sarafina's was full, I walked around to Cameron and Lilith.

Jordan never left my side. His weapon was in his hand, pointed at the ground. He listened to updates through a small transmitter in his ear.

Sighing heavily, Cameron said, "It sucks to be worth so much money, doesn't it, Ellie? People without a lot don't realize we always have a target on our backs."

"It's not all bad."

"Last year, when Dad took over that pharmaceutical company, Mom and I got all kinds of threats. All he ever wanted to do was publish good books. He's really good at making money." He paused and I watched him swallow hard. "I hope you'll still want to ride with me, play video games, and stuff."

I put my hand on his shoulder. "Cameron, *nothing* would make me not be your friend. Having a friend who understands the paranoia that's part of every minute is comforting."

"Do they taste your food if you go out?" The sad truth was that he was serious.

"Sometimes. It doesn't get easier to have your wings clipped, but I'll tell you a secret. A lot of the frustration is lessened by the *good* you can do for a *lot* of people who don't have what we have. Helping other people in need is what having money is all about. I take it seriously and I hope you will, too."

Cameron walked around Lilith to stand beside me. Clearing his throat, he said, "Ellie, I'm young but I'm also smart." I smiled and agreed. "When you were h-hurt last year, Katie…she came from that, didn't she?"

I nodded with my heart in my throat.

"I thought so. You're amazing to have her. It wasn't her fault. I think of you as a role model. You *never* quit, Ellie. I'll never tell anyone but I respect you more for loving her like you do."

"Th-thanks, Cameron."

"And I'm just saying, if she grows up like you, I call dibs on an arranged marriage. I'll be ten years older and that's not so bad, you know? When she's in her twenties, I'll probably still look good. I'd take great care of her."

I put my hand on his shoulder. "The thought of you being my son-in-law in twenty years makes me happy. You're like family anyway. Ten years difference in age is nothing. Men need the extra time to grow up, so their brains match their bodies."

"Har, har. You're so *funny*, Ellie."

We leaned against the wall and sipped bottled water Jordan handed us with a smile. "You're always welcome here, Cameron. You're funny, smart, and mature for your age."

"Thanks. If I was older, I'd sweep *you* off your feet." Jordan valiantly stifled a sharp bark of laughter, unable to look directly at me. Cameron grinned. "As it is, I'll wait for Katie. I have to sow my oats first, do all my manly growing up and all."

Jordan struggled with his laughter and it felt amazing considering why we were sitting where we were. I imagined the teasing I'd get later when the others heard about this.

We relaxed and chatted, making the best of being in a panic room. Half an hour later, we received the all-clear and my bodyguards escorted us to the main house.

Bianca's first sentence to me was, "I brought Katie and Robyn. No worries, little mama."

I released the breath I hadn't realized I'd been holding.

Robyn brought me Katie and Cameron settled beside me

after his parents assured themselves he was okay.

"She's going to be a stunner. Totally my future wife."

At our parents' shocked faces, he promptly informed them of our deal and had all our folks smiling.

"Katie, you'll find me annoying in your teens but one day, when you're about twenty, you're going to take one look at me and swoon dramatically *in love* with yours truly."

Katie laughed at her future fiancé loudly and Cameron grinned. "Already you have the tools to wound me. Diabolical."

Jonas came in a short while later and searched until his eyes landed on me. He visibly relaxed and gave me a smile.

"There was evidence of a car sitting for a long time on the other side of the boundary wall. Someone had a ladder against the side, sat with a pair of binoculars. A couple of gum wrappers but no used gum."

Fiaaz entered and ground out, "We traced the tracks to the paved road a mile over. The car could have gone any of three directions from there. I have cars fanning out."

Jonas told Jordan, "We need Tom at the house tonight."

His brother nodded. "I'll see if he's out of the bunker yet." The young man was learning underground tactics.

Turning to my dad, Jonas added, "I've increased the patrols to every fifteen minutes and the ground force will use horses to cover more ground silently than we can on foot."

With a nod to my parents, he moved to stand behind the couch. He told Cameron quietly, "Thank you for keeping a clear head. You helped us protect you and Ellie."

"Thanks for doing the protecting." The boy held out his hand and Jonas shook it with a sincere smile.

My security team wanted me back within a perimeter they checked and re-checked a dozen times a day.

Saying my goodbyes, I allowed myself to be lead to the armored SUV out front and driven to my home. I held Katie wrapped in a Kevlar hooded blanket.

The net around me would be tighter for a few days until the threat was either neutralized or dismissed.

Padme exhaled roughly when we entered the garage and the door lowered. "I love the estate but that house is a monstrosity to truly seal. There are so many rooms and external entrances. I love your snug little house, Ellie."

"Me, too."

"Tom should be here for dinner. His training group were on radio silence in the bunker. I'm sure he'll need sleep and food before he heads over."

Two hours later, we gathered around the table and Si entered the dining room with Tom behind him. He looked worn out.

"Tom. Sit and eat. How was the training?"

He smiled tiredly. "The worst part was being stuck in a twenty-foot square for three days without showers and having to do our business in a bucket." Releasing a slightly hysterical laugh, he added, "It was *hot* down there and we *stank*. I can still smell us. I'm glad that's over."

Lowering into a seat beside Padme, he said, "I ran the specs you sent over."

Her eyes widened. "You were supposed to be *resting*. I didn't mean for you to do it *today*!"

"This is important." He took a long drink of water and looked at me. "Ellie, I've been triangulating the separate locations where the guys I refer to as *shithead squad* rallied. There were about a dozen I found through the cameras."

I nodded. "This is probably a reporter though."

"No," Jordan and Jonas said firmly.

Padme added quietly, "It wasn't a reporter, Ellie."

I tilted my head with a frown. "How do you know?"

Every member of my team stared at the table and it was obvious they didn't want to give me the details.

Tom's eyes met mine. "Tell me what you know, Tom."

"I believe it's the eighth man. I'm sorry, Ellie."

Inhaling carefully several times, I whispered, "You've been tracking him."

"At the dead center of the abduction hideaways, there's a run-down housing development. There was a suspicious house fire a decade ago that left a disabled woman dead. Her son withdrew their money the day before and disappeared. He was about sixteen at the time."

"You think it's the same guy?"

"He tangled the trail. There are some connections that

might not be him. He changed his name and appearance several times. I could be *wrong*, Ellie…"

His voice trailed off and the skin on the back of my neck stood up. "Tell me. It's alright, Tom."

"I think Adam Schafer is the eighth man."

My heart stumbled. *Theresa's medical assistant.*

A man who spent *months* inside my house, who had *access* to me and my baby, who *touched* me several times.

"How? He was vetted by *three* teams."

"He's a psychopath and he's smart. He changed names several times in the last few years but he immediately takes his exams to get medical jobs. He has a residence in Ohio but I doubt he's ever lived there."

"Legitimate references, Ellie," Padme added. "Verifiable employment. No criminal record and he aces psych exams. He got past everyone."

Through gritted teeth, I asked, "What does he *want?*"

Jonas's hand was a fist on the table. "They found the corner of a condom wrapper and spermicide on the wall about where a man's hips would be if he stood on a ladder."

I stared blankly at him. "What? I-I don't get it."

Bianca explained quietly, "The pervert climbed the ladder, leaned over the top with binoculars, wrapped his tiny pecker in a condom to keep from leaving DNA, then wanked off while watching you, Ellie."

With a low hiss Padme added, "Taking all the evidence of

said wanking with him. The creepy son of a bitch."

"Wait…wait." I took several breaths to calm down. "Someone watched me and masturbated?"

Bianca nodded once angrily.

Everything inside me recoiled in revulsion.

"Then his goal isn't *money* or a *story*. It isn't anything but to *get* me. That's what we're fucking dealing with…some asshole's obsession. He wants to-to…"

I stood from my chair so fast, I knocked it over. I couldn't breathe. It was the same motive as the men from last year.

We were dealing with a man who wanted to use my body; someone who wouldn't care about taking money to go away.

The Hydes stood beside me and suddenly my memory was there. Not clear, not solid. I'd been dealt a major blow to the head. Nothing more than flashes, still pictures, small pieces.

But, oh my god, it was far more than I needed or wanted.

While I was semi-conscious they used my body brutally, in every way possible, laughing at Jonas as he tore open his flesh trying to get loose.

Bound with ropes and chains that held him in a position to *watch* what they did while unable to *protect* me.

Tears streamed down his face above the dirty rag they shoved in his mouth and tied in place. His body beaten bloody but no less desperate to get to me.

In my quiet dining room, surrounded by my team, and safe together, I met his eyes and witnessed the pure rage he carried from that awful event.

Numb, confused, I whispered brokenly, "Oh, *Hyde*…"

My body crumpled.

* * *

A light glowed softly on a table across the room. The rest of my bedroom was dim and the house was silent.

I blinked several times to clear my thoughts.

Jonas's voice came from the side of the bed and I turned my head to look at him. He knelt on the floor, head down, his hands clasped on the bed beside me as if he prayed.

"I didn't want you to remember. I hoped you *never* would. I'm sorry I didn't protect you. Sorry I didn't st-stop them. Forgive me, Ellie. Forgive me." His forehead dropped to the bed and wracking sobs shook his frame.

I turned to my side and cupped his hands in mine.

Jordan sat on the edge of a chair in the far corner of the room. His elbows rested on his knees. His head bowed.

"There's *nothing* to forgive, Jonas." I stroked my hand through soft golden hair and whispered, "Did you kill them for me?"

He lifted his damp face and met my eyes with a brutality that should have scared me but didn't.

Stroking his hair again, I smiled tightly. "Did you make them suffer for me, Jonas?"

"I made them scream until their voices broke. Tortured them and bled them slowly." His voice was a growl. "When I was covered in their blood, Jordan put a bullet in their groins and one between their eyes."

I moved closer and rested my forehead against his.

"They died *hard* for what they did, Ellie. I was scared for my sanity because I enjoyed it. I punished them for *their* part in what happened…punish me for failing to protect you."

I fisted my fingers in his hair and made my voice hard. "You didn't *fail* me, Jonas. You aren't *omnipotent*. You can't be everywhere at once…not even if there are two of you."

Stroking from his brow to his cheek, I murmured, "Evil men see evil done. I survived, you survived, Jordan survived. They didn't. We *won*, Jonas."

I pressed my lips lightly to his.

His arms crushed me to him, his hand held the back of my head. "No one will hurt you again, Ellie. You'll make good memories to replace the bad ones. I want to be part of them."

I soaked up his touch for a long time, struggling to ask for what I wanted. I was embarrassed to say the words, to tell them what I needed.

"Jonas, I'm afraid of the dark. I wasn't before. When I sleep alone, my mind tortures me. I didn't have nightmares last night, sleeping between you. I know it's a lot…that it's not appropriate."

He stroked his hand down my back. "We'd love to help you

keep the nightmares away. We'll change."

Touching his lips to my temple, he stood.

Watching them leave the room, I went to change into sleep shorts and a soft tank top. After I brushed my teeth and hair, I braided it and climbed beneath the covers.

I was lethargic from the stress and emotional input of the day. Angry that my first day *touching* and *being touched* by the Hydes was ruined by some piece of shit.

I was almost asleep when the twins appeared on either side of my bed in basketball shorts and t-shirts.

They put their weapons on the nightstands and slipped under the blankets beside me. I sighed deeply and rolled to my back so I could hold their hands.

I was asleep before the covers fully settled over their bodies.

Chapter Thirty-Four

Moonlight shone on the vibrant landscape painting hanging in my sitting area and for a moment I was confused about the presence of the two bodies in bed with me.

My upper body was stretched against the chest of one Hyde brother, my legs tangled with the man behind me.

In the dark, it was impossible to tell which was which.

I looked at my palm spread flat on a hard male stomach, skin to skin since his t-shirt rode up on one side. Firm muscle that radiated heat. I wanted to explore but I wasn't brave enough.

Not in this. In this arena, I knew nothing.

I started to pull away when a large hand covered mine. A voice gruff with sleep murmured, "You can touch us, Ellie. We won't touch you without your permission but you can touch us as much as you like."

He lifted my hand and kissed my palm before replacing it on his stomach. I swallowed deeply before sliding side to side, marveling at the muscle beneath the skin.

Resting my head on his shoulder, I slipped my hand higher. I felt the puckered scars from the bullets he took for me. Firm pecs and an almost imperceptible layer of chest hair.

The flat of my hand skimmed over his nipple and I heard a sharp intake of air. Pausing, I did it again and received a rough exhale. My fingers traced the lines of his collarbone, thicker than my own, and outlined the hollow at the base of his throat.

Lifting my eyes, I said softly, "Jordan."

He smiled and I smiled back shyly, pulling my lower lip between my teeth. After a long moment, I raised myself on my elbow and kissed him lightly.

A small moan escaped his throat when I raked my hands through his hair and cupped the back of his head. He didn't try to grab me or attempt to control the kiss.

I took my time, learning masculine lips, touching stubble beneath my fingertips.

When I pulled back, his eyes met mine. One Hyde or two, I'd never love another man the way I loved them.

Disentangling my feet from Jonas, I turned over to meet his eyes. I raked my fingers through his hair. The moonlight gilded the lighter strands shot through the darker length.

I followed the lines of his face, learning him by feel. I gave him the same kisses, filled with trust, I gave his brother.

Identical with exception to the wounds they sustained over a lifetime of fighting, it should have been dizzying having two men in my bed.

If there were only one Hyde, I wouldn't be afraid. Fear at there being two didn't seem to make sense. I fell in love with twins from the start.

There was no fear, no hesitation to touch them.

After a long time, I laid down on my back between them and they rolled to their sides. Their breath was warm on the skin of my neck beneath my ears.

"Who were you before you convinced the world you were the same man?"

They crossed their arms over my stomach and I soaked up the warmth of the contact. Like many twins, they shared their story, filled in gaps for each other, and took turns talking.

It was soothing, like a lullaby, their identical voices flowing from one side then the other, until the inflection of every word mesmerized me.

"We were born outside Melbourne. Our mother was on vacation. It was her first time away from her wealthy family in England. She ended up pregnant by a rancher who knew an easy mark when he saw one. She hid it from her parents, afraid they wouldn't allow her to keep us."

Calloused fingertips stroked my torso through my shirt and I didn't think I'd ever been so relaxed.

"She found refuge with an elderly couple. They saw her through the pregnancy and labor but she didn't survive our birth. Major Rothendam and his wife kept us."

I frowned. "What about her family in England?"

"Her parents refused to abide bastards in their prestigious line and told the Major he could do whatever he wanted with us."

I gasped in outrage.

"They raised us for several years on the farm where he retired after forty years of being a soldier. When we were ready for school, he enrolled us in military academy."

"Were they kind to you?"

"Always. They never had children of their own and considered us a miracle. We wanted to make them proud so they'd never regret taking us in. They died within a few weeks of one another when we were sixteen. The Major of a heart attack and Missus to a car accident."

My fingers gripped their forearms. "That must have been devastating. I'm sorry."

"We spent the summer at the farm, seeing to their animals. We thought we'd drop out to care for the land they loved. A few days after Missus funeral, a lawyer arrived to tell us we'd inherited everything. We received a letter from them that asked us to rehome their animals and return to school. They paid for it in advance so we had no excuse."

"You kept the farm?" The brothers nodded. "One day, we should visit. I'd love to walk the land you played on as children."

Their hands hugged me closer. "We haven't been back in two decades. After they died, we stayed at school year-round. We started trading places to see if we could. With twins, if you don't see them together, people forget there's another one."

I snorted at that. "I know that feeling. I'm half-crazy some days backtracking and reminding myself there are two of you."

"Is it getting easier, Ellie?"

Nodding, I said, "There are times it feels like I've always known and others I get confused. It's better every day." I stroked their forearms. "Tell me more."

"We were excellent soldiers, diligent students. We graduated at the top of our class and received our inheritance when we turned eighteen. Unsure what we wanted to do, we invested most of it and joined the military."

"It was already familiar," I guessed. "Do you have photos of you then?"

"Very few. After school, we gathered our documents and locked them in a safe. We buried it on the farm."

Glancing at Jonas, I murmured, "The military wanted you to be one man from the start." He nodded. "Did it...*hurt* to give up your individual identities?"

"At first. Essentially, we each lived half of a single life. It became familiar as the years passed. The pain dulled."

"Until we met you, Ellie. Having only *half* a life with you was suffocating. It felt like prison and it was one we made." Jordan sighed. "We started arguing. That was unusual."

"I'm sorry."

"We did it ourselves, Ellie." Jonas stroked my cheek. "Painted ourselves into a corner and didn't know how to get out." Going up on his elbow, he stared down at me. "Then Natalia insisted on introducing you to *Trois*."

I blinked. I replayed our conversation in my mind and my

eyes went wide. "She *recognized* you."

"At first, she wasn't certain but she suspected we were the men she met at a similar club in Amsterdam years before. Even in such places, we had to be careful. The outrageously wealthy usually have men like Leo who know us as one man."

"I thought she wanted me to feel comfortable becoming a *member* but…she was seeing how I'd react if I found out about you." They nodded. "Fascinating."

"We actually fought one another over coming clean to you several times, Ellie. Harper and Elijah were…problematic but it was the Bradshaw brothers who threw us into panic."

Staring at the ceiling, I grinned. "I imagine. You were definitely *closer* when they were around."

Jonas laughed. "I was damn glad when those two were off the market for good. All the happiness in the world and all that…just not with *you*."

Laughing, I nodded. "So, you buried your lives and became one man in the military."

"After three years of serving all over Europe, the CIA tapped us for service." Jordan snuggled closer to me. "Over the next six years, we met and assembled the team you have now. Disillusioned after a particularly dirty assignment, we went off-grid and formed our own network."

"Mercenaries with a gentle streak," I said.

Jonas kissed the tip of my ear and I shivered. "A few years later, we interviewed your parents at Salt Flats. At first, we weren't going to tell them there were two of us. Your mother inspired our trust and they agreed to keep our secret. They waxed poetic about you but we all expected the worst."

Jordan tweaked my nose. "We figured you'd be a spoiled brat. We weren't prepared for the woman you are. We forgot you were our employer. You were Ellie. You quickly became *our* Ellie and life got a lot more complicated."

My smile was self-mocking. "I almost died the first time I met you. I doubt I could have handled the visual input of you side by side from day one."

They laughed. "It was easy to fall for you, Ellie. You were too young, still are honestly, but it didn't matter. We were afraid to scare you, to lose your trust, so we waited…until the worst happened followed by months of guilt and regret."

"There was no reason for guilt. I know what you went through that day as well."

"We didn't want you to hate us and wondered about starting over, with everything on the table, to see how it went."

My fingertips absently traced their fingers, hands, and wrists. I cleared my throat and gathered my courage.

"I could ask a *million* questions but the primary issue is separating you in my mind. I'm not sure what to do. I can't…there's no way for me t-to choose between you. It's why I put distance between us. Then there's Katie and all of that. It makes it hard to think."

The brothers propped themselves up to better see my face. Jonas frowned. "What do you mean about Katie?"

"All of *what*, Ellie?" Jordan added.

I didn't want to say it. How could I? While I struggled with my thoughts, both men watched me intently.

"I had to keep her," my voice was barely audible. "I couldn't let it all be disgusting and painful. I never want her to know."

Jordan stroked my cheek. "You took a horrific act of violence and turned it into a precious little girl who'll never know a day in her life without unconditional love. To us, she's *your* daughter. We adore her, Ellie."

I nodded and glanced at Jonas. "Ellie, you thought I wouldn't *want* you after that day."

The lump in my throat threatened to choke me. "It's one thing to *know* someone has gone through something like that. It's different to *witness* it. That's always been the worst part for me. That you have those images in your mind. I- I'm embarrassed."

He pressed my hand to his chest, his eyes closed. He opened them and stared deeply into mine. "I've never felt such hatred, such rage, as I felt for those animals. I thought you stopped breathing. You were throwing up, bleeding, unable to focus or keep your eyes open."

His breath hitched and he rested his forehead against mine. "Each time you approached consciousness, you *fought*. Gouging their eyes, ripping them open with your nails and teeth. Most of your injuries came from the force necessary to contain you. They had no humanity but you *never* quit."

I slipped my hand between us to cup his face.

"They punished you because you wouldn't break, Ellie. The last thing you said to them was, '*Hyde will gut you. You'll die screaming as your organs hit the floor. My name will be the last thing you hear.*' That's exactly what I did. I tortured them, I gutted them, and I watched their faces. Before Jordan put the final bullet in their brains, I told them, '*This is for Ellie. Rot in hell.*'"

I couldn't hold back my gasping sob.

"Never, not *once* since the beginning of that nightmare to this moment, have I considered you *less*, Ellie. You survived the worst that can be done to a woman and it only made me love you more."

I cried hard and the brothers held me through it. Twins, bodyguards, men I loved.

The relief at lancing the infection of shame and degradation was immense. They never let me go as I sobbed out everything that hurt me, haunted me, for almost a year.

When I had nothing left, they wiped my face with a cool cloth and wrapped me between them.

"Sleep now, Ellie. It's time for your fresh start."

Gradually calming mentally and emotionally, I held them to me as they pressed close. I welcomed the chance to sleep, to rest after a purge held off for too long.

Even as I slipped away deeply, they continued to hold me.

Chapter Thirty-Five

Waking the next morning, I smiled.

Jordan and Jonas were with me, twined around me until I didn't know where one of them began and the other ended.

They were sealed to me, protecting me even in sleep. Hardened fighting men, fourteen years older than me, twins who masqueraded as one man to the world at large.

I loved them.

There were no nightmares but that wasn't why I knew I had to keep them.

My love grew even stronger after our night together in my bed. A bed that had never held one man, much less two.

I had to keep them and I wasn't sure...how that *worked*.

Jordan's face pressed against my upper back and my face was under Jonas's chin on his chest.

Several times during the night they spoke of their love for me and I believed them with every cell of myself.

I *wanted* to believe them but it was more than that.

It was *years* of their protection. The tears and rage that professed I was *not* just another assignment. It was the vengeance they carried out on my behalf.

Their need to see my attackers in the ground. That they didn't return to me until one threat to my safety was put to rest.

In my mind, I recognized them as two men. My heart considered them one and the same.

They shared *one life* for so long, was it so difficult to believe they could share *one woman?*

There was a whisper deep in my mind, *"Are you enough?"*

"I can practically *hear* your mind racing, Ellie." Jonas's deep voice rumbled beneath my cheek, roughened from sleep.

Jordan kissed the skin of my back above my tank top. "Your heart is *pounding* with your need to overthink things."

I couldn't help but smile. "You do know me pretty well."

Their arms tightened on me, their bodies moved closer. I doubt they even realized they did it.

I closed my eyes, soaking up the tactile sensations of them surrounding me. I registered their warmth, the slight rasp of the hair on their legs against my smooth ones, the scent of sandalwood and man, their deep breathing.

With a sigh, I stretched and accidentally brushed against their erections. They sucked air sharply through their teeth and immediately edged their hips away from me.

I knew *nothing* of men, and they knew that about me. At least, nothing healthy or normal. I never got that chance.

My innocence was lost on the dirty floor of a shack and

there was nothing I could do about it now.

"You don't have to shield me like that. I-I never dated because of the money. Insulating myself became a habit. It didn't mean I wasn't lonely, that I didn't wish things were different."

I cleared my throat. "In the first few months at school, the seven seemed to be everywhere I went, always asking me out. I was polite but indifferent. I didn't want my parents to order me back to the estate so I didn't talk to anyone about them."

Swallowing carefully, I went on. "Then I realized you were watching me. Again, under strict instruction, I was supposed to report it but I didn't. You could have been gathering information for a kidnapping but I didn't think so. I started expecting you to be there. Hoping, really."

I thought back on the first few weeks when Hyde became part of my life. "I found you attractive from the beginning. As the days passed, it was easy t-to fall in love with you. I felt silly, childish, and completely out of my depth. I still struggle."

"We're in love with you, Ellie."

"We have been for years."

I absorbed the statement that left me no doubt about their feelings and shook my foundation. "I can't choose. Obviously, I *know* you're two men. Emotionally, I can't differentiate between you."

"Ellie…" Jordan lifted his head, listening. "Robyn is coming downstairs. Katie must be awake."

With a nod, Jonas said, "We'll talk more later, Ellie." He leaned down and kissed me lightly then rose from the bed. Jordan turned my face and kissed me, too.

Then I was on my feet, standing between them. The top of my head came below their chins. They smoothed my hair and clothes, nudging me toward the bathroom.

I had to know one thing at least. "Answer one question and I'll wait to talk. Do you *expect* me to choose between you?"

As one, they replied, "No, Ellie. We don't."

Drinking in the sight of their tall muscular frames, I slowly closed the bathroom door and stood there in stunned disbelief.

I could keep them *both*? What did it mean? Would they alternate days they spent with me?

Would I be with them *together*?

Inhaling deeply, I thought about being wrapped between them while I slept. I replayed the image *without* clothing and felt a blush burn up my chest and face.

Was that nervousness or anticipation? I felt warm all over and my nipples puckered tight.

I wasn't an idiot. That was *anticipation*...and *curiosity*.

* * *

The next three days passed much the same. I dealt with charity work in the morning, swam with Katie in the afternoon, and had dinner with my team in the evening.

Padme and Tom were sequestered in her command center

and I rarely saw them. Si reported they were untangling the tech trail of my suspected stalker.

"Are they *eating?*"

My badass chef smiled. "I check on them regularly."

"Thank you, Si. Keep me posted and let me know if they need anything. They'll be vitamin D deficient by the time they come out of there."

Every night was spent talking to Jonas and Jordan as they held me between them.

I avoided too much discussion of the future because I felt the timing was shit with the eighth man still out there somewhere.

There were questions but they could wait for now. I contented myself with a million questions about their pasts.

They were gentle with me as they'd always been. They refused to push me, refused to let me take things further than kissing and touching them.

"All of this is new to you, Ellie. You deserve to take it all in, adapt at your own pace. We're happy to wait, to hold you, to give you time to acclimate."

They made no moves to touch me intimately and held firm to their statement that I remain in *absolute* control.

I knew there was concern about the psychological and sexual trauma I experienced and loved them for it.

Still, there was nothing about them, separately or together, which inspired the terror or disgust I felt during flashes of memory of my attack.

The only fear I truly had was not being *enough*.

Not one to entertain a false sense of modesty, I knew I was reasonably pretty and had a lot to offer. However, I also knew without being told that the Hydes had experienced the best and most exotic of women in their lives.

Where they might have to deal with my occasional post-traumatic stress, I couldn't shake the feeling that I was competing with every woman in their pasts.

It gave me an unfamiliar and unwelcome lack of confidence.

Alone in my bathroom, I pulled on my sport suit and a sundress. I loosely secured my hair in a messy bun.

While the bathing suits I chose for myself weren't overly revealing, my scars were visible and they embarrassed me. I might need to consider one-piece options going forward.

Sighing, I left my room and the Hydes led me downstairs after gentle kisses. I walked to Katie's playroom and my daughter smiled at me over Robyn's shoulder.

The nanny was settling in well. She was clever and tended to laugh more than the rest of us. It was a wonderful quality around my daughter.

Having seen her spar with Si and Padme, I was also certain of her skills. She could keep Katie safe.

I gathered my daughter's warm little body against me and inhaled deeply of her powder-fresh pink skin. Her eyes sparkled with happiness and I snuggled her gratefully.

Robyn gave me a soft smile and busied herself straightening up the space dedicated to the older child Katie would quickly become. I couldn't wait.

Walking with her to the kitchen, I chatted with her. "Good morning, sweetheart. What shenanigans can we get up to today? Should we try out the new water floatie?"

Jordan and Jonas stroked their huge hands over her tiny head. She graced them with smiles and giggles.

"Careful, Katie…save the big guns for important battles." She thought it was the funniest thing ever. "Your eyes are like Grandma's. My sweet darling."

I tried to prep her bottle with one hand and Jordan took Katie with a smile.

"Let's give your mommy the use of *both* hands, what do you think?" She squealed happily and held a fistful of his hair.

I made her bottle and Jonas took the opportunity to make me a shake with the prepped ingredients Si always left for me.

Robyn entered and grinned at the scene. "So much hustle and bustle." She stroked a finger over Katie's ear as she passed.

"Can we make you a shake, Robyn?"

"No, thank you. We've been up a while. Katie *loves* the sunlight in her castle tower. She's a real dawn to dusk girl. Her eyes open and she's already smiling."

"Like her mother," Jonas said with a smile.

I snorted. "Not anymore. I've gotten lazy." Walking around the counter, I waved the bottle at Katie and she giggled.

"May I, Ellie?" Jordan held out his hand and I placed the warmed formula in it. "I've always wanted to try this."

Jonas put one hand on my shoulder and held my shake in his other. "A good time for you to have something as well."

We sat around the table and chatted about the day. Bianca entered the room and cleared her throat delicately.

I glanced up, immediately taking in the look of alertness on her face. "Ellie, you can't leave the house. Not even the patio."

Jordan carefully handed Robyn my daughter and the Hydes straightened at my sides.

"What happened?" I asked.

"Tom is tracing an email Padme received through your corporate address. It's been bounced all over the place."

I looked at Robyn. "Please take her out of earshot. I know it's crazy but I don't want her infected with ugliness. One of the team will brief you once I know what's happening."

The nanny nodded and stood immediately.

I ruffled Katie's pretty curls. "I'm sorry, honey. Robyn?" She paused. "Stay with Si for a while, alright?"

"Of course, Ellie. We'll help make bread."

The moment Robyn disappeared into the kitchen, Bianca led the way to Padme's security room. It was unlit but the glow from the multiple screens gave it an eerie glow.

"Good morning, Padme. Tom. You guys look exhausted."

"I'm sorry, Ellie. I fucking *hate* bringing this bullshit to your attention." Tom murmured at her side and she nodded with a sigh. "I don't have a choice."

I put a hand on her shoulder and squeezed gently. "Let's get it over with."

She nodded, resigned. "This *garbage* was delivered to one of your corporate emails. A bouncing program has it rerouted all over the damn world but I have no doubt Tom will crack the last few locations soon. He's up to forty-nine so far."

Taking a deep breath, I said, "This guy's serious about hiding."

Tom mumbled, "Too fucking bad. We'll get him anyway. Piece of shit little pervy bitch." He looked up startled. "I didn't mean to say that out loud."

Despite the seriousness of the situation, I smiled. "You're hysterical and so serious, Tom. Never censor yourself."

Padme turned to face us. "While we trace, we all need to be on the same page. I'm sorry, Ellie. I-I wish you didn't have to see it but I know you do."

Bianca stood stiffly with her arms crossed. Fiaaz joined us and Padme played the video attached to the email.

It was less than two minutes in length. The voice was disguised and the man never showed his face.

The image zoomed in on me as I rode across the flats on horseback. Occasionally, the camera angled down and showed the man masturbating.

There was a ladder in the shot and the man's penis was

covered with a condom. He gave sickening commentary throughout.

"You're beautiful, Ellie. I want you. See what you *do* to me? What happens when I *see* you? When I *touch* you? I jack off several times a day and *every time* I think about your pretty tits, your tight ass."

The camera moved back to me and there was the sound of moaning while he watched me. "I want to touch you again. I know what happened to you. I wouldn't do that. With us it'll be *making love*. Oh yes, yes! Just thinking of your pussy around me…oh fuck, I'm *coming*. Feels so good."

The video ended with the man ejaculating and climbing off the ladder as Jonas went still in the distance. "Always interfering! I *hate* them. You're *mine*! All *mine*, sweet Ellie."

There was the sound of a car door opening but he kept the camera pressed to his side. The engine started and he placed the recorder on the seat, lens down, as he sped away.

The fool continued to narrate. "I come so hard when I think of you. Soon, I'll be able to come inside you, all over you. I can't *wait*. No one can *touch* what's mine. That would make me so angry. I never loved a woman before you. The rest of them are whores. Not you, not you. I love you, Ellie."

Unable to stand another second, I threw up in the trashcan by the door. Four hands held my hair back, handed me a glass of water, held a cool towel against the nape of my neck.

Jordan and Jonas massaged my shoulders and whispered soothing words that eventually calmed me.

I stayed over the trashcan until I knew I had nothing left.

"Sorry about the gross in your space, Padme."

"Girl, please," she whispered.

When I knew I could speak, I drank more water and straightened. With certainty, I whispered, "Tom was right. It's Adam. I'm sure of it."

Chapter Thirty-Six

The Hydes held me tightly. "How do you know, Ellie?"

"He said he touched me before. H-he's *seen* me, *touched* me, during exams. He was *always* trying to touch me. No matter how violently I reacted. I imagine he's behind the massage therapist trying to get photos of me."

Clenching my fist against my thigh, I hissed, "It's him, I'm telling you. I wasn't looking at his equipment. The sicko can't make me do that. There's a skin tag on his upper right thigh that's almost clear."

Padme typed furiously in the background and gave a hiss of triumph. "Good *spot*, Ellie! We'll use it for definite identification once we take him the fuck out."

Tom nodded beside her without looking away from the screen or slowing in his typing.

Jordan called Theresa on speaker while Jonas held me tightly to his side. "Hey, Theresa. Hyde. Can you confirm if Adam Schafer ever showed up to your new location?"

"Hold a sec. It's been so busy here. I forgot about him, to be honest." The sound was muffled as she questioned a few people. She came back a minute later. "He never showed. My original assistant came back to work and I didn't miss him."

"I doubt you'll hear from him but if you do, call us. We believe he's stalking Ellie."

"Oh, shit. He did seem too fixated on her but I thought it was an innocent crush. I'm sorry. Keep me posted."

"Thank you, Theresa."

Jordan disconnected and Jonas said to the room, "We need his fucking location. I want him in three hours."

Tom responded, "Yes, sir."

"Wait. Wait a second." I pulled my phone from the pocket of my dress. "I *have* his phone number. He made me take it, remember? It's our best chance. Trace it."

Taking a deep breath, I scrolled to it and dialed before my team could object. I placed the call on speaker.

Adam answered after a few rings.

Jordan took a small recording device from Padme and held it to the phone as my tech people typed furiously.

"Hello?"

"Hi, Adam. It's Ellie Fields."

"Ellie! Wow, it's so good to hear your voice." He made my skin crawl but I was seeing this through until the end. "I can't *believe* it's only been a few weeks since I saw you. It feels like a year. Does it feel that way for you?"

Closing my eyes, I replied brightly, "I've been too busy to call before now. How are you?"

His resentment came through clearly. "Everyone wants *too much* of your time, Ellie. Katie, your security people, even your parents. You need boundaries and I'd make sure you had them. You don't need to cater to all of them."

"That's nice of you but I'm alright. Maybe spreading myself too thin sometimes. I should take a vacation but I don't think that would go over very well. Everyone would worry."

Adam gave a sharp bark of laughter. "You're one of the richest women in the world, you can do whatever you *want*. A vacation would be good for you."

There was a long pause. "I liked you from the moment I met you, Ellie. I knew you liked me, too. It was an honor being able to care for you."

Swallowing my bile, I managed, "Th-thank you, Adam."

"You *did*, didn't you? Like me from the start?" There was a sickening pleading tone in his words.

Glancing at the monitor and recalling his video, I barely managed to reply, "Sure, I did. Y-you were a great…comfort to me."

Padme signaled the rest of the team to gather around her.

"Do you mean that, Ellie?"

"Yeah." I needed to keep him talking. "I was, uh, sad to see you and Theresa go."

"Theresa shouldn't have left you so soon! She should have made you her full-time concern."

"She had a life and a career, Adam. She took a long time

away from her family for me and I was grateful." I paused a moment before adding, "I bet I took you away from *your* life, too. I'm sorry about that."

"I'd give up *everything* to devote myself to your care, Ellie. No one would take care of you like I would. Those *bodyguards* are no good for you. I saw how you looked at them, how they looked at you. You can do so much better."

"The Hydes have taken care of me for years. They're as close to me as family. I can't imagine life without them."

"Family? They *want* you, Ellie. Come on! They're not like your *brothers* or anything."

I smiled at Jonas. "No, they're definitely not."

"You're not seeing past their tough guy exterior. Guys like that aren't what you need. I don't know why your parents don't replace them."

"They're the *best* at what they do, Adam."

"They *smother* you! I can see what you really need. You're lonely and I'd make it my life's work to make sure you were never alone again, Ellie."

"I'm not lonely. I have my parents. My team is like family and I love them. No one smothers me." I gripped the phone with white knuckles, goading him. "I have my sweet little girl."

"You shouldn't have had Katie, Ellie!" He yelled into the phone and he panted rapidly. Jonas and Jordan held me tighter. "I'm sure you love her but to keep the spawn of the men who *raped* you."

I growled into the phone, "She's an innocent *child*."

"She'll *grow up*, Ellie and what then? I did a DNA swab. I know which one is Katie's father…"

"Don't, Adam! It's not important." I shook violently.

"It *is* important. Don't you see? You should give her up for adoption. Her father was the *worst* of them. He was the one who sliced open your back and so much worse."

Dread settled like ice around my heart. "How do you know what he did to me, Adam?" My body was numb. "Did you see a *recording* of my attack?"

There was a long silence and I thought he hung up.

"I shouldn't have said that, Ellie. That's one thing I *never* should've said. Fuck! *Fuck!* Why did you make me say that? I need to think."

The call disconnected and I released a shriek of fury. "Find him. Find that fucking recording. I want to know it's destroyed. That's not haunting my child."

Tom hissed, "He's pinging at a motel five miles away but I don't fucking *trust* it. He'd never be so careless."

Padme nodded beside him. "I agree. He's checked in under one of his prior names and there's a car rental as well."

Silence drew out and Tom announced, "Traffic cam across the street shows the rental still in the motel parking lot but I'm telling you, he's not fucking *there*. It's too easy."

"Protocols set by Samuel and Monica Fields dictate we transport Ellie to the main house for additional security."

Jonas considered and shared a look with his brother. They nodded and announced, "Let's move. Keep us posted and let's get this asshole locked down."

Jordan was on the phone with estate headquarters and the entire compound moved to high alert.

We left the secured tech room and Jonas barked orders to the house as Bianca appeared with a change of clothes for me, my riding boots, and a bulletproof vest.

I stripped and changed in the kitchen and grabbed supplies for Katie that Robyn quickly threw in a diaper bag.

"Straight to Ellie's suite in the main house. Padme, you're monitoring all systems from your station there."

I frowned. "You have a station at the house?"

"Always separate from known living quarters. Impenetrable." Jordan took my hand and led me to the garage.

Tom ran from the house and tugged Jonas aside. They whispered together for a minute before my bodyguard clapped the young man on the back with a nod.

Robyn laid down in the cargo area with Katie bundled against her belly and I bent to kiss my daughter's curls.

Fiaaz moved to cover them with a Kevlar blanket as I got in the backseat with the Hydes on either side.

"Down, Ellie." They maneuvered me to the floorboard and covered me. "Five minutes."

I nodded, familiar with the insanity of high alert.

Steel laced the voices of the men who always touched me with gentleness.

"Si, oversee retrieval. Reports every fifteen minutes."

We drove to the main house and into the garage where it was complete chaos.

Padme separated from our group and the Hydes shielded Robyn and me as we took the rear stairs to my old suite.

My parents waited there with frantic expressions.

The instant we entered the room, my mother ran for us, hugging us in relief. My father laid his hands on my head.

"I'm sorry you're dealing with this again, Ellie. No one is going to hurt you this time."

Jonas and Jordan pulled me toward the hall as Robyn handed Katie to my mother and lowered them carefully to the sofa. I noticed my daughter was still fully wrapped in a Kevlar blanket.

"We need to check every room on this floor and coordinate with the house staff. Don't leave this space. Arm it and we'll be back in ten minutes."

I nodded. As the door closed, I flipped a switch and took a deep breath. Everything in the suite would be audio and video recorded until they keyed the re-entry code.

I listened as they gave orders to the rest of the team as they moved away.

Turning, I took a step toward my parents when the foyer closet door beside me opened.

Adam pressed a gun to my temple and pulled me back to his chest.

"Don't move, Ellie."

Chapter Thirty-Seven

Several thoughts slammed rapid-fire through my mind before I stilled like the docile lamb this psychopath needed me to be.

I could have disarmed him.

I could have killed him.

I waited. I had questions.

Robyn positioned herself in front of my mother and Katie as she was trained. My father moved shoulder-to-shoulder with her. I met his eyes and gave an almost imperceptible nod.

His expression told me he was more furious than panicked.

Adam chuckled. "Good. You understand I'll take what means most to Ellie if you don't do *exactly* as I say."

Information flooded my brain and I understood so many things as he took the time to lean close and inhale the scent of my hair. *Gross.*

"Do you want Katie to *live*, Ellie?" he asked softly.

I nodded.

"We're going to talk in your bedroom. Make some

decisions about our future. Once you hear what I have to say, I hope you'll agree we belong together."

A hard light entered his eyes. "If you don't, I'll be unhappy."

We wouldn't want that.

He pulled me backward into the bedroom I slept in when I was released from the hospital.

"Close and lock the door." When I did, he stepped away and gestured at the side of my bed. "Sit down, Ellie."

I did so.

"Your reaction pleases me. I've watched you fight. I imagine you could have *tried* to take my gun. That you didn't tells me you have feelings for me as I suspected."

As calmly as I could, I asked, "How did you get in?"

"That was the *easiest* part. Living here for months gave me an inside track on the workings of the estate. I came in with the laundry service three days ago. I knew it was only a matter of time before they traced your *stalker.*"

He imbued the last word with a hint of disbelief, as if his actions were above all that. He rolled his eyes.

Folding my hands in my lap, I looked him right in the eye. "What do you *want*, Adam? If it's *me*, you've got a fucked-up way of courting a woman."

The skin around his eyes and mouth tightened. "I wouldn't have had to *do* this if those assholes followed the fucking plan from the beginning!"

Tom was right about everything with this guy.

I wanted information. "I didn't go to school with you, Adam. I'd have *remembered* you."

"Thank you, Ellie. That means a lot. It really does."

He smiled and I laughed at how easy it was to stroke his fragile ego. One hand on his hip, he gestured with his gun hand. It looked *ridiculous*.

"I was in post-graduate studies. I supplemented my income by tutoring. Mostly jocks." He shook his head as if I should empathize with what he'd had to go through. "There were a few of them who impressed me with how they thought. We became friends. Surprisingly good ones."

"A boys-only club?" I asked snidely.

"Sort of. Sometimes, we let women join us. Those were the *best* days, Ellie." Bile rose in the back of my throat. "That's when we knew we'd be friends for a *long* time."

I ignored the crawling of my skin.

"One night, we talked about you."

"Really? What interested you about *me*?" I couldn't believe how easy it was to seem sincere with this guy.

"They *all* wanted you, Ellie. As close as we were, I knew they weren't good enough for you. You needed a man of *brilliance* and *cunning*. Someone who could truly appreciate being married to one of the wealthiest women in the world."

"It was about money then?" *Not a surprise.*

"At first, I admit." Adam smiled and I gave him an

imitation of one. "Then I wanted *you*. Your body was fit, healthy. You're pretty. I knew I'd enjoy fucking you."

I ignored the way my stomach flipped at the thought.

"Then you sent your friends to kidnap me."

"They were only supposed to take you. I didn't want you *hurt*, Ellie. Part of that was my fault. I trusted them too much. The plan was simple to me but they were too stupid to understand you were different than the others."

"The other women you kidnapped and gang-raped?"

He went bright red. "Don't say it like that! That wasn't what it was at all!"

"How was it then?"

"The women before you don't *matter*, Ellie! They were *nothing* compared to what I wanted for you and me."

Struggling not to laugh, I said, "Tell me about your plan."

"They were supposed to take you to an abandoned building I scoped out. They were supposed to keep you confined."

"Why take me in broad daylight?"

"You were never out alone at night. We figured out how to take most of your team out of the equation." He winked at me. "They *thought* we'd share you and your money like we had all the others but that was never my intention. You were going to know me as the man who *saved* you."

"You were going to be a hero?" The very *idea* inspired hysteria deep in my gut. I fought it down. "You were going to betray the members of your club? I thought you were *best* friends."

"They weren't as important to me as you, Ellie." Adam's eyes glazed as he stared over my shoulder. "In your gratitude, we'd have been married. You were *mine*. We belonged together."

He ran his hand over his groin and I saw he was hard. He was so twisted, it was almost surreal.

Agitated, he paced back and forth in front of me. "Watching you and that *bodyguard* bring down all seven of them, I don't believe I'd *ever* been so angry."

His look was one of *disappointment*. "You *infuriated* me!" he screamed at me then instantly calmed. "Then I realized you *thought* you were defending yourself because you didn't know the plan I had for us."

"Of course. I'm *so* glad you see that." He didn't notice my sarcasm.

"I got rid of two of them before they went to prison. They were the *stupidest* ones. They wanted to bring up my name and tell the police my plan. I had no choice."

Adam laughed and I controlled my flinch. "The two who died in prison threatened to tell their lawyers about me and appeal their conviction. They were halfway through their sentence!"

He gestured wildly with his gun. "If they were patient, loyal, they might have lived. It's easy to bribe prisoners to kill another inmate. Prison is a *dismal* place."

"So, *you* killed four of the seven. How clever of you."

You're one shit-bag crazy squirrel.

My stalker smiled with so much superiority, I was glad I'd already thrown up earlier.

"Thanks, Ellie. You're good for my ego." He resumed pacing. "The original plan was still sound. They were supposed to shoot your bodyguard, use a tranquilizer dart on you, and carry you out on the access road so Padme didn't see you."

He shook his head and sighed as if they'd done nothing worse than teenagers caught drinking.

"They fucked up as *usual*. With all the blood from hitting you, they didn't think they could get you out of the park without being noticed. They panicked. They dragged you and the *twin* bodyguard into the shed. I couldn't *believe* I never knew Hyde was a twin. That made me so fucking *angry*."

"I didn't know until I was released from the hospital. Does that make you feel better?"

Adam immediately brightened. "It really *does*, Ellie. I mean, if *you* didn't know, it doesn't seem a lack of intelligence was the issue at all. Wonderful to hear."

He crouched in front of me and took my hand. I fought my body's reaction with everything I had and let him touch me.

"Ellie, my darling…they weren't supposed to *touch* you. They told me they'd been without a woman for *years* in prison and they were *desperate*. It had been so long since they hunted."

"So that *excuses* what they did to me?" There was acid in my voice and I wanted to kill him with my bare hands.

"You were *lying* there. They recorded everything once you were on the path. You were *tempting*. Even with the blood, you were delectable."

"They *brutalized* me, Adam." I felt incredible rage but kept it out of my voice.

"I know. I know they did and I'm truly *sorry* about that. They were just going to try a little of you but they got carried away. Nothing could be done by the time I found out."

I schooled my expression carefully as my blood *boiled*.

He shook his finger, *reprimanding* me, as he said, "You fought and made them angry. When you started fighting, they paid you back for what you put them through."

I wanted to take his head off. "What I put *them* through?"

"You *rejected* them, sent them to *prison* where they were messed with by other inmates, and pretty much *ruined* their lives. They only roughed you up a little the first time. Their punishment was overkill."

"Only you've already told me you *kidnapped* and *raped* other women so all of you deserved more than prison time."

His eyes widened in surprise that morphed to anger. "Don't say things like that, Ellie! It was a misunderstanding! A situation that got out of hand. I could kind of understand their anger with you."

"You can understand why three men would attack me, Adam? You understand why they shot one of my bodyguards, tortured the other, raped me, and beat me within an inch of my life? Huh." I nodded with a smile. "Thanks for being so *understanding*."

Adam frowned. "You can't be so black-and-white about it. You're a gentle *soul*, Ellie. You'll forgive me in time."

"You have a recording of my rape, Adam."

He rushed to explain, "I'm the *only* one who's ever seen it, Ellie. I swear. It's safe and sound."

"How can I trust you?"

"You can! You'll realize that." He smiled. "The other three aren't even part of the plan anymore."

The nut still thought he had a plan.

"Having trouble contacting them?" I asked lightly.

"I guess they're in hiding but it's just as well."

For the first time, my smile was genuine. Adam responded instantly, leaning closer as if to kiss me.

My words froze him. "They're not in *hiding*, Adam. My men hunted, tortured, and shot them before getting rid of the bodies."

There was no fear or regret in his expression. Nothing but an honest bewilderment he hadn't known they were dead.

"And guess *what*, Adam?"

He held my hand like a lover. As if he had the right to touch me. My other hand was free.

"Wh...?"

I punched him in the throat hard enough to crush his airway. The gun clattered to the floor as both his hands went to his neck to get oxygen that no longer flowed freely.

I brought my feet up and mule-kicked him across the room. The moment he hit the floor, I straddled his chest and pulled the dagger from my boot.

The one Bianca handed me in the kitchen of my house.

Lowering my body until my face was three inches from his, I smiled as he clawed frantically at his throat.

Padme would later say my voice was *hellishly* seductive. "This is as close as you'll *ever* get to my body. While I'm fucking *real* men, you won't even be a *memory*. By the way, a man with a *tiny cock* should never, ever record himself jacking off."

His face turned purple and I watched him with interest.

"There was *nothing* about any of you that would've made me choose you. Self-absorbed, sadistic misogynists don't turn me on. Die knowing you're being executed by the object of your obsession. Tell the devil Elliana Monica Fields sends her regards. Rot in hell, you sick fuck."

I drove the knife upward through his ribcage as Si trained me. I saw the instant his heart stopped, a look of shocked horror etched on his face.

Standing, I said to the room, "I'm done. Get someone in here to clean this piece of shit off my carpet."

I took two steps away before changing my mind, turning back, and delivering a kick to the dead man's balls as hard as I could.

The door opened and I ran to Jonas and Jordan. *I loved them.* I'd always run to them. They held me hard.

"The moment you left to check the floor, I knew Tom told you he was in the house. One of you always stays at my side."

They nodded and I could see the tension ease away.

"You could have shot him from the entrance in the bathroom. You could have gassed the room. You could have *saved* me." I leaned back and smiled. "Thank you for letting me save *myself* this time. I needed to know everything."

They stroked my hair, hugged me tight, and buried their faces at my neck. I could *feel* their relief.

"I need to hold Katie. I understood the plan but I was still terrified for my parents."

In the main space, my parents grabbed me almost painfully hard. I could feel the bulletproof vests they wore under their clothes.

"He wasn't leaving here alive, Ellie," Mom whispered brokenly. "One way or another, he was going out in a body bag. Watching you walk into that room with him, I thought my heart would stop."

"I had to be *sure* he was the last of them. I had to know every step. It's the only way I could know it was over."

From a trapdoor in the ceiling, two members of my parents' personal security dropped. They were heavily armed. With a salute to my dad, they walked into the hallway.

Bianca entered with my little girl in her arms. "Sorry for the bait and switch, Ellie. We didn't know what he might have been recording."

"It was perfect and I knew she was safe with one of you." I kissed Katie a hundred times, running my hands over her to assure myself she was truly safe.

I wasn't sure my parents would *ever* let us go.

Hours later, when my stalker's body was removed and my stomach growled, we went downstairs for a dinner that went on forever.

My family was together. My daughter was safe. My team gathered and the Hydes sat at my sides.

Cook, as usual, outdid herself.

Chapter Thirty-Eight

End-July 2015

For two weeks, I traveled with my team. Robyn stayed with my parents to guard Katie and keep her on a schedule.

The rest of my personal security went along.

I missed her every minute but our time apart was worth it to ensure my own brutal experience would never *touch* her.

Several people joined us courtesy of Hollow that the Hydes vouched for but I'd never met. Elijah called me personally to let me know they were arriving with additional supplies.

A pair of cheerful friends from Ireland named Gear and Finn, a massive individual they called Roar, and a smaller man who didn't stray from his side named Ashok.

One was a redhead who landed in front of me and said, "I have it on good authority that you're joining the *two dicks, one chick* club. Welcome! The annual dues are ridiculous but we get the *cutest* fucking t-shirts."

"Uh. Hi." I was out of my league.

"Too much? Should I have stuck with my first choice of *girl ballers?*" She pulled at her wild curls. "I always *doubt* myself! I need to learn to *trust my instincts,* you know what

I'm saying?" Hands on her hips, she stared at me. "I've frightened you. I can see I've caused your spit to dry up. I'm Tawny."

She held out her hand and I shook it. Pulling me close, her deep green eyes stared into mine.

"Hmm. Your eyes are *purple* with a touch of darkness. Hot." Without looking away, she added, "Boys, all the props. Bring her 'round and let us show her how to crack the whip."

Her smile was slow. "You hold *all* the power, sweet thing. That's what you need to know. They might be bigger, stronger, and older but you hold them in the palm of your *seriously* silky hands. What moisturizer do you *use*, girl?"

"M-my mom makes it from almond oil and fresh lavender." I blushed to the roots of my hair.

"Frealz?" I nodded and she held up one of her palms to show me. "Think you could hook up a bitchy redhead with a tendency for weapon callouses?"

"Yes. I'll send you a couple of jars. She makes a lot."

Putting her arm around my shoulder, she turned us toward the Hydes. "You're like...a Texas debutante and shit, huh? Born and bred in the Lone Star state and *filled* with honey."

"I honestly have no idea how to answer any of that."

"Red. Break Ellie in slowly." I didn't know which of the brothers spoke. I couldn't look away from her face.

She looked at me. "Ellie and I are cool, Jonas. She'll think about this convo later and laugh to herself." With a smacking kiss on my cheek, she released me and clapped her hands sharply. "Let's hunt some motherfucking perv digs."

We visited every location with even a remote link to Adam or one of the others. There were two trailers along the west coast, an old warehouse in the middle of nowhere in Arizona, and more than a dozen storage units scattered between the estate and my old campus.

Everything was removed from each location and Red's team returned later to burn the structures to the ground or douse them with chemical agents to strip biological evidence.

The woman apparently *loved* burning things down.

Anything related to me was incinerated but we kept the driver's licenses of more women than any of us could contemplate.

Tom added them to his growing database. Sometimes, he shed silent tears. I sat with him and explained the guilt he carried didn't *belong* to him.

"You did more to try and help these women than *anyone*. We never imagined there were others. Think about what you want to do and we'll help them however we can."

His green eyes were huge in his pale face. "Thank you, Ellie."

"You were crucial these last months, Tom. I can't tell you how grateful I am that we met when we did."

"I'm glad I could help. I wish…you never went through any of it. I wish I could have stopped them."

"I'm okay. They won't hurt anyone else."

He sat back and folded his hands in his lap. "There are always more people like them out there, Ellie. Always people hurting other people."

"That's an awful truth. Another truth is there are always people like you in the world, Tom. Doing what you can to stop them, to save as many as you can."

Nodding, he said quietly, "I-I love the estate. I've never had such a stable life. I don't want you to think I'm ungrateful."

"Hollow wants you on his team." It wasn't hard to figure out the way his people grilled the young man.

"You...know? About him?"

"For a long time." I sighed and hated that the world *needed* people like Hollow who in turn needed people like Tom to slosh through the muck and ugliness that seemed to be *everywhere*. "You'd be an incredible asset. He's a good man."

I reached out to touch his forearm. "You'll accomplish a lot of good with him and his organization." I smiled. "He knows quality. He only takes the *best*, Tom."

"I feel disloyal after all you did for me."

"You *earned* it. You helped me close a violent chapter of my life. Follow your instincts and you always have a home with us if you want or need a place to be still." Inhaling, I added, "Get a list from him of what you need and I'll see you have it. Stay in touch so I know you're alright."

"I will. You're amazing, Ellie."

"So are you." Patting his arm, I stood. "Let's give all these women some closure. I'm sure they've lived in fear." I smiled. "It will give you some much-needed closure, too."

He nodded his head once and started typing furiously. I wanted to ruffle his dark hair but I didn't. I wanted to hug him but I decided against it.

I looked at him and saw the ten-year-old boy he used to be rather than the grown man he was with prodigy-level computer skills.

He was one stray I couldn't keep.

Stepping out of the mobile unit into an abandoned warehouse with the Hydes, I said, "Get him on the phone. I want assurances about Tom's safety. I'm not sending him to die."

Jonas nodded and walked away on his cell. I glanced up at Jordan. "Food and I need to call Robyn."

The last storage locker we found in California was dedicated to me. It was filled with pictures, many taken through the windows of my old dorm. Videos recorded through the cameras hidden around my room.

Adam purchased outfits, sex toys, and books he planned to give me. My name was scrawled on dozens of gift-wrapped packages.

A metal lockbox held mementos from the other members of his gang, probably for safekeeping while they were in prison.

Driver's licenses and personal effects of women, some of whom I recognized from my college campus.

There were letters between the eight men spanning several

years that were written in code. Tom offered to decipher them but I didn't want the words in his head.

None of the women reported their attacks. A combination of fear and shame kept so many victims from the justice they needed and deserved.

Victim-blaming was still alive and well.

The women we knew about deserved peace of mind. They needed to know they didn't have to live with the fear of seeing their rapists on the street or wondering if they'd be taken again.

Padme and Tom found current addresses for most of the victims whose worlds were shaken apart by sexual violence.

Some disappeared, others fell into substance abuse, and two committed suicide within months of being brutalized.

The IDs were wiped clean and returned to them from a random post office. Each envelope held a note.

The men who took this from you are dead. They will never terrorize you again. Don't let them take another moment of your life.

In the future, Tom could give me recommendations about therapy or financial assistance they might need. While we worked that out, we wanted them to know they were free.

Everything else was destroyed and we returned to Texas with Hollow's team in tow.

Less than nine miles from Elysian Fields, we located a trailer Adam purchased after Katie's birth.

Inside, we found his laptop and countless images of me. Padme and Tom worked together to sift through the garbage the man hoarded on his hard drive. It was horrific.

Multiple images from my attack as well as video taken by one of my rapists on his cell phone were Adam's most frequently accessed files.

I didn't look at them.

I asked the Hydes not to look at them.

Padme sobbed as she and Tom ensured none of his media had been broadcast or shared. Both doubted it and I prayed they were right.

The thought of it being used by other sick individuals as fantasy material made my soul freeze with dread.

"Ellie, he thought of you as *his*. He wanted to keep his fucking *treasure* to himself." Growling, my assistant added, "His ego wouldn't have allowed it. We'll keep checking but…I'm pretty confident."

After we leveled the trailer, I rented out a restaurant in Dallas and celebrated seeing the last of the eight men who impacted too many years of my life.

My team wouldn't rest until they were certain every single crumb of information about myself or my daughter was expunged and destroyed.

I felt as if I could *breathe* again.

Cutting into my steak, Tawny was suddenly at my side, whispering in my ear. "With all this behind you, it's *play time!*"

She crouched and I loved the way all her curls were haphazardly piled on her head. "You ever have questions or need advice, you ring me up."

"Okay."

"Next time you're in New York, we party. I'm *tons* of fun."

"I can tell that about you."

Grinning, she whispered, "You're *such* a lady."

"I try to be." I added, "Thank you for your help. I truly appreciate it. All of you are wonderful."

"I love to get my arson on." She winked and stood, staring between the Hydes. "I like her. Bust out the fireworks."

She wandered to the other end of the table where she perched on Bianca's lap. I watched her with my head tilted.

"She's the most liberated human I've ever met." I met Jonas's eyes. "Deadly?" He nodded with a smile. "Huh. I like her." After a long pause, I told Jordan, "I wish we found her first."

He leaned toward me and murmured, "You'll have plenty of chances to visit. She and her men are members of *Trois* and another club nearby."

My eyes went huge. "A club…in Dallas?"

Jonas scooted his chair closer to mine. "It's much harder than *Trois* but the same rules apply and anonymity is guaranteed."

"We wouldn't take you in without a mask," Jordan added.

I took a sip of wine. "What do you mean *harder*?"

"Bondage, public flogging, and more," Jonas explained.

"All participants are consensual adults but it might be too much."

"There's a lot of nakedness, spankings, and even displays of public sex." Jordan looked concerned.

I stared between them. "You've been there?" They nodded. "Would you take me? I want to see it."

"Rest for a few days and then, yes." Jonas held my gaze. "Our dynamic isn't like much of what you'll see there, Ellie. Still, it's closer than *Trois* and exclusive."

Hours later, we parted ways with Hollow's people and made our way back to the estate. Tom gave us a salute when we dropped him at his studio in the security compound.

Everyone was exhausted and felt covered in slime from the grueling trip. Robyn suggested I take a full day to recover while she remained with my parents and I gratefully agreed.

I vaguely remember showering and brushing my teeth. I don't remember climbing in bed or being joined there. I slept for eighteen hours with Jonas and Jordan curled protectively around me much of the time.

Too exhausted to talk, I soaked up their presence. I slept deeply, without any dreams at all, and it was marvelous.

Twice, I drifted to the surface of consciousness to use the restroom and wondered about Katie. I felt guilty for spending so much time away.

When Robyn returned to the house, Padme brought my daughter in to sleep beside me. Freshly fed and changed, I snuggled her close and drifted to sleep again.

The Hydes alternated checking on the house and remaining beside me with Katie guarded between our bodies.

I was out of it when they held her to me to kiss before returning her to Robyn near dark the next day.

Around midnight, my body decided I finally had enough sleep. Inhaling deeply, I blinked to get a fix on my surroundings and adjust to the lack of light.

Katie was no longer in the room but the Hydes were stretched out on either side of me, their arms crossed over my torso and their warm breath ruffling my hair.

I laid my hands over theirs, sighed happily, and felt more than heard two masculine chuckles.

My smile felt too big for my face. "Closer. You're warm and obviously as bad as I am about kicking off blankets."

Without hesitation, they sealed their bodies more firmly against me and tightened their arms. Long legs lifted, their bare feet settling warmly along my own.

"That's much better."

We laid there snuggling for a long time and none of us felt the need to fill the silence.

A sense of deep contentment, of things being exactly as they should be, settled into my spirit.

A horrible chapter of my life was finished and I was ready to embrace the next phase.

I told them quietly, "I've been thinking. We should take things slow. Get to *know* one another, spend *time* together. Enjoy some making out. Eventually, we can talk about *living* together and I'll introduce you to my *family*."

Their laughter filled me up. I wanted to smile and keep smiling.

"Oh *wait*...we've done all that." They nodded and hugged me closer. "Never mind, then." I sighed. "I guess that means we should shower together and you can sex me up in the manner in which I'd like to become accustomed."

Jonas said against my shoulder, "Ellie, it would be our *pleasure*."

Chapter Thirty-Nine

Jordan pulled me off the bed while Jonas went to start the shower. I clipped my hair on top of my head as they stripped away my sleep clothes.

They kept our bodies close and I knew it was to make me feel safe, to help me adjust to their presence. I trusted them but appreciated the *thought* they put into touching me.

By the time the water warmed, we were naked, and I was kissed out of my capacity for coherent thought.

The kisses now were different than the ones I received before, and there was almost a sense of desperation to them that I felt as well. They reined themselves in to avoid frightening me.

They didn't frighten me.

The moonlight shining through the high windows provided enough light to take in the visual impact of their nude bodies.

I'd never seen a fully naked man so close before and my mouth hung open a bit taking in two excellent examples of the species.

Their hair was ruffled from sleep. Broad shoulders and thick chests tapered to narrow hips and long legs. A light dusting of chest hair faded into a trail that pointed the way to thickly veined cocks nestled in trimmed pubic hair. Their balls hung heavy and tight between slightly spread legs.

Jordan turned to enter the shower and I was amazed that the view from the back was equally as enticing. He turned and smiled over his shoulder at my little gasp.

I stepped into the space with Jonas behind me. Their hands moved slowly, focused on keeping me comfortable and at ease. They took in the sight of *my* body as thoroughly as I was absorbing all the details of *theirs*.

Fingers reached out to stroke my hair, hold my hand, and trace the curves of my body without aggressiveness.

They kissed and nuzzled even as their erections slid against my wet skin. A tremor worked over me and I felt as if every hair stood on end in anticipation.

Whispering my name in the damp air, strong hands slicked over me from the front and back, the scent of my body wash hung delicately around us.

They didn't leave an inch of my skin untouched and I could hear myself panting as their hands passed smoothly between my legs in tandem.

I held myself up with a vise grip on the shoulders in front of me. My head rested on the shoulder behind me, my eyes closed as I soaked up the sensations created by the touch of four hands coasting over me.

I was in sensory overload.

Cooler on the front of my body, my eyes raised heavily to watch Jonas rinse me. He gathered me close and Jordan rinsed my back.

The brothers traded holding me to wash themselves.

"You're…so beautiful." I could hear the reverence, and the self-doubt, in my voice.

They heard it, too.

Wrapping me tightly between them, they said, "You're not allowed to overthink any of this. Not one person in our lives, separately or together, ever affected us as you do. No one, Ellie. You hold all the power."

People kept telling me that but it was hard to believe.

Stepping from the shower, they dried my body and wrapped me in a towel while they dried themselves.

I couldn't drag my eyes away from the simple realization that men did things differently than women. Even in the way they dried off after a shower, their hands were faster, rougher.

It struck me as long-overdue knowledge.

Jonas scooped me up, planted a gentle kiss on my lips, and laid me down in the center of my bed. Jordan pulled my hair from beneath me.

They took their places at my side, stretched out, heads propped on their hands. I realized immediately that the Hydes intended to take their time.

They passed my mouth back and forth, kissing me for long minutes. While one kissed my lips, the other stroked my hair, planted little open-mouthed kisses on my neck, and played with my fingers.

My hands explored them, drifting over warm skin. Unable to contain my curiosity another moment, I trailed my hands down their torsos and wrapped my fists lightly around their cocks.

They threw their heads back with barely leashed control.

"That feels good then…" I said into the darkness as I traced Jonas's collarbone with my lips. "Good to know."

I moved to Jordan's pectoral, licking once over the tight nipple. Their hands fisted in the towel still wrapped around me.

I whispered, "It's alright. I'm okay. Please."

Jonas rested his forehead against mine. "Ellie, if you don't stop touching me, I'm going to lose it."

Jordan lowered the edge of my towel and took my nipple inside the wet heat of his mouth. I arched at the previously unknown sensation with a gasp.

It pushed me firmly against his mouth and increased the pressure of his suckling.

Jonas repeated the attention on my other breast and I released them. They edged their bodies further down the bed and slipped the towel from under me.

Stroking my hands over their silky hair, I couldn't muffle the soft moans escaping me.

Fingers, light as butterflies, trailed a path over my ribcage, abdomen, and hips. Across my pelvis, directly above my mound. The lines of me were traced with hands and followed by lips that kissed me everywhere.

A sensation I didn't recognize at first built inside me. It was something I never experienced with another person. Gathering strength beneath questing hands, their mouths touched skin that suddenly felt too tight.

Dipping lower, outlining the sensitive folds, my hips rocked up of their own accord, and pleasure slammed into me like an arrow from a bow.

It stole my breath.

They stared up the length of my body as the tension slowly let me go. "It's so different than when I'm alone."

My eyes felt heavy but the greens and blues in their eyes reflected the low light in the room.

"You deserve all the pleasure we can give you, Ellie."

"This is about making your first time *everything* it should be." I started to state the obvious and Jonas lifted his hand to place three fingers over my lips. "Your *first* time, when you give of yourself willingly, that's *now*."

"We plan to make sure you remember it with happiness," Jordan murmured. "And maybe a blush or two."

They rubbed their cheeks over the skin of my pelvis and I sighed. Raking my fingers through their hair, I whispered, "I've always loved your stubble."

Planting kisses on my hips, I could see their smiles. "We noticed that actually." Jordan lifted his head. "Unless we had events, we stopped shaving in the evening for you."

"Such a small thing to someone else…but it slays me."

I lifted my upper body and they met me with kisses. Warm

hands cupped the back of my skull as they traded my mouth back and forth.

Keeping my hands on them, I rested my cheek on Jonas's shoulder and whispered, "When did you know I loved you?"

"When Jonas was shot at the Delkin party," Jordan told me as he kissed his way up my neck. "We wondered before but the way you reacted left little doubt."

I nodded and kissed them desperately. "Fear was a constant companion after that night."

"Don't be afraid, Ellie." Jonas gently pushed me to my back and Jordan kissed his way down my torso. "Every close call, every scar, every moment of pain or rage or sadness, is worth it to be close to you, to see you smile, to hear you laugh."

He gathered my upper body in his arms and kissed me. I held him tight but wanted to crawl into his body with him.

While his mouth devoured mine, Jordan kissed my nipples and continued lower to settle his shoulders between my thighs.

His kisses on my most sensitive flesh made me gasp into Jonas's mouth. A finger slid through my folds and I moaned.

"Soak it up, Ellie," he whispered against my lips. Hugging me, he moved his body and added, "Watch him. You need to *see* everything, *feel* everything."

Positioning himself slightly behind me, he held me and raked his fingers through my hair. His mouth trailed along my shoulder and up my neck.

I stared at Jordan and he stared back at me. He circled the entrance of me with the tip of his finger as he sucked my clit between his lips.

The whimper I released sounded desperate, needy, and Jonas's hands moved around to cup my breasts.

His thumbs stroked over my nipples and he murmured at my ear, "Every moment is about you, Ellie. It's about the joy, the freedom, to touch you after *years* of longing."

I was awash in sensation, unsure what to do or if I was reacting in a normal way. I felt amazing but selfish and thought there was something I should be doing for them.

Jordan lifted his mouth from me. "Let yourself feel and experience. Take everything we want to give you."

Jonas held me closer. "Let us please you, Ellie. Let us love you. Our pleasure is heightened by yours."

I watched fingers circle gently over my clit. The sight was so stimulating that it caused a shiver to race up my spine. Jordan smiled and I tugged my lower lip between my teeth.

Lowering his mouth to me, he held my gaze as he licked, sucked, and nibbled flesh that trembled from his attention.

Turning my head, I stared at Jonas and he kissed me roughly. I returned it as if my life depended on it and he groaned. One hand around the back of his head, I let the other rake through Jordan's hair as he took me apart with pleasure.

My breathing sped up, my heart raced, and as the climax

crashed over me, Jonas told me, "I love you, Elliana."

Gasping, I said, "Jonas, I love you, too."

I sealed it with a kiss and he held me so hard I wondered that it didn't hurt at all. He kissed along my jaw, buried his face at my neck, and I felt no doubt about his feelings.

Raking my fingers through Jordan's hair, he lifted his face to watch me as he stroked deeply into my body with his fingers.

"For so long, we waited to love you and it's humbling that you're open, responsive to all we want to give you, Ellie."

I pulled him to me and he came willingly. Our lips met and I tasted my body on his. Strong hands gripped me, as if afraid to let me go for a single moment.

Raising his face, Jordan stared into my eyes. "I love you. I never loved a woman before you. I'm glad you were the first."

"Really?" I asked softly.

He nodded. "Life was too precarious. The way we lived, it wasn't something that seemed possible. You changed all of it, Ellie. You made us think about the future."

Stroking my fingers over his jaw, I said, "I love you, Jordan."

Taking my hand, he placed it over his heart. I felt it pounding under my palm. "Since the first morning I watched your face light up when we all had breakfast together, you've made my heart race. None of us ever imagined you'd want such a thing."

"Everything about you was new to us, beautiful to us." Jonas nuzzled my cheek. "Being *wanted*, being *needed*, it gave days *meaning* they never had until we met you. Loneliness, isolation, they slowly crept in and we hadn't noticed. Not until you made us part of your life."

Blinking against tears, I hugged them as hard as I could. "I was so lonely before you. I wondered if it would ever be different."

They kissed me, over and over, until I was breathless between them. Their fists tangled in my hair and mine in theirs.

Then Jonas kissed his way down my body and Jordan moved to sit behind me. He hugged me to his chest.

"Watch him, Ellie. Take all the pleasure. We want you to be ready so there's no pain, no fear." His lips trailed down my neck and back again. "Touching you, tasting you, is heavenly."

Jonas settled between my legs and rested his face on my inner thigh as he explored me. I whimpered.

"Do you like how that feels?" he asked.

I nodded and watched as he lifted, his lips worshipping every fold and suckling my clit. He alternated between gentle open-mouthed kisses to flat passes with his broad tongue to tiny flicks that made me squirm in need.

Jordan held my nipples between his thumbs and forefingers, tugging and rolling them.

The multiple sensations were almost too much. Never had I felt such pleasure from the touch of my own hand.

Fingers thrust deep, curling inside me. I knew he was preparing me for so much more and my heart pounded.

At my ear, Jordan whispered, "How do you feel?"

"A-achy, needy, desperate," I answered honestly. His cock pressed against the crease of my ass and my hips circled to feel more of him.

He hissed, "*Ellie...*"

I rocked my hips against a hot mouth that shredded my ability to be demure or coy. "Please. Please, Jonas."

Raising his face, he stared at me, his fingers stroking rhythmically to the movement of my hips.

I felt as if he could see *everything* about me – who I used to be and who I could become – and wanted all of it.

It was liberating.

"Let me please you. Let me love you." I didn't recognize the hoarseness of my voice. "I need you."

Jordan said, "We want to love you into the new phase of your life and give you good memories to overwrite the past." He placed a kiss at my temple. "Are you ready, Ellie?"

"Yes. Yes, please."

His hands never stopped moving on my breasts and Jonas worked his fingers urgently inside me. The way I panted into the quiet room should have embarrassed me but it didn't.

Their touch was everywhere, reaching a heart that ached so

long to love them, to touch them in return.

With a long moan, my body arched as I careened over the edge of bliss again. I wasn't afraid, there was no doubt. I knew they'd see me safely to the other side.

"Now," I said between gritted teeth. "Now, Jonas."

There was the sound of plastic tearing as Jonas crawled up my body and kissed me with a desperation I returned. I held his face as he positioned his cock at the entrance of my body.

He hesitated and I knew he wondered if they were moving too fast. "I need you, Jonas. I want you inside me."

"Ellie, if anything gets to be too much…"

I put my fingers over his mouth. "I trust you. I want this. I want all of it. You won't hurt me. You don't frighten me. Don't make me wait anymore to feel you, Jonas."

The thick head of his cock pushed inside me and I tensed for a moment at the unfamiliarity. He stilled instantly.

"Don't stop. Please don't stop."

Slow, steady thrusts as he held my gaze built the tension in my entire body. Being held between them as Jonas pushed his way inside me was surreal.

When our bodies were sealed together, he stilled and spent almost a minute kissing me as his breath panted against my cheek. His cock throbbed against flesh that felt everything.

"Roll us over, Jonas." The request took him by surprise. The brothers froze. "I need both of you. Our first time, it has to be all of us."

I didn't know much about men or sex or relationships but there was a part of me that knew I had to show them they were equal to me, that I loved them both with all of myself.

"It can be…intense, Ellie," Jordan whispered behind me.

"I imagine." Turning my face, I stared at him. "Show me."

Jonas rolled me and I straddled him. I was shy about how open and exposed I was but I held myself up by my hands and stared down into a face I knew better than my own.

Jordan left the bed then the room.

My hair was a thick curtain around us and he gathered it, dropping all of it over one shoulder.

"You're fucking stunning, Ellie."

"So are you. In all my fantasies, I never imagined this would actually happen." Jordan returned and climbed up on the bed. He kissed my shoulder and I turned to look at him. "I missed you. I'm glad you're back."

I focused on kissing and touching Jonas, struggling not to move on him, as two lubricated fingers circled the tiny entry of my ass.

Jordan whispered in my ear, "It may feel strange at first. There may be pain until you adjust."

"It will be worth it."

His finger pushed inside, shallowly stroking until he slipped passed the ring of muscle. I moaned at the pleasure/pain.

I wondered what it would feel like to have them filling me.

He added more lube and another finger, going deeper, curling his fingers inside me as I circled my hips for more of everything I sought to experience.

"So tight and hot. A paradise I can't wait to feel."

Staring into Jonas's eyes, I said, "Jordan. Lube your cock and take me. I can't stand the suspense."

My inner thighs were slick with my own release easing from my pussy. The room was beginning to lighten with pre-dawn sun and I didn't want to wait another second.

"Your cocks filling me up. That's how I want to start this new day." I looked over my shoulder. "Now, Jordan."

When I heard another condom wrapper being torn open, I wanted to sob in relief.

"Please take me." I *sounded* weak but *felt* strong.

"*Ellie.*" It was all Jordan said as the head of his cock pressed into my ass and he worked himself deep.

Filled completely, held between them, I closed my eyes. "Yes. This is what I needed."

I doubted there could be a more sexualized position yet I felt loved, cherished as they held me, bodies tightly pressed to my front and back, and started to move.

They worked in counter-thrust, one withdrawing as the other entered. I could feel their friction against the thin wall that separated my two entrances.

I knew within seconds that I'd want this, need this often.

At first slow and gentle, they gradually built the speed and strength of their thrusts into me. Taking me, claiming me, making me theirs in a way I never expected.

I reveled in the way the wildness made me feel.

For every touch, kiss, bite they gave me, I returned my own. They loved me, fucked me, into my new life.

I screamed when I came but there was only one word I was coherent enough to remember. "Hyde!"

It drove them into a frenzy and I moaned as their cocks shuttled faster, harder in and out of me.

Every cell, every nerve reached for them as the world stopped for one beautiful perfect moment and there was only *this*.

They groaned my name into the room as they came, their hot release filling the condoms. On and on, they drove themselves as deep as they could get and rode orgasms that made me proud to have facilitated.

I held them to me, wanting every second of the experience etched in my memory. There were several minutes of silence as air sawed in and out of their lungs and their hearts pounded against my back and chest.

"Ellie…"

"Our Ellie…"

They eventually pulled out of me but I was mindless and boneless by that point. Too tired to notice or care that they cleaned my body of our fluids.

I whispered, "More…"

"Rest first...then as much as you want, as much as you can handle. Sleep, Ellie. Sleep knowing how much you're loved."

I slipped into unconsciousness with a long, pleased sigh.

* * *

The sun was high in the sky when I woke. I felt the warm breath of one of my men on my neck but it appeared the other was gone.

"Jonas is playing with Katie but we wanted you to sleep."

He climbed from the bed and padded naked to the bathroom. I heard water running a few seconds before he came back to crouch beside the bed.

"Time for a nice soak, Ellie. Are you sore?"

"A little but I like it." He took my hands and pulled me up. His arms were hot on my skin and I hugged him for a long time. "It's daytime. You're still here. I didn't dream it."

He dropped kisses on top of my head. "Neither did I, Ellie."

One more squeeze and he led me to the bathroom. Holding my hand, he helped me lower into the warm water. I sank to my shoulders with a moan of happiness.

Jordan planted a kiss in my lips and left the room.

I knew the moment Katie was near me. Her smell of baby powder and perfection got me every time. Opening my eyes, I smiled at her naked baby self being held in front of me.

"I made sure the water was cool enough that she could join you." Jonas knelt beside the tub with a grin.

I took her happily and nuzzled her face while she cooed little baby sounds at me. I lifted my knees and sat her butt on my tummy so she could lean back and see my face. Sprinkling water on her belly made her squeal with excitement.

"She's beautiful, Ellie. When she laughs, I wonder what life would be like without her…and can't imagine it." He smoothed a damp hand over her curls. "We couldn't love her more if she were ours."

I pretended there weren't tears sliding down my cheeks.

For the rest of the day, I settled back into life on the estate. It was strange after the weeks we spent on the road cleaning up the last pieces of filth from my past.

I did some coordinating with my corporate assistant and saw Tom off into his new life with more than a little fear.

Several times during the day, I caught myself daydreaming about the night I spent with the Hyde brothers.

Jonas and Jordan guarded me quietly while I worked but I caught them looking at me hungrily more than once.

Mom came by to visit but my dad was gone until the following weekend. We chatted for a few minutes over lunch but I was distracted, zoned out.

"Darling." I startled at the sound of her voice and she chuckled. "Take a few days off. We'll catch up once you have a minute to…catch your breath."

Her expression told me she could see the difference in me and likely knew the cause. My blush was nuclear.

"I won't torture you…for now."

She kissed my cheeks, gave the Hydes a mock salute, and let herself out to her waiting security team.

As the sun set, I read to Katie before tucking her in snugly. Diva curled up happily beneath the crib and refused to leave. I grinned and headed downstairs to the dining room with the Hydes behind me.

Before we entered the open space, they whirled me around and pressed me between them. Just like that, I responded to their touch.

"Eat *quickly*," one of them whispered. I have no idea what I ate or what my team discussed or how long it took to wrap up the meal and return to my bedroom.

I was certain, however, that whatever Si made was delicious.

When the house was quiet, I showered and paused before pulling on pajama shorts and a tank top.

Quirking my mouth in the mirror, I said, "Who are you kidding?

Instead, I smoothed almond oil and lavender moisturizer all over my body. It was the only outfit I needed.

Opening the bathroom door, my men turned to me in sleep pants and raked their eyes over my body from head to toe.

With a smirk, they pushed the pants down with their thumbs and kicked the fabric away.

I was already breathing harder, my heart pounded, and the folds of my pussy were glazed in expectation.

"More." It was all I said. It was all I needed to say.

It was *exactly* what they gave me.

Chapter Forty

One year later...June 2016

In my lifetime, there were only two real fights with my parents.

The first was when I refused to compromise about going to an out-of-state college.

The second came when my mother *insisted* I marry one of the Hydes to avoid awkward questions and provide my future children legitimacy.

Shockingly, the twins were on *their* side.

They explained several points rapidly, stopping me before I could storm out of my father's den.

Alternating sentences the way they did sometimes, I lost track of who was speaking but it didn't matter because I was mad at *both* of them.

"You're being unreasonable, Ellie. Your parents are right. You can't walk through your former life as if *nothing* has changed. You have Katie and there's a very *real* chance you could get pregnant again despite precautions."

I stared between them blinking rapidly.

I'd never considered the thought of pregnancy because I already had Katie. Suddenly, I understood the use of condoms when we were together and felt woefully *young* again.

"I'll go on birth control…"

"It's not a guaranteed solution."

"Well!"

"Ellie. You're technically marrying *Jay Hyde*. It's our joint identity. We don't want your money, we have no intention of giving up your protection, and want you as safe as possible in every way we can provide…including your pristine reputation."

"I'm not having a different name than Katie. She'll feel alone."

"Not if you give us the privilege of adopting her." The room went silent. I put my fingers over my lips. "Katie is a year old, Ellie. She could realistically pass as our child."

"What if she found out the truth?"

"We fall back on the AVF story if that happens. We've been with her since birth, have no children of our own, and already consider her our daughter."

"Do you even *want* to get married?"

"We don't care about paper, Ellie," Jordan said quietly. "We want to love you for the rest of the minutes we have left on this planet. That's all that matters."

Jonas gestured to my parents standing a few feet away. "It takes so little to put their minds at ease. A small compromise that changes *nothing* about our life together."

After an hour of pressing the point, I agreed.

Another fight raged immediately after when the Hydes demanded a prenuptial agreement that made my blood boil.

No matter what happened, they wanted it in writing that they didn't get *one dime* of my money.

It was unheard of and I refused to entertain it.

"Now you're being stubborn, Ellie. It's up to you to protect what your family built. This is happening because you're going to know that *every time* we touch you, *every time* we tell you we love you…it's *you*, not your *money*."

Growling, I turned to my parents, "Arrange a wedding however you see fit. The courthouse sounds perfect. Write the damn prenup the way they want it." I prepared to leave and said over my shoulder, "Triple their salary."

"Ellie!"

The Hydes called my name as I stormed out of the house and climbed in the back of the car with Fiaaz behind the wheel. The brothers walked to either side of the car and waited.

He said conversationally, "A little fight then?"

"Take me home. I'm mad."

"Uh…"

"Oh, alright!" I unlocked the doors and they slid in on either side of me. "You can ride with me but I'm furious."

The moment we pulled into the garage of my house, they were out and Jonas lifted me into his arms. "Arm it, Fiaaz. Tell Robyn we'll be along shortly."

"You put me down and let me yell at you."

"Of course. The moment you're behind closed doors in your soundproofed bedroom."

He carried me there and set me down. I went to my desk and typed angrily for an hour. Jordan left and returned to report that Katie was sleeping but asked for the pool after her nap.

I nodded but otherwise ignored them and continued working.

From the corner of my eye, I watched Jordan reach behind him to lock the door. Without a word, they crossed the room in coordinated steps as they so often did.

Jonas pulled out my desk chair and sank to his knees in front of me. He didn't take his eyes from mine as he pushed my sundress up my thighs and lifted one of my legs over the arm of the chair.

"I'm still angry," I told him.

"That's okay, Ellie," he replied as he pulled my panties aside and lowered his mouth to folds that were already wet.

My head dropped back on the chair and Jordan stroked my cheek with one hand as the other pulled his cock from his jeans. "Pleasure will ease your stress and you can yell at us again later."

Leaning forward, I sucked him deep and he groaned. "Ellie,

your mouth is heaven."

I hummed around the length and felt his palm circle the back of my neck. He held my head still as he stroked slowly in and out of my mouth while Jonas stole my ability to think.

Neither of them were in a hurry but I couldn't hold back my orgasm as two fingers stroked deep inside me.

They lifted me from my chair, stripped away my clothes, and cleared the desk. They laid me across it naked. That they were still dressed always destroyed me and they knew that.

Jordan sat in my chair and took over eating me while Jonas stood on the other side of the desk and thrust into my mouth. He leaned over to suck my nipples.

"Every inch of you tastes incredible, Ellie. Little cherry nipples." I moaned around his cock and he hissed, "I love when you suck me."

A year of fucking two men changed a woman. They explored what I liked and taught me about myself.

I discovered I loved when they talked to me during sex and they found intense pleasure watching me masturbate.

With a low growl, his thrusts slowed and he pulled back. "I'm not coming in your mouth. I want your ass."

They sat me up and Jordan rolled a condom over his length. Holding me, they settled me over his lap with my legs over the arms of the chair.

"You're so *deep* like this, Jordan," I whispered.

"You have no choice but to enjoy the ride." I gripped the

back of the chair as Jonas stepped behind me. His latex-covered cock was cool and slick with the lube from my desk drawer.

Lengthy preparation was fun but no longer necessary. They took my ass regularly so there was no pain or discomfort. I knew the shape and feel of them in every part of my body.

Jonas pressed inside carefully, rocking back and forth until he was buried to the hilt. He whispered at my ear, "You have the sweetest ass, Ellie. I never want to leave it."

"Take me hard. Fuck the mad out of me."

They grabbed my shoulders and hips and started to move. I was so open, dead weight, and they took their time, drawing their orgasms out as they slammed me into one that almost made me pass out.

Then they braced me and fucked me *hard*. Driving into my body until I was mindless with my need to come.

Jordan kissed a line up my neck and over my jaw. "You ready to explode?" I nodded, unable to speak. "Come all over my dick while I fuck the warmest, slickest pussy in the world."

I started to shake and they went harder.

"Ellie, I love how tight your ass grips me." He kissed across my shoulders. "Like a goddamn fist."

I collapsed limply over Jordan as they shoved me into an orgasm that didn't *stop*. They filled me up, held me close, and murmured how much they loved me.

After a short nap, I woke up in the center of my big bed

with them stretched out on either side.

I could tell they cleaned me up like they always did after sex. It took me awhile to get used to it.

"There you are. Nice nap, sweetheart?"

I grinned at Jonas. "You fucked me stupid."

They laughed and Jordan kissed me nipple. "Funny. You always fuck me brilliant."

"I'll never get enough of you both touching me, wanting me, loving me." I pulled them closer. "I love you. Sometimes, it feels like an obsession."

They stroked over my still-naked body. "May your obsession never, ever fade, Ellie. Ours won't."

Then my men took me up one more time and it was better than the roller coaster at the fair, all those years ago when I realized how much I loved my beautiful bodyguard.

My Hyde.

One of them whispered, "Hang on, Ellie."

Then the drop came and I closed my eyes with my hands over my head. This time when I wished it could go on forever…

It did.

Epilogue

October 2016

There were many things the man the world knew as Hollow was grateful for every day he opened his eyes.

One was having a family who continued to love him despite his mistakes, his rage, and that he too often pulled away from them.

Another were the friends who never hesitated to rally for every cause, no matter how dangerous, no matter the odds.

There was one person who would forever be at the top of his list. The only man who knew the horror he endured as a child because he had endured it as well.

Elijah entered the warehouse and took a seat beside him at the command center. For almost a minute, the silence dragged out between them.

Finally, the man of few words said, "You can't continue like this and I know you know that."

"Did he send you?" Hollow asked softly.

"No." Green eyes met his directly. "Brie did."

It was almost impossible to conceal his surprise. "Brie…?"

Elijah gathered his thoughts, considered his words carefully.

"You claw at the scabs. Reopening the wound again and again." He shook his head and his blonde hair picked up the low lights. "You refuse to forgive…"

"No." Closing his eyes, he whispered, "I…"

Clenching his jaw and his fists on his thighs, he breathed through the very real stress that having the conversation caused him.

"I lie when I say I won't forgive her for what she did."

Elijah frowned. "You refuse to forgive *yourself*."

"Why did you come, Elijah?"

"They know I'm the only one you'll listen to." Elijah's smile was gentle and it struck to the heart of him. "I'm cautious about how I wield such power. In this, I agreed it was needed. Things can't continue as they have."

"I'm fine."

"Another lie. One I've told many times myself."

Hollow stared at the man across from him. A man known around the world as the deadliest human being.

It had never mattered to him.

When Hollow was eleven, Elijah saved him. Eviscerated the man who tortured him sexually for five years without anyone in his life realizing what was happening.

Several years older, already a champion in renowned fighting competitions held for the fiercest men and women from every continent, Elijah had *never* been a child.

Hollow's childhood was taken from him by the man his father trusted most, the man who was also Elijah's father.

He doubted either of them remembered innocence.

What began as a hero complex steadily transformed into a deep love for the person who pulled Hollow back from the brink of destruction again and again.

"You have so much now, Elijah. Don't worry about me."

"You're worth saving," he said again. "If you can forgive her, if you can look beyond the past, you deserve to make her yours."

"She doesn't deserve such a fate, Elijah. She deserves so much more than I can ever give her."

Elijah reached inside his jacket and removed a folded piece of paper, holding it out for him to take.

Hollow took it in confusion and unfolded it.

A *memory* was depicted in a detailed sketch and it made him gasp. In the bottom corner was a date and Brie's signature with a little heart.

He would have been almost eighteen. The girl in the sketch with him was two years younger. It was before he left home the first time. Before drugs took him out of his own head and granted him false peace for a little while.

"Do you remember that moment in your life?" Elijah asked softly. "Brie draws what she sees. Based on the date, she would have been about fourteen. Based on the angle, she probably drew it from a second-floor window in her parents' home. Do you *remember*, Hollow?"

Blinking back tears he didn't recognize at first, he nodded. "I remember." His voice was hoarse.

"She loved you before you left. She loved you when you returned. She loves you still."

"No…"

"Don't lie to *me*, Hollow. Not to *me*. There have never been lies between us."

Meeting his gaze, he replied quietly, "There have been a few, Elijah. None that I can't live with."

"I'm sorry."

"No, you're not. You can't help who you love and you should never apologize for it. For a long time, I was angry. The way he *was*, the way you *allowed* it." He lifted one shoulder in a shrug. "Brie made it better for both of you and I'm glad. I…resent him less."

"He loves you."

"He *tolerates* me. Some days, I tolerate him as well. As much as he knows, he still knows nothing." Looking at the image in his hands, he smiled at how talented Brie was. "She captures emotion stunningly well."

"Love is a magic that draws her."

"I'm inoculated." He tried to hand back the sketch but Elijah shook his head.

"Brie found it in her things and insisted I deliver it when I saw you." Inclining his head, he added, "She wrote a note on the back. Said you'd understand."

Turning the heavy paper over, he stared at the word *hope* written in charcoal.

Controlling his breathing, his heart, he murmured, "Why not give it to Isabella?"

Elijah's smile was slow. "She assured me Izzy has plenty."

"Why did you *come*, Elijah?"

"Because I love you, Hollow. Not the love you need but love nonetheless."

The words filled him with joy and agony simultaneously.

Elijah leaned forward, his elbows on his knees. "Before Brie entered my life, I felt I'd reached an expiration date. Every day exactly like the one before it, stretching out endlessly, painfully, in front of me."

"*Elijah…*"

"She changed everything because she loves me as the man I *am*. Not some perfect ideal. Every scar, every mistake, every moment that made me who I am…she loves me."

He stood up and put his hand on Hollow's head, stroking through his hair as he had when he was a boy who followed him around like a puppy.

"Stop rescuing everyone else for long enough to rescue yourself. Let her in, let her wrap her love around you, and *drown* in it." He bent and pressed his lips to Hollow's temple and added in a whisper, "*Please, Hayden.*"

Then he walked from the warehouse.

Hollow stared at the sketch for a long time.

Eventually, he shut down the lights, armed the building, and went to bed. The silence *pounded* in his mind.

Turning his head, he stared at the sketch he'd propped against the lamp on the bedside table.

After an hour, he couldn't deny what he needed. He stroked himself, remembering the way Izzy used to feel in his arms.

The way she *looked* at him. The way she *touched* him. The way she *loved* him no matter what he said or did to her.

He came with a gasp, her name a groan, and stared at the ceiling for hours. There were no easy answers to the questions that raced around his mind.

He had no clue what to do with himself.

It was time to figure that out. He'd punished himself, and her, for more than two decades.

He wondered if love had an expiration date.

The Barter System Series

Read the entire series now!

The Barter System Prequels
The Barter System (Book One)
Hudson (Book Two)
Backstage (Book Three)
Liberation (Book Four)
Radiance (Book Five)
The Barter System Companion – Volume 1
The Barter System Companion – Volume 2

Author's Note:

Before we head into "**The Hollow Universe**," you should read "**The Barter System**" series. You don't *have* to but since many of the characters in my anchor series will make an appearance, it's a great idea. You have a *lot* of ground to cover so…start reading!

About Shayne McClendon

If you're looking for stories that tug at your heart, make you laugh out loud, and sometimes make you cry so hard you need a giant box of tissues…look no further than books by Shayne McClendon.

She's a prolific author (more than 8 million words and counting) known for dramatic, steamy, enthralling fiction that will grab you and not let go until the last page.

A nomad at heart, Shayne currently lives in America's heartland with her dog, cats, and two grown children.

She listens to the voices in her head because their ideas are (almost) always awesome. Coffee consumption is too high, amount of sleep is too low, but the words always feel just right.

Be sure to like her <u>Always the Good Girl Facebook page</u>, or visit her at <u>Always the Good Girl</u> and join for your free story!

Shayne currently has more than two dozen books that range from heart-wrenchingly romantic to captivating non-stop heat. Explore them on the next page!

Shayne McClendon

Also by Shayne McClendon

Dramatic Romances
Completely Wrecked
The Hermit

Sports Romances
Love of the Game
Hart of the Matter

Country Romances
Yes to Everything
Somebody
Gravity
Break Down Here

The Barter System Series
The Barter System Prequels
The Barter System
Hudson
Backstage
Liberation
Radiance
The Barter System Companion – Volume One

The Great Outdoors Series
Sunny's Heart
Permission to Come Aboard
Permission to Land
Special Delivery
Embrace the Wild

Short Story Anthologies
Quickies – 2014 Edition
Quickies – 2015 Edition

Romantic Comedies
Always Delightful

Special Acknowledgments

For my friend and longtime personal assistant, Jana who never lets me fall on my face.

For Rhonda and Sheryl who are changing the way my words are presented one book at a time. You've given me incredible peace of mind. Thank you.

Without the help of these women, I'd fail.

All the love in the world,
Shayne

Shayne McClendon

Made in the USA
Middletown, DE
23 July 2017